T0149123

ESCAPE TO AN AUTUMN PAVEMENT

ALSO BY ANDREW SALKEY

Fiction:
A Quality of Violence
The Late Emancipation of Jerry Stover
The Adventures of Catullus Kelly
Anancy's Score
Come Home, Malcolm Heartland

Poetry:
Jamaica
In the Hills Where Her Dreams Live: Poems for Chile 1973–1980
Land
Away

Children's novels:
Hurricane
Earthquake
Drought
Riot
Jonah Simpson
Joey Tyson
The River that Disappeared
Danny Jones

Travel books:
Havana Journal
Georgetown Journal

ESCAPE TO AN AUTUMN PAVEMENT

ANDREW SALKEY

INTRODUCTION BY

THOMAS GLAVE

PEEPAL TREE

First published in Great Britain in 1960
by Hutchinson
This new edition published in 2009 by
Peepal Tree Press Ltd.
17 King's Avenue
Leeds LS6 1QS
England

ISBN13 Print: 978 1 84523 098 2

Printed in the United Kingdom
by Severn, Gloucester,
on responsibly sourced paper

INTRODUCTION

THOMAS GLAVE

Among the twentieth century's Caribbean-originated writers who at one time or another emigrated to Britain – C.L.R. James, Samuel Selvon, Beryl Gilroy, Wilson Harris, George Padmore, Claudia Jones, and George Lamming among them – Andrew Salkey remains one of the most arresting and original. While numerous Caribbean writers of the period expressed their anger about and opposition to British colonialism in the West Indies, British racism, and the often traumatizing plight of Caribbean emigrants in England – as their descendants did later in the century and continue to do today – none assayed as bold a journey into explorations of sexuality, and the possible homosexuality of a Caribbean man in particular, as did Salkey in *Escape to an Autumn Pavement*.

Here, accompanying Salkey through his crisp, often terse, prose, we encounter a London that is at once familiar, public, yet revealed as a terrain of secrets, of vulnerabilities as emotionally charged as they are profoundly and (for a little while, at least) unspeakably private. This is the city of Hampstead Heath and Piccadilly, but also of ardently experienced, sometimes ambivalently propelled desire felt by one man for another, and by a woman and man for each other – the sorts of complicated, interracial and intercultural desires that here anticipate the more overt sexual experimentation to come in the later 1960s and 1970s. It is through these complex and compelling attractions that we soon come to know Johnnie Sobert, the novel's sardonically articulate, deeply conflicted Jamaican protagonist who, by his own description, is 'Middle class. Or so I've been made to think' (p. 15).

Escape to an Autumn Pavement places us squarely in the London of 1960-61, fifteen years after the end of World War II and nineteen years after the German *blitzkrieg* of London and several other cities in Britain that took more than forty thousand lives in the capital alone, and whose results were still visible in vacant bombsites. At this time, Britain still maintains colonies in the Caribbean, Africa, and Asia, though with increasing dissent and resistance from the colonized. Johnnie Sobert's London is the increasingly racially uneasy, twilight-empire city that, twelve years after the arrival of the famous *Empire Windrush* ship (with emigrants mostly from Jamaica and other parts of the Anglophone Caribbean), reveals an increasingly African-descended – and specifically Antillean – population. It is a metropole that continues to house the royal family and parliament, but also more West Indian night clubs such as the one in which Johnnie works in Oxford Circus, squarely in the heart of the face-shifting city. In 1962, only a year after we meet Johnnie, Jamaica, accompanied by Trinidad and followed four years later by Barbados, will become an independent nation no longer formally beholden to 'Mother' England.

In *Escape*, we share the observations of a shrewd critical Caribbean man's eye – an eye deeply sceptical of the 'Mother' country and its pretensions and hypocrisies – in Johnnie's typically witheringly ironic comments on English citizens and life:

> Astringent faces in the queue; behind me clock-faces, all with tea-time written over them – tea-time past and tea-time to come. What a good shot of Jamaican white rum wouldn't do for them is nobody's business! Come on, now, we must learn to love our neighbours as ourselves. Learn to be tolerant (good word that! A damn' good British-made word!) (p. 38)

As *Escape* progresses, Johnnie's acerbic observations about English and Caribbean people and society loom as the insights of someone powerfully unsettled not only sexually, as his continual self-questioning and pondering of possible attraction to another man – a white Englishman – increases, but also geographically and psychically. He is an urban London outsider far from the Caribbean 'home' about which he feels a profound ambivalence, yet to which he still feels in some ways a deep emotional connection. He makes this clear in a passionate critique of Jamaica's class difficulties in a revealing conversation with Fiona Trado, a white Englishwoman who discloses to Johnnie that she has a romantic/sexual 'past' with a Nigerian, and is presently – restively – wife of the man who collects rents for the rooming house where Johnnie lives:

> There's no middle-class bit where I come from. Yet there's a sort of behaviour which adds up to it. Which damn' well strangles everybody. The thing doesn't exist, yet a tight bunch of people move and hope and act as if they're being guided by it... Surely it takes much more than a hundred and twenty-eight years after the Abolition of Slavery for a middle class to evolve? (p. 50)

Later in the novel, in a sequence of reflections on his difficult relationship with his father ('the old man'), Johnnie's reflections on the Jamaican middle class and the implicit reasons for his 'escape' from that context become even more trenchant:

> I suppose [the old man] had the right life saved up for me. The life of endless respectable pursuits and conventional patterns of behaviour. Not that the old man would have insisted. But 'the others' would have prescribed a girl three to four shades lighter than myself. Respectable people are married people. Shade's the thing. Could very well be the reason for my coming to England where I can get a girl a million shades lighter than myself. Just to show the Jamaican and Panamanian middle-classery where it gets off. (p. 81)

This anger and restlessness, manifested in Johnnie's unyielding desire to question and critique the painful realities left behind at 'home' and the newer, more immediate inconsistencies and peculiarities everywhere about him (including the erotic and platonic possibilities that arise in the Oxford Circus night club where he works as a waiter, and the interactions between other

West Indians whom he meets there), marks the sharpening of a Jamaican consciousness in conflict with the emergence of a Caribbean-British hybrid one. This is a way of being that today could be correctly termed black British: an identity comfortable with both blackness and Britishness, derived from the deeply complex perspectives of both, that squares with the fact that blackness and Britishness are not mutually exclusive. In Johnnie, the result of these convergences and tensions is a kind of insider-outsider eye that, throughout the novel, wields a wicked ability to skewer characters and situations. Among the most hilarious and disturbing of these is a moment with a drunk white Englishman who casually chats Johnnie up outside a pub one early evening, starting with what can only be described as a decidedly odd conversational opening, the strangely intimate imperiousness of which reflects the colonial relationship between them: 'Where d'you come from, young man?… Come on, answer smartly, now. I won't bite you, you know' (p. 40). After learning that Johnnie is Jamaican, the Englishman tactlessly remarks, 'You've got some very beautiful women, haven't you? Wonderful skin. Nice high backsides. Strong devils, I bet?' In a subsequent moment both shocking but also grotesquely comic and revealing, this man frankly declares that he would like to 'get my hands on one of those nigger wenches. Delightful people!' (p. 41).

It is also fascinating to note *Escape*'s anticipation of, and conversation with, the conflicts expressed in Derek Walcott's famous poem 'A Far Cry from Africa,' published in 1962, a full two years after *Escape*'s publication. Walcott's poem centres on the anxieties raised in a 'fractured' consciousness (similar to W.E.B. DuBois's African American 'double consciousness' theory, espoused nearly sixty years earlier) that, from minute to minute, migrates uneasily between the 'West' and an historically remembered and embraced Africa. In this tense exchange with Fiona, Johnnie notes:

> '…I walk around London and I see statues of this one and the other… I see litters of paintings in your museums and galleries. St. Paul's. The Tower. All of them. There's even Stonehenge!

And d'you know how I feel deep down?… I feel nothing at all! And yet, I want to feel just a little something.'

'But why?'

'Why? Because Africa doesn't belong to me! There's no feeling there. No bond. We've been fed on the Mother Country myth. Its language. Its history. Its literature… We feel chunks of it rubbing off on us. We believe in it. We trust it. Openly, we admit we're a part of it. But are we? Where's the real link?' (p. 52)

Walcott's ideologically and personally risky poem garnered considerable attention after its publication, but it is useful and important to remember that several other Caribbean writers, Salkey prominent among them, began the conversation/question that centred on the realities of and longing for Africa – the other 'Mother' – and 'here', 'there', and 'home'.

Keeping in mind Salkey's formidable skill with precisely honed language – language that, sometimes playful, sometimes grave, and often ambiguous in regard to (homo)sexual and romantic desire, frequently veils as much as it discloses, opting for implication over direct statement – it is Johnnie's intriguing, ostensible attraction to another man, and what is gradually revealed about that man's feelings toward him, that offer some of the most fascinating moments in *Escape*. All of this is bravely rendered by Salkey in an era when the word 'homosexuality' was barely mentionable, and the homosexuality of a Caribbean person literally unthinkable. An interracial homosexual relationship between two men that involved actual love and romance was surely even more beyond the pale – as, in many instances, remains the case today.

Reading *Escape to an Autumn Pavement* again, as Peepal Tree Press has fortunately made it possible to do with this reissued edition of yet another path-clearing Caribbean work in the Caribbean Modern Classics series, I remain grateful to both the author and the Press for making Johnnie Sobert's story available to an entirely new generation of readers, among them Caribbean readers, Caribbean queer readers, queer readers everywhere, and innumerable others. It is not unrealistic to imagine that Andrew Salkey would not only have been pleased with this gorgeous new edition of his novel; I believe he would have applauded, and perhaps, as Johnnie would have been inclined to do, even have laughed, sardonically yet with appreciation, out loud; then invited us all to Johnnie's Oxford Circus West Indian club for a round of good Jamaican white rum, glasses raised with Johnnie's, to resounding and emphatic cheers.

Finsbury Park, London
January 2009

There is always something rather absurd about the past.

MAX BEERBOHM

Time present and time past
Are both perhaps present in time future,
And time future contained in time past.

T. S. ELIOT
Four Quartets – Burnt Norton, 1, i–iii

I do not know!
I do not know!
I do not know what time is at
or whether before or after
    was it when –
but when <i>is</i> when?

DAVID JONES
The Anathemata – Keel, Ram, Stauros, VI

Although all the characters and situations depicted in this novel are fictitious, I'm obliged to point out that the character called SHAKUNTALA GOOLAM might, indeed, cause some offence in that, quite unwittingly, she has been given an improbable Indian name. Apparently, SHAKUNTALA and GOOLAM belong to different worlds.

After naming her, I learned that SHAKUNTALA (Sanskrit) is Hindu, and GOOLAM which is properly GHULAM (Persian) is Muslim. Because of this I should like to say that there has been no attempt on my part to embarrass anyone, or to utter propaganda on behalf of Hindu-Muslim Unity, or anything of the sort.

In the first instance I plead ignorance, and in the second innocence. If I'm allowed a third I plead invention. As it is, SHAKUNTALA GOOLAM barely exists in name, therefore, she has no other life and exerts no influence whatever beyond her appearance as a minor character in this novel.

A.S.

BOOK ONE

NOTES IN THE PRESENT
FOR A TIME PAST

1

The name's Sobert. Johnnie Sobert. Jamaican. R.C. Middle class. Or so I've been made to think.

There's hell below my room. A small Hampstead bedsitter. Private tenement kind of hell. Six rooms below mine: an Indian, not a Trinidadian Indian, just an Indian, the kind that caused Columbus to make his *fortunate mistake*; and four Londoners.

Ménage?

No. Just people.

And that means simply: one fainthearted student love-spree; an unmarried married couple; a low-breathing, fish-faced chauffeur with a whom-have-you-been-sleeping-with glaciated look who drives a fleshy, overdressed, upper-middle-class tramp between Golders Green and Knightsbridge when she has to visit her hairdresser who is half man and half problem child; and the owner of the house, a jagged, sophisticated dragon who reigns on her damp throne and who insists that more people ought to listen to the Third Programme and talk less about Colonial Development and Welfare schemes.

*   *   *

'Why are you so angry, Mr Sobert?' the dragon on her damp throne asks me.

'I dislike the Third Programme and I adore the idea of C.D. & W. That's why.'

'But surely, Mr Sobert, you're different from the others I've seen working in the Underground.'

'And on the dustcarts,' I offer, assisting her Old England benignity.

'Yes. And those on the dustcarts, as you say. Surely, they have some sort of childlike right to be angry and resentful. Not you.'

'Mrs Blount.'

'Yes?'

'Do you feel the same about the Covent Garden porter?'

'An English porter, you mean?' Cunning hesitation. Inclination of neck. Flick of fingertip and wrist. 'Yes. Yes, Mr Sobert. I most certainly do.'

'A childlike right to be angry, eh?'

'Mr Sobert, you're making quite an issue out of this, aren't you?'

'My chip on the shoulder, Mrs Blount. A small one from my well-preserved forest.'

'Never thought of you in that way before, I must say.'

'Really? Why?' Trying to catch her tone. Hope it upsets her. Hope it makes her livid. Might make her laugh instead. Couldn't care less, actually. Her face seems blank. Didn't register.

'Well, you seem so…'

'I know, Mrs Blount. *So different.* Isn't that what you mean?'

'Do I detect a little feeling of the eternal outsider in your voice, Mr Sobert?' She assumes her role of Titania, and holds it.

'No. May be a little bit of the Colonial Office, Mrs Blount. May be a touch of Kenya, or for that matter, a dash of…well, never mind the rest.'

'You are angry, aren't you?' A well-timed chuckle. Pause that refreshes.

'Wouldn't you be?'

'I can't say. This is one of those rather impossible questions, don't you think? I would imagine some people might try to answer it.' Hesitates again. 'Pure folly, really. I don't think I should risk it, at all.'

Another lump of silence. Bigger than a mere pause. Not refreshing either.

'More tea, Mr Sobert?'

'Thank you, no.'

The old dragon pours herself number three. And, of course, there's no use wishing that she'll choke, because she's not the type to, in any case.

'I'm sure we'll be friends.'

'Why, Mrs Blount?'

'Well, for one thing, you're so intelligent, Mr Sobert.'

House-owning bitch!

★   ★   ★

The third time I pass the Indian on the stairs by the toilet, she speaks. The thing actually speaks!

'Where you come from, Sobert?'

'A place damn' far away from India, Miss Goolam.'

'Yes.' Sounding uncertain. A little perplexed. Thick piece of curry, aren't you?

'Where d'you think?' I ask.

'The Jamaicas?'

'Yes.'

'You have some Indian blood in you, Sobert? Yes?'

'A touch.'

'What you do, here?'

'Here, where?'

'In this country.'

'Dream and try to pay the rent to our gracious queen!'

'Why you call Mrs Blount our gracious queen?'

'Well, isn't she?'

'You not too well, Mr Sobert, perhaps?'

At last the messy little job showed some respect. What's she, after all? A student of something or the other. Law, I bet. Crazy state of affairs! Coloured territories (shameful epithet that) in the near future will be thick with wigs and gowns and silks, dear God, and not a damn' soul qualified to look after a simple thing like the land – nobody worries about Agriculture in mainly agricultural countries or islands. Dirty thing, the land! Not for middle-class aspirants! Import a Scot or Welshman. He'll make the necessary plans. Damn' good builders of bridges, canals, factories, etc.

'Of course I'm feeling well.'

'You don't sound it.'

'Never you mind whether I sound it or not. What are you studying, or is it a secret between you and Nehru?'

'You must be mad! What has Mr Nehru to do with my studies?'

So it's Mr Nehru, eh? You are a little leech, Miss Goolam Chops.

'You owe everything to him, I would say.'

'Nothing at all, in no way. My parents pay for me.'

'Nothing at all?'

'No. And I repeat to you that my parents, for my entire stay in this country, pay for me.'

'And a fat lot it'll do them. D'you really think you'll ever let them get anything out of it? Will they be any better off for sending you to England?'

'What's the meaning of all these questions? I don't think it's your business, Sobert!'

So it's Sobert again, little Miss Prawn Curry!

'Never mind. What are you reading so far away from your martyred parents, Miss Goolam?'

'You are a strange man, today,' with narrowed eyes. Pause of Indian pride and joy. 'I am reading Economics, if that is of great interest to you, Sobert.'

'And who told you to, Miss Goolam?'

'I decided.'

'All by yourself?'

'Most certainly, yes.'

'You have a boy friend, I suppose?'

'You suppose correctly.'

Not a bad effort beneath that great swaddling expanse of sari. Must see her for a little chat. Perhaps when we cross paths at the toilet, again.

★   ★   ★

Fish-face and I seem to be the only ones who use the bathroom with any regularity. Fifth meeting in two weeks. Haven't spoken before. He's trying hard to beat me to it. Beat me to the bathroom, I mean. Moving towards the door rapidly.

'Oh! So sorry,' Fish-face risks.

'What for?'

'We're always meeting at this point, aren't we?'

Tender chuckles from Fish-face. Long fingers with manicured nails. Third-class citizen with a first-class citizen's gram-

mar and accent. Harrods dressing gown. May be Aquascutum.
Or even Burberry. Could be a Christmas present from the tramp
for services rendered on the road. I wonder what his driving is like
under pressure?

'If you promise not to be long,' Fish-face ventures.

'That's all right. I'll wait.'

'I'm right below you. Snape's the name. The old lady calls me
Dick on her off days.'

'Mine's Sobert. John Sobert.'

'Where did you get that Welsh accent, Mr Sobert? Or is that
rude?'

'Not from Wales, I don't think.'

'But it's decidedly Welsh.'

'It's been described as decidedly Northern Irish, as well.'

'I hope you don't mind talking about it? It's rather puzzling,
really.'

'I know.'

'Look, I only want to wash a few socks and handkerchiefs. I
could use the basin.'

'Fine by me. Few towels to do myself.'

'Jamaica, is it?'

'Humm.'

'Shouldn't think you get a fair break with our wretched
climate?'

'It's a bit new.'

'New! Weird. Weird as hell, if you ask me.'

I like old Fish-face. May be he isn't such a fish-face after all.
Hell of a lot of socks. Initialled handkerchiefs, and all.

'Served with a few of your chaps during the war. Difficult
customers.'

'So I've heard.'

'Nearly always in trouble. Must have been beastly for them,
though.'

'Why?'

'Well, you know what I mean. Not their war. Not their
climate.'

'They weren't forced to join up, were they?'

'That's true, too.'

19

Must find out more about Fish-face. No. Dick. That's better. Let us give the nice ones a bit of respect and affection. Obviously a very fallen bird. I wonder if he's *that way*, really?

'Oh, by the way. Ought to give you a tip about the old lady. She's dead suspicious! Wants to keep Britain clean, you know. You know the position, don't you?'

'No. I don't, Dick.'

'Well, you've had a few girls upstairs rather late, haven't you?'

Aha! Here it comes! Dick is a bit of a Fish-face when all's said and done. The whom-have-you-slept-with look's coming into those chauffeur's eyes of his, now.

'I had two friends, night before last. Yes.'

'The old lady complained about your dancing girls, and all that.'

'I suppose she was expecting a ritual killing right over her head, eh?'

'I wouldn't put it that way, Johnnie. It's all right to call you Johnnie, isn't it?'

'Sure, Dick. Sure.' Pause. Reflection. 'You say that the old lady complained? Strongly?'

'How many girls, Johnnie?'

'One. And her husband. Friends from back home. Met them at a West Indian club and brought them back here for a chat.'

'So, you didn't…'

'Of course not.'

Most peculiar moment, this. The look on Dick's face wants to tell me something. Very badly, most urgently. Can't make out whether he's glad or sorry.

It's a telling look, all right. Something has pulled him up smartly, or on the other hand, satisfied him – made him assured. Why should I worry, anyway?

'Better be careful. The old lady's a hawk when she wants to be.'

'Tell me, Dick, what's the score about our Miss Goolam?'

'Nothing out of the ordinary. She's got a lovely time of it, actually. The eternal student, sort of thing.'

'Has she been at it for a long time?'

'Long enough to have produced three economists, if you ask me.'

'It's like that, is it?'

'In a way.'

'In what way, Dick?'

'Well, you know the sort of thing – parties galore, trips to the Continent, boys, weekends, the lot.'

'She didn't altogether fool me. Thought she had some sort of life. I don't think she likes me. How about you?'

'Oh, we get along. Year in, year out. We've both been with the old lady for the better part of seven years.'

'I gather, tell me if I'm wrong, that she's rather the old lady's girl. Is she?'

'That's a peculiar question. What sort of an answer do you want, Johnnie?'

'They're both Third Programme, aren't they?'

'Oh, that!' Giggles. Giggles mixing with the squelchy noises of wet cotton and soap flakes. 'Yes. They do meet there. But only once in a while.'

'Pretty little effort, Dick. Why haven't you snapped it up? Seven years is a long time.'

'Never gave it a thought.'

'Don't you believe in East meeting West and may be even more?' Another tense look. His eyes narrow and then relax. In a flash.

'I'm not prejudiced in any way, Johnnie, except perhaps in one way: I can't stand poverty. Poverty of any kind.'

'You're fixed all right, aren't you?'

'I've got a job, if that's what you mean.'

Here's another tense moment. Perhaps, the most tense of all three, since we've met today. Must find out more about Dick. He's definitely not a fish-face. Anxious? May be. Has all the nervous energy of his class, or rather his class come-down-to-ground-floor level.

'Yes, I suppose that's what I mean.'

'How about you, Johnnie?'

'I wait on tables in a night club. Three-to-eleven affair in Oxford Circus.'

'Sounds interesting. What's the chance of my getting a job?' Shy chuckle. Yet warm and affectionate.

'You wouldn't like it, really.'

'How d'you know?'

'Well, for one thing it's a West Indian –'

'What's wrong with that?'

'Nothing's wrong.' Pause, nervous, caught-out kind. Dick's all right. Made a silly slip there, didn't I? 'Lots of G.I.s, pros, and the rest. Damn' nice boss, though.'

'The pros and G.I.s aren't nice?'

'Didn't mean it that way.'

'Did you know, Johnnie, that you've got more prejudice than you'd hope for!'

'Think so?'

'Oh, yes. More than you realize.'

'I'm sure I know where I got it from.'

'Where?'

'Never mind.'

'Guess I'd better hold on to my prejudice against poverty and leave you to yours. I'd love to see your place. That's if I can get in.'

'Don't see why not. I can sign you in as my guest, any old time you want.'

'I suppose I'll be frisked before they admit me?' Good-natured giggles.

'Not for offensive weapons or dope. Only for the necessary, may be. Must keep the cash register busy, you know, or else.'

Basin is unplugged. Gurgling screams of soapy water. Flashing hands. Dick departing.

'Watch the dancing girls, Johnnie! See you again.'

★   ★   ★

Sunday morning. The unmarried married couple's sitting-room door is ajar. They collect the rent for the old lady. They scrub for the old lady. They sometimes cook for the old lady. They bank for the old lady. They spy for the old lady. They hate the old lady.

Let's hope I can get through here. Ought to be able to get by them without mention of last week's non-payment. They know I'll pay. Who're they to take a stand about lack of honour or lack of responsibility, or – ?

'Is that you, Mr Sobert?'

'Yes, Mrs Trado.'

'Come in for a moment, will, you.'

Furniture. Nice hire-purchase look about it.

Sexy-boy Trado is sprawling in an armchair. Quite obviously reading *The Observer*. Quotes Ken Tynan the way a Jamaican peasant quotes the Bible. Sexy-girl Trado is toying with the handle of the old lady's vacuum-cleaner. Also sprawling in armchair number two. Carpet by mantelpiece a trifle threadbare; just the spot where jolly Trado takes his stand after a hard night at the pub and lays down the law on anything *The Observer* had already made clear to him the Sunday before.

In the left-hand corner, a delightful tortoiseshell cat, curled protectively against the thick Sunday-newspaper atmosphere. Multicoloured cushions. Ubiquitous Penguins, little reviews, Thomas Manns, Evelyn Waughs, and precious back numbers of *Horizon*.

Oh, man! Am I not glad I'm a bloody waiter!

All protective colouring. All that keeping up with the dead literary Joneses – museum bait.

'Well, Mr Sobert, aren't you a little behind, this time; last week's and now this week's?' Greta Garbo Trado croaks.

I'm sure she got that husky projection from standing in the queue outside the Everyman in last week's downpour. Culture martyr!

'I'm sorry, Mrs Trado. Tomorrow evening. As soon as I leave the club. I'll let you have both weeks.'

'You do come in rather late, but I suppose we'll wait up for you.'

'I'm sorry.' Not really sorry, at all. And who is she fooling when she talks about all this 'rather late' business? Bloody night hawk! Never puts out the light before four most mornings.

'Look, Sobert, old chap! We can't very well tell the old lady that we're sorry, you know,' pipes up Evelyn Waugh Trado. 'We rented you that room because the old lady wants the money. We aren't asking too much of you, are we?'

You're asking nothing, Thomas Mann. You're just talking too damn' much. That's all. Nice mess of contradictions, you are.

Boy with scruples; boy without! Boy with an intellect; boy without! Man who's married; man who isn't!

Ignore him.

'If that's all, Mrs Trado, may I leave now? I've got to go –'

'You haven't, you know,' pipes Horizon Trado once more. 'What you really have to do is try not to let this sort of thing happen again.'

Ignore him. He's lonely. He's anxious. He's insecure. He's bisexual. He's unhappy. He's anything. For God's sake, just don't do anything stupid. Hold on, boy!

'You see, Mr Sobert,' his wife tries to slip in again, 'we've had more than our fair share of students and their arrears in this house. Positively nerve-racking. Mountains of debts. The chap who had your room left us at the dead of night. He even moved pieces of the old lady's furniture. Arrears, twenty-seven pounds. And, of course, don't get us wrong, but one always finds that coloured tenants are prone to this kind of thing.'

'One hears the same stories about Finns and Falkland Islanders, too, Mrs Trado.'

'Damn' nonsense!' screeches Trado. 'This sort of vandalism is obviously a coloured student's idea of ragging or something. He gets some sort of political satisfaction out of it. Sort of Colonial versus Imperialist!' He seethes and rests. Ten seconds. Up again. Renewed strength. 'Sobert, we're watching you closely. No funny tricks, now.'

Can't let this jackass get away with all this! Might as well jump him and be over with it. Surely, it's the only way to deal with a crap hound like Trado. Of course, there's no use behaving like a *civilized chap.* No use behaving the way my mother would want me to, responsibly and politely; the way she would be proud of; the way a *little gentleman* is brought up to behave; the way up to the bloody stars! I'll just mess his face about a bit; and as I'm about it, I might as well smash his little library-cum-castle of a room. Won't touch Mrs Trado, though. Wouldn't do to –

'I do hope you've understood what I've said, Sobert? There aren't many houses in Hampstead that would have your kind; you know that, don't you? You must try to meet us halfway. After all, we are running a hell of a risk as it is. And besides, the old lady –'

24

'It's all right, Gerald. I think Mr Sobert realizes our position. He has promised to settle up on Monday. I'm sure he won't let us down. Will you, Mr Sobert?'

'If he does, he'll be spoiling his own chances. As far as I can see, there's no problem. It's purely a matter that rests with his own sense of responsibility.'

Pulpy pause. The room is swimming. Ubiquitous Penguins fuse into a greenish-red blur. Trado takes up the tirade once more.

'Another thing, Sobert…Your entertaining visitors after eleven o'clock is something I consider quite cowardly. You were told when you applied for the room that the old lady strictly forbids lady visitors to call on gentlemen tenants after seven in the evening. She also forbids gentlemen calling on lady tenants after the same hour. You were told all this, and yet you've had women in your room as late as two o'clock!'

'Gerald, could we discuss that matter another time? I'm sure Mr Sobert understands.'

'Does he? I wonder?'

Hit him! Hit him murderously hard and be done with it. Bash whatever little brains he has left and feel like a man afterwards. There's only one way to get out of this with any satisfaction, and it is done with a touch of violence. Not enough to land in prison. Just enough to restore the balance of power. That's all. Drive him a nice one in the mouth, and two swift ones in the guts. There are other rooms. All over the same precious Hampstead! Hit the bloody man!

'Where are you going to? Sobert? Sobert!'

Ignore the ass. Ignore him and his blasted question. Do what you have to do. Do it!

'Sobert! I'm talking to you! Come back here!'

'Oh, Gerald. Leave him alone. Let him go. You've been quite beastly to him. As a matter of fact, I think you've gone too far. Far too far, Gerald!'

Climbing the stairs to my room. Climbing away from at least six months in somewhere or the other, rent free. Door knob feels like Trado's head. Cold. Round. Easily destroyed. Wrenched off and discarded at the back of the house.

Climbing away from Trado? What's caused me to behave like an idiotic nigger-coward? My mother? No! Not at all. The result would be different. I'd be simply a *civilized coward*, then. A rather whitewashed nig with lots of *coolth*!

Of course, he's in the right. He's only asking for two weeks' rent. He's the lawful collector of two weeks' rent. That's all. I owe him three pounds. No, I don't! I owe the old lady three pounds. He's still asking for what's his: the old lady's, I mean.

Didn't have to ask for it in that way, though. Of course, he didn't have to! And he damn' well knows that, too. And little does he know I know that he knows.

There aren't many houses in Hampstead that would have your kind. On whose behalf is he really talking? How dare he represent anybody! Ponce with an approved accent!

Ought to rest for a while. Get ready for work in good time. Seven to ten, tonight. Thank God quickly for that! Still, might make a few tips. Help out with the Trado crisis. I'll have to borrow a fiver. Off whom? Better touch the boss. Poor rich Sandra. Poor white Sandra with a West Indian-G.I. world in her own native Oxford Circus. I wonder if a fiver's too little a touch for the first time? Might not get it, at all. Ten quid's too much of a surprise. Better come clean; better play it from the shoulder: owe rent…two weeks…can't pay…a bit ashamed about it…please! That ought to be all right, really. My salary's a damn' good… Good what? Good for whom? Sandra? Sheer crap, that! Sandra lends me ten – she pays me two a week. What kind of jackass would she be to entertain such a bastard of a risk? No. I'll ask for five. And I'll tell her why I need it. I'll tell her that I need the extra two to see me through. I'll promise to pay in two weeks. *Bank of England; I promise to pay the Bearer on Demand the sum of Five Pounds – serial number and signature of the Chief Cashier.* And it's no dream. It's my great big fat slice of decency. Honour (Boy Scouts' and Girl Guides' style). Of course I need it. Who doesn't need to be reassured constantly about things like integrity, paybackableness, honour, the-shape-of-the-real-gentleman-to-come. The trouble is that a real gentleman seldom has to borrow a fiver for a thing like rent.

Forget Trado and get ready for the fiver.

Trado's not even the front page of *The Times*.

2

A West Indian night club in Oxford Circus; must cling to something West Indian – coward enough not to try elsewhere. Two pounds a week and four thousand miles away from…five pounds to get in three hours…working and begging in a breath.

'Hey, Johnnie!'

Pretend not to hear. A second call, a better tip.

'Hey, Pres! Johnnie!'

Gracious G.I. flattery. Pres for President. Me, a president. Of what?

'Hey, Johnnie! Two on the rocks and a lager. O.K.?'

'Coming up, Sarge!'

Coming and hoping the tip's nice and fabulously American overseas. The G.I.'s St Francis of post-Hitler Europe; the five pounds for everybody's rent. Bloody thought!

'Thanks, Pres. The lager's for the chick. Rocks for us, over here.' Pause. 'Now, what about one for you, Johnnie?'

'Thanks, Sarge.'

'Crazy, man! Drink a…drink what you want, for Pete's sake, Johnnie.'

'A Scotch all right by you?'

'Cool, Johnnie! What's the grab in all?'

'Eleven shillings.'

'Great! Here's a crisp ten and a silver one to go with it. And one-and-sixpence for you, my man. Right?'

'But you've offered me a drink already, Sarge.'

'Won't get rich that way, Johnnie. No, sir, you simply won't.'

'Just thought you…Thanks, Sarge.'

Crawl back to the bar. Biddy pours ginger ale into a whisky glass and I raise it and thank St Francis, again. St Francis smiles and says: 'Cool, man! Cool!'

Sixpence goes into the till. Two-and-six into my pocket plus one-and-six tip; and ginger ale into a gurgling belly.

Biddy turns her dollar-sign eyes towards me and bleats, 'I'm a woman, Buster, and I know how to take a G.I. or any other man for that matter, but you waiters certainly know how, don't you?'

'Jealous?'

'What's eating you, Johnnie?'

'The age of innocence.'

'Oh. You're in one of those, are you. Don't pay to be nasty, you know, Johnnie. What's wrong?'

'Nothing.'

'Nothing means something. "So-so" means not a damn' thing. "Sort of" is the same thing. All that Jamaican language display simply ruins me.'

'You're American enough for a blasted Cockney. Aren't you?'

'All right. Never mind. Don't throw your chips around the floor. Customers might get splinters.'

'Seen Sandra?'

'Look, Johnnie, I serve the drinks here. Sandra pays me. Pays you, too. That's all I want to know.'

'All right, all right.'

'In trouble, Johnnie?'

'Yes and no.'

'Money?'

'Yes.'

'How much?'

'Mind your own business. You're only the barmaid. Remember?'

'How much, Johnnie?'

'You haven't enough, in any case. Thanks all the same.'

'I said, how much?'

'Five pounds.'

'When are you paying it back?'

'Why?'

'I asked you a simple question.'

'All right. I'll pay back a fortnight tonight.'

'Good deal. I'll let you have it in a sec.'

'Why're you doing this for me, Biddy?'

Pause. Dollar-sign eyes melt into eyes. Strange softness results across her face like a flush of fever-bumps.

'Don't you know why, Johnnie?'

Helpful distraction coming up like a windrush.

Great liquid rustle of taffeta! Dior! Affluence! Assurance! And in walks Sandra. Up to her chin in the good life. And swoops up to the bar.

'And why have you two got on your Good Friday faces? What's the till reading, Biddy?'

'Just a minute, Sandra.'

'How's our favourite waiter?'

'Fine, thanks, Sandra. Fine.'

'You don't sound sure about that. Nice and depressed, again eh?'

'Not really.'

'Haven't heard from home?'

'It's not that.'

'O.K. What d'you want this time?'

'Well...'

'Well, what? How much?'

'I don't like asking you this sort of thing, Sandra. Honestly. But...'

'How much?'

'Five.'

'Until when?'

'Fortnight.'

'All right. Done.'

Biddy returns. Tells Sandra that the till reads £13 10s. 6d. Sandra says something about 'the bloody Sunday trade'. Then:

'Let Johnnie have a fiver, Biddy. Put a slip in the till, will you!'

'But Sandra, I just prom— All right.'

Silence and loud stares between the two benefactresses. In matters of this sort, all women have the same age, the same agelessness, same softness, same vulnerability. And God knows that I'm not playing Biddy off on Sandra. For that matter I'm playing neither of them.

'Thanks, Sandra. Thanks a lot.'

'That's all right, Johnnie. Hustle some of those low lifes in the corner over there, will you. Tell them a kip's impossible without paying dear for it. And push the "shorts", for God's sake.'

'Right.'

Two weeks to repay a debt which has to be earned on two floors, ground and basement, between fast Fridays and faster

Saturdays. Will have to employ the King George nig's coolth and aplomb to extract the necessary from a roomful of Uncle Sam's nigs. Nig against nig! It's a game of split cultures played at low level, very low level. All Nigs Unite! Sounds silly, enough, doesn't it. Almost as bad as that Wright writer hoping to be embraced in West Africa and not even getting an invitation to dinner. What did he expect? Absolute recognition. And smelling of Old Spice, Wrigley's Gum, Arrow linen and Old Crow. The South's damn' far away from Paris! Damn' far away from West Africa. Poor privileged prospector. What did he really expect to find, anyway? A slice of very green pastures crawling with Cadillacs! All Sam's chillun waiting for the great black – sorry off-white – writer to preach *pax vobiscum* to them.

The air's so clean now that Sandra's fiver is almost as good as repaid. No conscience.

My God, if Trado ever saw that table over there, he'd drop dead. Six. Three like Trado and three like me. All six keenly aware of the business in hand. Oodles of petting and sweating. Not a single soul is odd bedfellow out. Trado, d'you know something? Tell you right now. Leave them alone; and me, too. The whole crisis is bigger than you. Older than you. And more human than you. All you've got to do is leave them to the lynching rope of the Southern States. They'll separate them, all right. The chaff from the chaff.

'Pres! This side, my man!'

'Coming up!'

Of course, I'm coming up. The enemy and I. We must use each other in this time of crisis. Must see each other's nerves. Each other's wives. Each other's arms. Each other's conference tables.

'Hey, Johnnie! What about getting me a little fix, man? Play it nice and creepy daddy. I'll see you right for sure.'

'Don't get me wrong, but I don't deal, Pres.'

President calls president out into the open for a little joy ride. 'Hey dig, Johnnie! I reckon, man, that you're an ice block, managing the boys when they get into town. You know? When the Base is behind us, man, you take care of us and pave the way to glory! Glory, man! Vous dig?'

'Look, Pres. I don't deal.'

'Can't you whisper a name?'

'No.'

'What about the Tin Whistle?'

'I didn't know he dealt in ——'

'Now dig, Pres. Grab me a fix from the old Tin Whistle and I'll see you go straight next time I'm in. O.K.?'

'I'm sorry. Must leave you now. Table's calling.'

Wonderful, tempting offer. When Pres comes down from the Base, next time, it could mean anything from a typewriter to a pair of cuff-links. Doesn't matter, really. Other risks in the sea. Lesser ones, too.

'Say, Johnnie, could you come over here a minute?'

Well-behaved English customer. Sorry, 'member', I mean. Only that kind in here. *Members only.* Terribly well tailored. Well-tied club tie. Well-perfumed young lady presumably from a well-ordered home in S.W. somewhere.

'Yes?'

'Johnnie, old man, can we arrange anything tonight?'

'The usual?'

'Yes.'

'When and how much?'

'Oh, not particular, really. Leave it to you.'

'Shan't be coming, though.'

'Oh. Why?'

'If you're a procurer, do you have to wallow in it?'

'Suit yourself. Lots of food and good stock of Scotch. And the other.'

'Is she in the *spread*?'

'Yes. She's game, little darling.'

'How many boys this time?'

'Up to you, Johnnie. Three or five.'

'Two boys are handy right now, I think. Want to meet them?'

'No. Trust you, old man. Anything you say.'

'Right. They'll be there. Better have a drink to kill the suspicion.'

'Fine. Scotch for the lady and a pink gin for me. And you?'

'Scotch, please.'

Poor, silly, pretty thing's going to be shown just how lavish night life can be! Just how lavish matters like debauchery and frenzy can be. Just how terribly good these black chaps are. Poor girl! Yet she might like it very much indeed. Hope so, for her sake. For her mother's sake. For her vanity's sake. For the sake of the black operator's vanity, too. Even for the sake of 'old school tie' and his prospecting manners.

Wonder what kind of slavery *they* would call this operation? White? Black? Off-white? Tan?

Must hustle harder. Time's running out. An hour to go. Same faces. Same coy disgraces. Before launching another offensive into G.I. susceptibilities, I'd better see how deep Biddy's wound is.

'Biddy, you crow, you! How much d'you expect to take home with you tonight? Leave a little in the till, for a float, will you!'

A wild off-the-mark entrance.

Biddy believes in love at any sight. Easily bought with all brands of tears. Hamlet's mother's tears. Brother Crocodile's. Alice's. Even precious G.I. tears.

'Why don't you take a flying jump, Johnnie! It would clean the air. But for good, man!' Biddy's Brooklynese is an item the United Nations Assembly ought to take seriously when contemplating closer relations between American Sam and English John. Give her half a chance and she'll get her jargon into the nearest approved dictionary. Smart girl, though. Likes tears and flowers. Southern Comfort and P.X. pocket books. Near-bums and near-crises. Likes people, I think, when all's said and done.

'Biddy, my love. Can you tell me why I stick it down here? Is it your ugly face and charming manners? Is it your love of black men? Your love of white men? Green and blue men? Is it your blotting-paper shoulder? Tell me, love.'

'Your chip's getting so large, man, that I can't see your face for the beam that's swinging in front of it. You're not normally like this. What's eating you?'

'I'll tell you in one word, Biddy. Compromise.'

'I don't follow.'

'I find that I can't go the whole hog with a damn' thing. Can't see a thing to its logical end. Every step I make, I'm constantly reminding myself that the mores are different.'

'Mores? What's that?'

'Habits and customs. You know what I mean.'

'You could have said habits and customs, in the first place. All right, go on.'

'You know something, Biddy? Mother Country as a catchword is no catch. One lies differently and for a million different results. Can't be too warm or free lest you're blacklisted as being irresponsible and madly *outside*.'

'Didn't you come over with too many expectations, Johnnie? After all, we are never aware of being a mother to you all. Maybe some Whitehall goofs made you out there feel the mother thing and believe in it. But not so with us in this country. Everyday English people couldn't care less. They themselves are in need of mothering just as much as you are. In any case, why should we really have this "open white soul" outlook? We're ignorant about you, and you expect too much. That's how I see it.'

'Nothing more to it, eh?'

'What more is there? We're all self-seeking, selfish, security-hunting types. Yours and mine. I guess you could call it one of the human things that we all have in common. Honestly, your type of West Indian always gets on my pip. Twisted like mad. You think this way this minute, then you slip off the next minute to some other point or the other. And d'you know something, Johnnie? The enemy, as you and your kind call us, isn't like that. Nearly all of us are as conservative as hell. Especially when it comes to accepting foreigners.'

'That's a strong offbeat word for British subjects, isn't it?'

'All right, all right. In a minute you'll ask me whether the American is a foreigner or not. And I'll say, No! N-O!'

'What's he, then?'

'He's the part of us that's made good. The youngest in the family sort of thing.'

'The one who didn't get into the Grammar School but made the University in the long run, eh?'

'What's that got to do with it?'

'Nothing, really. I was just thinking of the kind of Englishman who's just as foreign in his own country as a Finn would be here. You know, the one cursed on the tongue. Your set. Even though you don't speak through your teeth. When he *makes good*, what happens? Isn't he a threat?'

'You're crackers, honestly! Just like Sandra as a matter of fact.'

'Crackers? Economics, Biddy! Money, money, money! Grasping lot! Of course you resent the American presence. But you like the aid it spews around, don't you? Why should little presences like the Africans or West Indians actually get your respect or regard? You can't get a bloody thing more out of them. Sugar isn't even a problem any more. Of course, I agree with you. We're crackers to believe in the Mother Country crap. We're crackers to expect...Oh! Never mind!'

'You West Indians do have a lot of Hyde Park in you, haven't you?'

'And you a bit of America, I suppose.'

Talking to Biddy is like talking to one's bathroom mirror. Everything you don't say or say comes back at you plus the reflection of one's naked body. Like talking to her, in spite of everything. Honesty is Biddy and Biddy's a damn' good policy for any taker.

Better wander around and work for a fiver – that's also a form of honesty, got in the dishonest way. The way of the immigrant worm.

I wonder why Biddy resents Sandra so very much. They have their own worlds, or their own tested idea of happiness on a bed. In a way, Biddy reminds me of Dick. Fallen stones who never caught the birds. The birds are still playing about freely. Just wait until their birds really get shot to pieces.

'Can I help anybody get nice and drunk on this very English Sunday evening? More Scotch, Pres? Lagers?'

'Hey, hold it now, Johnnie-O! You was just puttin' down a mess o' living there. How's about a repeat, man? Send me, Mr Poet-Man! Send me!'

'All right. I'll make out, Pres, as though you haven't even heard it for the millionth time.'

All jobs done well are done by actors. Could be in prison. Anywhere. If you can't play the fool or Hamlet you're just a bloody cipher as far as the job's concerned. Here goes for the millionth and first time!

'Not altogether dejected and rejected cousins of Old England and incidentally sons of your own very Un-United States of America. I'm here to see to your innocent livers and unbloodshot eyes. Trust me, and within the hour you'll all be feeling positively reckless. Shockingly snazzy!'

Loud cadaverous applause. Nig entertains nig at first nig's expense. (O.K., so you say that it can be done by the Japanese or the Swedish or the French – but when a nig does it to a nig the parody's outrageously Third Programme.)

'Hey dig, Johnny! Dig! We'll be wanting a whole shoot o' Scotch and beers, man. Take the count and get something for yourself. O.K.?'

'Thank you, Pres! Thanks.'

Christ! Who's worse? The pestilential Trados of Hampstead, Swiss Cottage, unphoenix-like Bloomsbury, Broadcasting House, W.1, or the Soberts of three hundred years' British colonial-activity?

At last, I've admitted it. We all operate from the same bloody motives. Behind our eyes, we're one! Hurrah! We're one! I've thought it at last! The whole human race is saved behind my own two eyes! *Hurrah for the intellect of a black man! Hurrah for the intellect of a white man! Hurrah for God's own intellect!* Crap!

'Everything all right, Johnnie?'

'Yes, Sandra. Slow and expensive. D'you want me to go downstairs, now?'

'No. Might as well hold on here. *The other* can cope without you. Music draws them in any case. Holding them up here is a toughie, isn't it?'

'Well, sort of. Calls for a little blarney and playing up to them.'

'That's your speciality, isn't it? Sometimes I think you're a Dublin man in disguise, Johnnie. I've listened to your line of patter and, believe me, you're the most.'

Whenever Sandra waxes G.I. it always sounds like the result of an American language course taken along the Tottenham Court Road. I'm the 'most'; the 'least' she means, really. The least of her worries, anyway. Perhaps the 'most' in entertainment and tax value to the club; but that's all. Lucky Johnnie! Got my fiver; got the pluck to plunk it down in the literary-review softness of

Trado's palm when the time comes. Getting a few tips; giving a few laughs; seeing the curious parade around the square for the millionth time. Things are great. I'm a very happy man! What more could I really want? Total independence for my little archipelago of a territory? More loans for the regional governments? More enthusiasm for the publication and sale of regional books within the region? More adult education? More exchange among islands of island-problems and debates? Of course not. I'm basically selfish. Couldn't-care-less hunter of rent money and bus fares kind I am, really. Not interested in the land, in agricultural improvement and development. Not conscious of nationalism and growth and pride and independence and wealth and the rest. Used to be interested in the Yankee dollar earned on farms in the South; interested now only in the punctured pound acquired by magic in industrial England. Who or what made me this way, I'd hate to say. Maybe I'll never know. Must ask Sandra if she knows. Or Biddy. Or Mrs Trado. Damn' well won't ask Trado, simply because he'd give me an answer which would be accurate and provoking.

'Johnnie?'

'Coming, Biddy.'

Weave a path to the bar through the tangled tracks of G.I. shoes, Dolcis cast-offs, empty, squelchy, cellophaned packets of Luckies, king-size variety of others; to the bar of delight and deceit. Stand easy and wait on the goodness of a troubled barmaid. Fire away, Joan of Arc Biddy!

'Will you call last orders, Johnnie? It's time, I think.'

'Sure.'

'Oh, before you go. Promise to do the bottles for me tonight. I get the shivers when the other does them. All right?'

'Sure.'

The other. The other waiter. Biddy certainly knows how to shorten things; how to speak racy dialogue; how to simplify matters of men and moment. Sandra, too.

'Time, please! Place your last orders! Last orders! Last orders, everybody!'

Last orders! Last tips, too. Last minutes to do any dealing, for some people. For others it's their last moments to arrange to make a G.I.

a temporary home with sweaty bedsheets and cracked porcelain. For Biddy, it means nervous fingers counting the night's takings. For Sandra, the same. She'll be checking not counting. And a little more. For Sandra it also means a problem of how to spend all the takings on the same night higher up the road in another palace for the sleep-shy population of owners, big bosses, straw bosses, starlets, and other would-be *News of the World* bait.

Bottles are being put away, one by one, expensive label after expensive label. Members are being hustled off the premises. Sandra's hour has arrived. The till's the real hero now. It's a sickly sweet pleasure to watch Sandra's anxious, explosive eyes. They seem to be saying: Rich for one night at the palace-doors, up the road; genuine waiter service, floor show, an Alpine menu in a trembling hand; death in every ashtray.

'Got the key, Biddy?'

'Yes. Just a moment, Sandra. In my bag somewhere.'

'Johnnie?'

'Yes, Sandra?'

'Going straight home now?'

'Think so. Why?'

'Nothing. I thought you had a little business to attend to.'

'Oh, that! No. Gave the boys the address and ducked out gracelessly. Haven't got to watch over them, as well, have I?'

Pause. Wry laughter. For one.

'Tell me. How did you know about it, Sandra?'

'Oh, I get to know most things. Have to, you know.'

Up comes poor, fortunate Biddy. Biddy and the important key. Always makes Biddy frightened. The key to the den of dollars and diluted Scotch. Biddy's the only one with a sense of keymanship in the establishment. So, let her be the keeper. Makes her a real person, somehow. Security and all the rest of the trappings.

'Here we are, Sandra. Ready?'

'Think so. How about you, Johnnie?'

'Sure.'

Key makes the final noise of the night and we're off. Sandra to her palace; Biddy to her dreams and keymanship; and I to Trado the Profound.

What a shock's in store for Parnassus Trado!

Ten-thirty, and Oxford Street with its squeaking silences under shutters. Wonderland beacons continue their ogling unashamedly with the traffic lights. Sticky, biscuit-sweet, soggy lovers huddle together in a make-believe which excludes Mom and Pop.

Can feel the presence of cash registers along the street. Mania for presences. But this is different. The moment is magic. The weightiness is different. It's haunting. Metallic buddha kind of weightiness. Plump and couchant, in a way. A threat. Hundreds of presences on both sides of the street. Yet it's always a joy to know that they're out of action and are unable at the moment *to make it off you*; to suck you in and spit you out minus your bus fare. Doesn't really matter, does it? They'll catch you early Monday morning, just the same. Catch you with their pre-National Service male attendants and pimply sales girls, their thin, grubby, last-night collars and cigarette-stained forefingers. They'll catch you with brisk American-style sales-patter salted intermittently with brash Cockney aplomb. And who doesn't really want to be caught at some time or the other? There's a nice warm feeling gurgling inside when you say: 'Look at this, my dear. Selfridge's for nine-and-eleven. Would've had to pay anything up to twelve-and-six along Regent Street.' And of course you've already docked two-and-seven off the twelve-and-six merely to feel nice and warm inside, haven't you?

Up Baker Street and heading for the bus-stop. Three No. 13 buses are playing tag in the opposite direction. Three times thirteen, thirty-nine. Thirty-nine steps away from Hampstead. Can't get a No. 13 at this hour without spending fifteen minutes in a mad daydream which helps to pass the wait away, as Biddy would say. What else would Biddy say? I wonder.

Astringent faces in the queue; behind me clock-faces, all with teatime written over them – teatime past and teatime to come. What a good shot of Jamaican white rum wouldn't do for them is nobody's business! Come on, now, we must learn to love our neighbours as ourselves. Learn to be tolerant (good word that! A damn' good British-made word!); learn to wait and wait and wait.

Learn to tighten the belt and taste honey in bread and water. No, son-son, a little gentleman never says such things. A real gentleman takes off his hat when he's under a roof. He gets up and offers his seat to a lady. He wears well-polished and shiny shoes. He speaks quietly in public places. He smiles when things are difficult. He smiles when things are worse. He smiles always. Tips his hat. Holds the door open for ladies to pass (note, 'ladies'). Always brushes his teeth three times a day, takes his church worship seriously. Takes a bride and not a floozie. (Where to? I wonder!) Takes his time when he eats. Masticates at least twenty times before swallowing a mouthful. Never gulps or ever swallows for that matter; merely coaxes the stuff to the back of the mouth and lets it slip down gently, almost imperceptibly.

A gentleman is the No. 13 bus, really. He's dreadfully slow in coming forward. Yet a gentleman is more than a bus. In wartime he serves, readily. He gets his gentle colonial ass scorched with bullets. He dies like a gentleman – boots highly polished, clean teeth, hair well parted, back erect, bills all paid-up, charitable thoughts about his worst neighbours, church dues up-to-date, a clean shirt on, tie in place, and a broad warm smile on his face.

Ah! The bus, at last. Not packed out, thank God. Up the street. Park Road. Lord's. Cricket, Lovely Cricket! *Great big dirty sawn-off petrol drums and calypso feet on hallowed English turf in celebration over a game which we taught them. How dare they! How dare they come here and crow over us. And in such a pagan fashion – drums, war dances and all! Filthy ritual! Nothing to do with cricket. Nothing whatsoever!*

Finchley Road. Swiss Cottage. John Barnes. Station. West End Lane. Heath Drive. Off before I'm reminded gently, 'Where did you say you wanted to go, sir?'

Down my street with the dream drifting away from me. Empty again. Pavement rises to meet me. Drains. Then no more drains. Man approaching with half the pub hauling him backwards. Sweet feeling that. Sweeter on somebody else's generosity. Man and I; we are, now, in direct line of pub-fumes. He gestures. Funny thing, that any time a drunk gestures it looks indecent. Even an outstretched hand looks like an offensive pose, a reminder of the phallus possibly. We're in line with each other.

Have stopped. His hand is floating all over my shoulder. Of course, he's not a Blimp. He's just mellow and looks terribly un-English. That's all.

'Where d'you come from, young man? Eh? Where? Come on, answer smartly, now. I won't bite you, you know.'

'I hope you won't. Jamaica.'

'Ah? Good place. Very nice people. Very nice indeed. Just left one as a matter of fact. Lovely teeth. Lovely teeth. Smiles all over the place.'

Look into a horse's mouth and you can tell his age.

He's as high as a kite.

'What the hell are you doing in this rain-sodden country of ours, eh? Student, I suppose.'

'No.'

Really warming to me now. A glowing intimacy.

'Tell me something. You've got some very beautiful women, haven't you? Wonderful skin. Nice high backsides. Strong devils, I bet?'

'Yes. Yes, of course.'

Pause that refreshes. Fumes. Miss the drains. How can I get out of this? Just walk away, of course. Simple. I'll do that.

'I say! Wait a minute!'

'I'm sorry, but I must go now.'

Tiny shuffle up to me. Hand, again. This time, right round the neck. Breathing's slightly asthmatic. Tobacco shirt-front. Dewlapped face. Eyes sunken and glazed. Stocky body. Three to four inches taller than I am. Not a giant by any means. I'm waiting. Not embarrassing, to me either. I'm rather amused in a way. Entertained is the better word.

'Listen, carefully. Couldn't you and I get a party going at my place? Not far from here. Flask Walk. All you'd have to do is get a couple of your girls to come along. I've got the rest. What d'you say?'

'Sorry.'

'Be a sport! Come on!'

'I must get home now.'

'You look like an intelligent chap. Surely it ought to be easy for you to arrange a party.'

'Another time.'

'Tell you what. How about Tuesday evening? At my flat.'

'Where's your flat?'

Slight pause. A new idea dawning.

'I have a better plan. Let's all meet in The Crown at nine and then I'll take you back afterwards.'

'Sure.'

'That's a date, then.'

'Fine. Tuesday.'

'Damn' good. Long to get my hands on one of those nigger wenches. Delightful people!'

Must remember never to drink in The Crown. Might meet this Flask Walk joker again. And that'd be too soon.

3

Approaching my little cabin in the fog with resounding footsteps along the cracked pavement. The club behind me and, in front, a fearless meeting with Trado. Bold swish-clicking noises of key in lock and leisurely pace up the stairs. Ever so sure of myself. Fiver in hand. Rent's under control.

I wonder if Miss Goolam Chops had a good, clean evening? No light under her door. Dick's away, I suppose. Driving out his guts in dead earnest. The old lady's in. Her smell is swirling around, all right. Around and around like Crusoe's pipe-smoke.

Up to my door, at last.

Turn of knob.

That's strange! Thought I had locked it. Search for key in pocket. Yes. It's there. Must have forgotten to use it. Yet, I seem to recall a clicking sound when I left to go to the club. Actually it doesn't matter, now. Door's open and bed's waiting.

Funny! Perfume. Where's that coming from? Couldn't care less. Bed. Can't be bothered to turn on the light. Sprawl across the eiderdown for a while. Tired like a workhorse, like an ancient marin…perfume's terribly strong! Smells like expensive stuff, too. Oh, well! Cross arms under the pillow and stare up at the camouflaged ceiling, a mosaic of curious shadows and shimmering lights sprinkled on the ceiling from the street-lamp blinking below the window-box. A very apt reminder of the results which the projector my brother and I made when we were children used to give us, when we held private showings to impress Mother on a Sunday evening. Poor Mother! Every new experiment would cost her at least two cinema fares and a shilling extra for nuts and ice-cream. The trouble was that our projector hardly did anything else but spill out light and shadow, simply because we never got around to making our own films. That's a laugh! We made a type of light and shadow cardboard lantern-slide, perforated all over; and that was as far as we ever got.

That crazy smell again. Smells like the perfume our double-whisky members wear to extension evenings at the club. I wonder how Sandra's making out with the takings? A nice cosy round of drinks ought to make a pleasant dent in the side of her handsome bag. Still, not to worry. There's always Biddy who'll fill it faithfully tomorrow. And me. And *the other.*

Funny! Feels like somebody's in the room with me. Distinct presence besides mine. Hold on to my easy panic for a while. Just nerves. Must be more tired than I think. Tired of bowing and scraping to an almighty lot of hedonists, lovelorn 'Presidents', drifters, hustlers, ten-bob ponces. Tired of Biddy's cow's eyes. Tired of the ginger ales and the slick hustling tricks. Tired of the masks. Tired of the cheap waiter's coat.

There's somebody in this room with me. I'm damn' sure of it. Perfume, again. Better sit up slowly and investigate. Sly look round can't hurt, can it? By the wardrobe first.

'Please, don't turn on the light!'

So I was right, after all.

'It's me. I must talk to you. I'm sorry about this, really. But, I couldn't sleep knowing that you were hurt by Gerald…by the things he said…the way he raved, and –'

'So, it's you, Mrs Trado.'

'Yes, Mr Sobert.'

I knew I had locked the door before I left. She must have used the copy in the hall, on the rack.

'Won't you be missed downstairs?'

'No. He's dead drunk.'

'Well, shall I turn on the light?'

'If you want to.'

'I think it might be best, considering the curfew.'

'Damn the curfew!'

'Fine by me. Damn the curfew as you say. Wouldn't you like to sit on the bed?'

'Thank you, I will.'

'Have you been waiting long?'

'A few minutes.'

'We'll have to talk quietly, of course. Wouldn't do to disturb the old lady below.'

An attempt at an easy chuckle. Doesn't come off.

'Damn the old lady, damn the curfew and damn everybody and everything.'

'You seem upset, Mrs Trado. What's wrong?'

Sucking silence. Somehow the perfume doesn't seem to be as strong as it was. Mrs Trado's quite obviously upset about something more than just her husband's tirade this afternoon. What could it be?

'I must tell you the whole story, Mr Sobert...'

'What story is this, Mrs Trado?'

'Well, it's about this afternoon's display of temper and horrid behaviour by Gerald.'

'I see.'

'You see, Mr Sobert, what you don't understand is this: Gerald resents everything about you. I suppose you'll understand when you've heard the reason for it. Well, to begin with: Quite a long time ago I used to be engaged to an African medical student who left me high and dry after his finals. He went off to the North of England. I traced him and found out that he had got nicely entangled with some dreadful Welsh girl or the other. In time, he left her as well and returned to Lagos. Gerald came into my life right after that. We were both caught up in a series of embarrassing situations...for one, he was married and penniless, and I was five months' pregnant –'

'But, Mrs Trado, d'you think you ought to be telling me all this? I mean, it's none of my business and –'

'That's just it, Mr Sobert. I was pregnant by Joseph – my "charming" African lover – and poor innocent Gerald thought that it was someone else. You see, I told him another story entirely. Well, anyway, the time for the showdown came and the baby was born. Everything was chaos. Gerald nearly killed me. My parents told me never to come near them again, never to write to them…'

'What happened to the child?'

'He's with an aunt of mine in Newcastle.'

'And the African?'

'Oh, he knows nothing about it.'

'I see.'

Bloody stupid thing to say, *I see*. What can I see, anyway? What else can I say to her? *Sorry*? Blessed lot of good that will do. No wonder Trado won't behave like a Brother Elk where I'm concerned. But, why should she hide in my room to tell me this? Oh, no! Not that. Of course not. I'm not her type in any case. No profession. No glamour to rub off on her. Slim chance she'd have to try a transfer on me if even she wanted to. I've got her wrong altogether. She's genuinely a good sort. Must have loved old Joseph, the witch-doctoring bastard! Guess she just wants me to know that I've got her in my corner. Better not say anything to hurt her. I'll listen and say the safe 'I see' and nod in the right places. Hope she can see me nod in the dark.

'Please don't cry, Mrs Trado. I know how you feel.'

'Do you? Do you really?'

'Yes. I think so.'

'And another thing, I'm not Mrs Trado. There is a Mrs Trado but I'm not her. Gerald sees to that. He no more wants a divorce than the man in the moon. All he wants with me is a nice cosy life in sin. Wash, cook, and sleep! And when he's drunk enough he either beats me or uses me as a sort of public convenience, or both.'

Better not say anything to that one. Let her go on. Trado the Strong Arm must have belted her this evening. Hope I wasn't the cause. Did she say anything in my favour? She seemed quite passive at this afternoon's party.

'Mr Sobert, all I can say is that I apologize about this afternoon.

Forgive us. Please. Gerald will meet his match one day. I'm damn' sure.'

Pause. A long wet pause. Gentle whoosh of perfume slips out and darts between us.

'Thanks, Mrs Trado.'

'Can't you call me Fiona?'

'Well – er – just for now, I will. Yes.'

'Good. It'll make me feel so much better, Johnnie.'

Fiona is a gentle name. Like Alice. Or like Vanice. Or like Felicity. Fiona. Poor woman. What shall I say now?

'I may call you Johnnie? Mayn't I?'

'Sure, Fiona.'

'All your callers ask for Mr Johnnie Sobert. Even Dick calls you Johnnie. Don't see why I shouldn't.' Tiny chuckle. 'What d'you intend doing in England?'

'Oh, anything really.'

'No plans?'

'Not yet.'

'Escaping like the rest of us, eh?'

'From what? I sometimes ask myself.'

'It's best to escape in your own country, they say. No passport. No passage to pay. No difference in climate.'

'Does sound good.'

'It's hell, actually.'

'Do you still think of Joseph?'

'Of course I do.'

'Have you forgiven him?'

'Could any woman in my position?'

'Don't suppose so.'

'Pride was his trouble, Johnnie. Pride, pure and simple. He had the whole of Africa on his back. He carried it around with him like a packhorse. I don't think he ever dropped it. Not even when he made love to me. At times, it would seem that he wanted me only as a sort of beating-stick for the white man's plunder of Africa, or something like that.'

'I think I understand.'

'And since we're on the subject, Johnnie, I might as well tell you that Joseph hated West Indians like poison. He used to refer to them as "halfies". He was always annoyed when I spoke to one of them at a party or at the Students' Centre. Somehow, I think he was envious of most of those with whom he had to study at the University. It was always, "A very clever Jamaican said…", or, "One of the privileged halfies made an ass of himself in the pub this evening".'

'Was he a clever man?'

'I think so. Got some gold medal or the other after his finals.'

'Doctors need a lot of tolerance and understanding from what I can gather.'

'I suppose he has got over a lot of his bitterness now. Success, you know. Makes us all more acceptable monsters.'

'Let's hope so. Nevertheless, I'd hate to have to go to him as a patient.'

'He was the first Negro in my life. And didn't I learn a few things about prejudice! D'you know, Johnnie, I'm being honest when I say that Joseph held more prejudice and rancour in his heart against white and black than you'd expect a despot to have. He was certainly an education to me. Quite an experience!'

'Oh, by the way, I've got the arrears. Would you like to have it now?'

'No. It would be better if you handed it over to Gerald. I don't think it would be fair for me to take away from his surprise and defeat, if you see what I mean.'

'D'you mean he doesn't expect me to have it by tomorrow?'

'Exactly.'

'I see.'

'Stay in this house long enough and you'll certainly see more! More than you'll believe, at that!'

A slight giggle and a draught of perfume. The meeting has gone on too long for comfort. She's so trusting and obviously pleasant that I'd better hold on and see what she's up to. I hope Werewolf Trado's still asleep. Hell! What if someone's listening outside? Someone like the old lady, for instance. What would I do? No lights! Tear stains. Fiona sitting on the bed beside me!

'Well, I must leave now.'

'Thanks for coming. I feel much better now that I know you're not –'

'I always wanted to have a chat with you, Johnnie, but what with the Gestapo system in this house, I've had to think better of it.'

'Gestapo system?'

'Yes. Don't you know?'

'What?'

'Well, for one, there's our dearest Shakuntala…'

'Who's she?'

'Miss Goolam, of course.'

'Is that her name? Really?'

'Hummingbird sound to it, isn't there? Then there's Dick.'

'No. Not Dick as well?'

'Yes. He's fallen from grace recently because he's refusing to play ball. But he was in, all right. Suppose he saw the folly of his ways and pulled out. You see, Johnnie, the old lady checks up on him, too. Poor Dick must have found out and decided that it wasn't worth it.'

That's a bit of a letdown. Yet he seems all right to me. Better watch out, though. But why should I? To hell with Mrs Witch-hunting Blount! She's not the only landlady in Hampstead. Think I'd like to blaze her for the sheer comfort of being considered one of her 'outsiders'. The time will come, no doubt. Maybe sooner than I think.

'Well, Fiona, thanks again.'

'That's all right.'

'May I ask a pointed question?'

'Go ahead.'

'When are you leaving him?'

'Gerald, you mean?'

'Yes.'

'Oh, I don't know.'

'It's like that, eh?'

'I suppose it is.'

Pause. Suppressed sighs. Tingling silence.

'Johnnie?'

'Yes.'

'In a way I'm rather like you, you know.'

'Yes. How?'

47

'I don't know where I'm going and I don't care a damn. The only difference actually is that I'm living in my own nasty country, and you're not.'

'Oh, but you're not right about the first part.'

'What d'you mean?'

'It's a long story, Fiona.'

'Will you tell me?'

'What, now?'

'If you want to.'

'No. I'd better leave it for another time, that's if you don't mind?'

Better go easy. After all, she's only asking a little thing. She's been good company. Fair and square with me and all that.

'All right, Johnnie. Another time, then.'

'Sorry. But it would be best if we met again…'

Hell. Hope she doesn't think I'm trapping her for a tryst.

'Under less pressure, eh?'

'Yes. Under less pressure.'

'Good…morning, isn't it? And thanks for listening. Thanks a lot, Johnnie. It meant a great deal to me.'

Creak of Blount's furnished bed springs. The intruder stands and surveys the cabin. Turns towards the door and turns around to face the bed again. She shakes her head and the spray of street light touches her profile and she becomes a silver coin for a moment.

'Before I go, I'd like to ask you one last question. May I?'

'Sure. Go ahead, Fiona. Hope it's nothing too difficult.'

Risk a smile in the dark. Ought to be worth six in the light if Trado were present. Smiles again. And now what's coming up? Fiona wanders across the room and stands in front of the larger of the two windows. She taps gently upon it. Turns to face me. Softly.

'Tell me, Johnnie, couldn't you do the same sort of thing just as successfully in your own country? And be even more comfortable while you're about it?'

'Do what thing? I've not mentioned what I want to do, have I? What's the "thing" you're referring to?'

'Don't be childish, Johnnie! Nobody bothers to take the journey that you've taken from the West Indies for sheer pointless escape. If you escape, there's always a plan at the end of it somewhere.'

'I see.'

Worrying silence.

'What are you going to do here that you couldn't do over there?'

'Live, I suppose.'

'Can't you do that in your own country? Surely, everyone manages to do that after a fashion. Don't they?'

'Not everyone, Fiona. Ask Gerald Trado, the Empire Loyalist, why! He's the type with the answer for that one. Besides, even if I don't have a plan, being here is plan enough for me. It's certainly education enough, among other things. Meeting a man like your Gerald soon provides all escapists with a bloody clever plan. Believe me, it does.'

'Bloodthirsty, aren't you?'

'Not in the least.'

'I'm sorry, but I did warn you. A pointed question! Remember?'

Gleeful chuckle.

'That's all right. I just tried to give you a fair answer.' Pause. No reply. 'Well, didn't I?'

'Did you, Johnnie?'

'I'll enlarge later. Right?'

'Will you really? I know your kind.'

'For God's sake, don't start thinking of me in terms of that witch-doctor of yours. At least he had a damned conventional plan. Pat as hell! Medicine can be most men's answer to travel to Britain, you know. Or the ever faithful Law. Or the factory job. Or street-cleaning.'

'Not so loud, Johnnie. Shh! Don't get upset. We can talk about it another time.'

'Sorry, Fiona.'

'We all have our sore point.'

'Yes. We have.'

Grey silence. Bleak breathing. And the shadows of Fiona's legs warping themselves across the armchair. Shouldn't have blown up like that.

'Look here, Fiona, I'll tell you what you want to know. Don't you think you'd better come back and sit down beside me? I might be tempted to blow up again.'

Mutual chuckles disperse the bleakness.

'Right, Johnnie. I will.'

'Can you imagine a middle class that doesn't exist, but is actually a part of the thinking of a people in a society? Oh, hell! What a bloody pompous way of putting it!'

'I don't understand you.'

'I'll explain.'

'Oh, wait a minute! You aren't going to tell me about middle-class morality, are you? Because if you are, let's not bother. Please. All I ever get from Gerald and his literary friends is an endless stream of speculations about their opinions on middle-class morality.'

'Morality? Yes. But not the middle-class bit. That's exactly what I want to say. There's no middle-class bit where I come from. Yet there's a sort of behaviour which adds up to it. Which damn' well strangles everybody. The thing doesn't exist, yet a tight bunch of people move and hope and act as if they're being guided by it.'

'I suppose it's my time to say "I see", isn't it?'

'Well, do you?'

'Not really, Johnnie. But how can I? I'm not a part of the society you're talking about. In any case, if your people think that they're middle class and they act, as you put it, towards that aim, then they're middle class. Aren't they?'

'How can they be, Fiona? How can they be when the society isn't ready for that kind of step forward? What we have is a suggestion of a middle class – the bare bones. A shadowy outline. Surely it takes much more than a hundred and twenty-eight years after the Abolition of Slavery for a middle class to evolve?'

'You sound terribly desperate, Johnnie. After all, we're not experts, you know.' Giggling teasingly. 'Before we jump to conclusions, we'd better consult a sociologist or the type best able to advise us on the matter. We might even ask one of Gerald's Brains Trust pals.'

I'll ignore that snub. Just press on and get it over with. She asked for it, anyway.

'That's my sore point, Fiona. That's my little monkey on the back.'

'But how has it affected your life over here?'

'It has affected my vanity. It has affected my conscience. When I look at your middle-class structure and I think of mine back there, I want to laugh and cry, all at once.'

'But that's not sensible, Johnnie! Britain's a nation of people, old and well formed. Too well formed, as a matter of fact. I can't see how you could possibly think of Jamaica in terms of this country!' Pause. Sweetly. 'But you're all right, Johnnie.'

'No. I'm not, Fiona. That's just it. Precisely. I'm the result of that misconception. That misconception plus what your gracious Gerald would call colonial endowment. Look! I'm unskilled. I'm puffed up with my own importance. I'm a drifter. A dreaming prig! And a coward into the bargain. A moral one, at that.'

'Isn't it a bit too easy to blame it on a frail thing like a system? After all, as you've said, a hundred and twenty-eight years isn't such a long time.'

'You mustn't get me wrong. Or rather, you mustn't get Jamaica's middle class wrong. There are a few families who're aspiring to a sort of middle-class position. In some weird way, these are ready for it. They have the necessary trappings, the deceitfulness, the narrowness, the smugness, the holier-than-thou attitudes – all this plus a deep-rooted working-class mentality. As far as I can see, working-class and slave-class skeletons-in-the-cupboard add up to the most ridiculous situation in the Caribbean Area.'

'That may be true, Johnnie. But how can that affect your life in England? You're removed from it now. Your values must have changed by this time. They might even be the same values that the English hold, for all I know!'

'My values haven't changed. Spotlighted, yes. You see, I'm an escaped product of this premature middle-class mess! With all the play-acting that goes with it, too.'

'Would you rather not be in your present position? Would you rather not be in it, at all?'

'What? Being neither one thing nor the other?'

'But, isn't that the West Indian problem? Not being totally anything identifiable? I mean, you're not Continental African and you're not anywhere near the other thing...'

'No real identity, eh?'

'Not as basic as all that, Johnnie. But almost. Don't you think? I mean, I listened to Joseph carefully when he talked about the African situation, and comparing his with yours, I can see clearly that you're in a vice. At least he has a solid reality which is his strength. His pride and joy, in fact. And my downfall, when he chose to use it as a weapon.'

'Where must I search for this reality, Fiona? Where does anybody actually come face to face with his national identity? Can you tell me that? Where?'

'That's difficult to say right off the bat, Johnnie, but, I do know that –'

'Listen to me, I walk around London and I see statues of this one and the other...I see litters of paintings in your museums and galleries. St Paul's. The Tower. All of them. There's even Stonehenge! And d'you know how I feel deep down?'

Pause. Sweating slightly. Clammy fingers. Fiona's silent and brooding.

'Well?'

'Fiona. I feel nothing. I feel nothing at all! And yet, I want to feel just a little something.'

'But why?'

'Why? Because Africa doesn't belong to me! There's no feeling there. No bond. We've been fed on the Mother Country myth. Its language. Its history. Its literature. Its Civics. We feel chunks of it rubbing off on us. We believe in it. We trust it. Openly, we admit we're a part of it. But are we? Where's the real link?'

'I don't know.'

'Why don't I understand and feel about things? For instance, the things I mentioned a while ago. Why don't I feel any pride and joy in them, as they say one ought to feel if you're linked? Can't you see that I don't belong anywhere? What happened to me between African bondage and British hypocrisy? What, Fiona? What?'

'Not so loud, Johnnie.'

'Yes. Not so loud. You're right. I'm sorry. I'm sorry for the umpteenth time.'

She shifts and the bed cries feebly. There's no more perfume. Just her body next to mine. I'm sure we feel the staleness of the meeting depressing us like a warning.

Our nervous systems are now sorting out all the implications of the night's information. After that, we're only two bodies blocking space. Embarrassment. Feverish delight gone. Lost. Lost in tossing waves of doubts and fears. Anxiety wins again.

'Must go now, Johnnie. We'll talk some more about our pet problems. Another time, eh?'

'Sure. Another time.'

She walks gingerly to the door and looks over her left shoulder. The darkness is wearing thin in the room. We look at each other. We wait. She smiles tenderly like someone offering alms.

'I shan't talk any more about the witch-doctor. I promise.'

'That's all right. I know how you feel. Can't say I blame you.'

'Good night Johnnie.'

A click and a feeling of nausea.

Why did I talk such crap?

4

Monday-morning mouth. Feels as if it had swallowed a pint or more of *white rum*, last night. Always feels that way when I've been upset and argumentative. Leather lips. Mouth feels and tastes like sand and petrol fumes mixed with dead saliva. Upset in the head, and your mouth and gut pay for it! Must be a moral in that somewhere.

Whom will I meet on the stairs? Whom will I meet on the crisis stairs? Better keep the arrears on me. Trado could be the first to break the duck. Down the stairs. Carpet's too lumpy to be green pastures all over God's heaven. Into bathroom like a thief.

Bathroom smells like a deserted soap factory – faintly funeral-parlourish, only not so well-kept. Groan and spit of tap water. I suppose Goolam Chops will be in here any moment now. Good, sweet, little overseas problem girl ought to be getting ready to go to her impressive lectures. Shakuntala! Shakuntala! Where can you be? I do so hope that you awaken to find your Indian big toe missing. *Shakuntala the fair, Shakuntala the lovable, Shakuntala the lily-maid of Delhi and Astolat, high in your chamber up a tower to the east, may you guard the sacred shield of the old bitch Mrs Blount which first she placed where morning's earliest ray might strike it and awake her with the gleam.*

Ah! Letters. Any for me? I wonder. Won't wonder for much longer. Just dry these messed-up eyes of mine. Dry, towel, dry. Dry. Toothpaste and soap, away. See if there's anything for me. Something turgidly dramatic about a postman. The messenger of death. The fortune-twister. Shakespeare loved his messengers, too. Always messing up a poor lover or somebody else. One for Miss Shakuntala Goolam, six for Mrs Blount, three, no five for Mr Gerald Trado, and an air letter from Jamaica for me.

Up the stairs; slip Goolam Chops hers under the door; and fly off to the cabin for a cosy read.

At Home,
18th June.

Dearest Son,

I haven't heard from you for some weeks, now. Is there anything wrong? I miss you so much, and pray that God will protect you and guide you to happiness and contentment. Remember that I've always found my answers in prayer, and I'm doing the same for you, my love, even though I know you'll laugh it off when you've read this letter. Please, pray at nights before retiring, son. I saw to it when you were a boy at home. You ought to be able to carry on without my having to be there to bully you into doing it.

I do hope you'll not let me down over there in any way. For the sake of all that's good and holy, please remember that you've had more than most. You know what I mean, don't you? Therefore, your behaviour ought to be rational and calm. Don't be blinded by the bright lights. Their enticements are just the same as those you've experienced at home. Their lights may be left burning longer. That's all. (Laughs.)

Be level-headed and cautious. Don't try to get something for nothing. It's too easy. And, besides, nobody's fooled. Think of the story I once told you about Honest Timothy and the four apples. Hungry but honest to the last.

Your brother, Percy, and I often talk about you and he has just passed by asking me to say hello to you. I'm sure he wishes you well. You two were never great friends, but your absence has softened Percy in a way. Do try to write to him, if only for my sake.

How's the job getting on? Try to give good service. And above all, son, see to it that you do not get involved in any political rows or, for that matter, any racial nonsense. You never had the intelligence and cunning to deal with either topic. For God's sake stay outside and mind your own business.

Do write soon to your

Mother.

P.S.

You haven't told me what kind of job you're doing. Don't you think that your own mother is entitled to know? Don't forget to tell me all about it in your next letter. I do hope it's something that we can all be proud of, and that you are happy in doing.

★ ★ ★

Pride of family name, first. And my bloody happiness, last, eh? Good old soul, nevertheless. Love her, though. Very dearly. Great work waiting on tables, if only she knew what it involved. All the maddening members' whims, all the scavenging. Deceit. Criminal niceties. Surprises. Social fireworks, damp ones, going off unexpectedly.

Back to the bathroom and complete the good wash. Check to see if I've still got the arrears on me. Down the stairs. Descending the apples and pears. Small stirring sounds coming up from the Trado kitchen. Tap water in bathroom still spitting reluctantly.

'Ah! The early bird!' Dick behind me.

'Early worm, you mean.'

'Why d'you say that? Who's after you, Johnnie?'

'The Trado bird.'

'Had a run-in with the great man?'

'Sort of.'

'Anything I can do?'

'No, Dick. Things are patched up, thank you.'

Wonderful to watch Dick and his little saucepan. Brisk house-wife movements while he scours it with detergent and metal pad. Soon it'll be messy again with scalded milk, I bet.

'Fix your own breakfast all the time?'

'Now and then, when I've got an early job. We might be going down to Brighton this morning. Brighton or Hove. Not sure yet.'

'Nice job you have, Dick.'

'Awfully boring at times, though.'

'What d'you do during free periods?'

'Sit and read. Or walk around a bit. Window shop. Clean the metal parts. Or tinker about with the engine.'

'Why?'

Oh! Did I go too far? That 'why' sounded a bit peculiar.

'Just asked for asking's sake.'

'How's the club?'

'It's there.'

'How's the bank balance?'

'Non-existent as usual.'

'No tips?'

'Comes a good tip, today. Nothing for a week after that. Comes and goes, you know. Depends on the G.I.'s pay day, really, if the raw truth be known.'

'What about looking for something steadier? Tried anywhere else?'

'Not skilled, Dickie boy.'

'That's no stumbling block. Others seem to manage. Doesn't seem to be a problem.'

'Oh, no? Ever tried applying for something you really like doing, and not having a piece of paper to prove you're skilled at it? Eh?'

'Bit of a dreamer, aren't you?'

'The curse of the immigrant classes, Dickie boy. Good intentions but no direction.'

'Have a cup of coffee with me?'

'I'd like to, but coffee's an enemy of mine. I'll come up and sit with you if you don't mind.'

Up the stairs. Dick in front carrying a dazzling saucepan like a sword to battle.

'I say! Is that you, Mr Sobert?' The voice of wisdom and understanding – Trado the Seer.

'Yes.'

'Just a minute, will you?'

Dick winks and tells me he'll be in his room. He turns slightly and whispers: 'Come up when you've slain him. I'll have enough coffee. Lesser of two enemies. Besides you'll need it.' Sly chuckle and off.

Does Trado know about Fiona's visit last night? I suppose he could have found her out. May not have been sleeping, at all. He could easily have been outside…

'Come in, will you.'

Sitting room with early-morning dreariness stamped all over it. Sour ashtray atmosphere. Tie and scarf wedged into the back of the seat in the sofa. Empty cigarette packets. Tens. Minors.

'I prefer to talk to you about this matter when my wife isn't present. And I think this is as good a time as any.'

Pause. He sits and I stand. Trado's obviously playing the headmaster and liking every moment of it, liking the tension he's building up, liking the anxiety he's supposed to be causing me, feeling the richness of the carpet under his big feet.

Reaches out for a packet of cigarettes. It's empty. Bless his little throat. He shakes the empty packet and tosses it away with the air of an exhausted business man.

'Now, Mr Sobert. I don't suppose you've got the rent yet, have you?' Sharp imperial ring in his voice.

'Here you are.' Calm, almost matter of fact hand-over of Caesar's goods. 'I'm sorry about the delay.'

'Oh, I see. Well, I…'

'By the way, Mr Trado, I'd be grateful if you'd see about a rent book for me. You could leave it on the table in the hall. It would save your having to climb the stairs to slip it under my door. Thanks.'

About turn. Walk casually to the door. Don't slam it. Leave Trado blissfully disarmed. God bless our gracious Sandra!

Up the stairs. No longer the crisis stairs. Better not break

57

into a run. Trado might hear it. Would spoil everything. Easy does it.

'That was quick!' Dick, over his shoulder; the rest of him crouching over the gas-ring. 'The coffee's not even made, old man. What did you use? An assagai?'

Broad laughter and release. This Dick's going to be a crazy friend of mine. Sure signs. Should I tell him the Trado story? He hasn't asked. If he does, tell him. I'd like to hear the Trado story from his own history of the house, though. Better hold on. We're all in battle. Guerilla style.

'Did you hear someone knocking, Johnnie?'

'No. Where?'

'The door.'

'May I come in?' Goolam Chops pipes up. Faintly heard outside.

'Yes. Come right in, Shakuntala!' Dick's voice circles the room.

Goolam Chops enters. Costly sari swishing here and there over the biscuit brown of her body. Brown inner tube of flesh barely visible round her waist. That's right, ignore me, Shakuntala. You can't disturb me today. I'm victorious and secure. Won't back down from a tussle with you, either.

'Dick, did you bring up my letter for me?'

Bring up, indeed. What's the Chops talking about? No doubt the contents of her clear little letter would make Dick vomit. Her mutton-curry affairs would make anybody bring up something or the other.

'No, Shakuntala. I didn't.'

'I thought it was you. I just wanted to say thanks. It was an extremely nice thing for anybody to do, don't you think?'

'Oh, by the way, d'you know Mr Sobert? Johnnie, this is Miss Goolam; Shakuntala, Johnnie.'

'I think we met already, yesterday. He's a rude man entirely, Dick.'

Trying to draw first blood, I'll chance, 'How entirely rude, Miss Goolam?'

'You see what I mean, already? He's a very difficult individual. Just as I tell you.'

She looks from Dick to me and back to Dick again.

'Don't you think she has a fine-looking brown frame, Dick? Reminds one of Delhi's answer to Marilyn Monroe, eh?' Second attempt to draw blood.

Rapid soprano sighs of disgust from Shakuntala and quiet appreciative chuckles from Dick.

'Johnnie's sold on you, Shakuntala,' Dick suggests.

A ranee-quick change of subject by Shakuntala. 'If you have the car this morning, you could give me a lift to India House, Dick.'

'No lectures this morning, Miss Goolam?'

'I can't see that being any business of yours, Sobert!'

Shakuntala scores. Dick to the rescue.

'As a matter of fact, I was going to ask the same question.'

'No. I don't go in until eleven-thirty today.'

'Well, Dick, it's now clear to us that it's not a case of the lady being unwilling to be lectured to, today, isn't it? You know, "Miss Otis regrets she's unable to dine today!"' Feeble comeback by me. Nothing happens.

'When will you be ready, Shakuntala?' Dick asks calmly.

'In a few minutes, Dick.'

'Right. The sooner the better. Might be going down to Brighton later on.'

Nothing to do, now, but leave the doubtful duo.

'Johnnie.'

'Yes, Dick.'

'What about some coffee?'

'No. Thanks all the same.'

'Want a cup, Shakuntala?'

'Thank you. No milk, please.'

'See you, Dick. Later. Running upstairs. Don't poison our jewel of the East. Mr Nehru mightn't take it lying down, you know.'

Not a quiver from Goolam Chops. As if I hadn't said a word. Outside and up to the cabin. Hope Dick isn't annoyed. Glad I've got Trado off my back for this week. Better have a good haircut. Might as well get rid of this pseudo-African hairstyle when the money's in. I wonder why it's so easy to let yourself go in a strange country? First the hair, then the morals. Sounds like something

59

Mother would have said. Sure she must have, at some time or other. Make up this cabin-class bed of mine. Looks like the wreck of the bloody…Fiona sat here. X marks the Trado spot. Like her. Like her very much. Suppose her witch-doctor Joseph ever knew that she told her story to a Jamaican intruder? What would he say? Fiona's a bit of a child in a way. A child with a coffee-coloured child in a…world. Stupid case of Africanitis!

There's something depressing about this eiderdown! I'd love to throw it out, right in front of a speeding car. Odd thought, for a victorious tenant. Still, it's a thought. Fiona, again. Joseph the rake. Wonder why she took the risk of coming up here alone and waiting in the dark for me? I mean, after all's said and done, she could've been raped. The way it's done in most novels set in the deep South. Negro contacts an unsuspecting white woman and the only noble thing for the Negro to do is to knock her for six straight over the bed head. If there's no bed, then he has to knock her flying over a pile of hay, or the famous woodpile, or a swamp, or…

The British 'nig' hasn't acquired that knack, yet. I'm sure it takes time. Nevertheless, Fiona's a damn' nice person. Like her very much. Not sorry for her, either. Just like her.

This eiderdown's the end. Lumpy and sprawling. Must have covered many a beating heart. Let's take it off and see the effect. No. It does something for the bed in its own odd Blount way. Leave the thing where it is.

'Mr Sobert?' Voice from outside. Sounds like Goolam Chops. 'Come in.'

'Mr Sobert, I would like to ask you a question.'

'Would you like to sit in this chair, Miss Goolam?' Should've put her on the eiderdown. They make such a cute still life. Both lumpy-headed and sprawling.

'I will. Thank you.'

'This is quite a surprise, Miss Goolam. What can I do for you?'

'Mr Sobert?' Pause. Too long. What's up?

'Yes.'

'Why don't you like me?'

'Oh, but I do, Miss Goolam. Whatever made you think I don't?'

'No. Seriously, Mr Sobert. I want to know why you're always

60

trying to say nasty things to me. A while ago, in Dick's room you were most savage. What's the matter?'

'I suppose it's my way of getting to know you, Miss Goolam …I don't know. Maybe. Maybe not.'

'What kind of mixed-up answer is that? It must be one thing or the other, Mr Sobert. Come straight out with it. Please.'

'Well, for a start, I just thought I'd loosen you up a bit. My first impression of you wasn't so favourable. Found you a bit starchy.'

Have to watch out. This is a brand new Goolam Chops. Quite sure, Dick must have put her up to this.

'Mr Sobert?'

'Yes, Miss Goolam?'

'Why don't you like Indians?'

Nothing like being bullied in return. Master stroke. How does one navigate out of this…? What's the quick, bright answer? What do I really feel on the subject? Nothing. Indians you meet and you leave like most people in the world. O.K. Sounds fair enough. Indians you meet and like. Same with most people in the world. Indians you meet and positively dislike. Same with most people in the world. Shakuntala's one whom I dislike and like, all in one breath. Answer like that simply won't do.

'Mr Sobert?'

'Yes, Miss Goolam?'

'You haven't answered my question.'

'I know.'

'I'll ask you again, Mr Sobert.'

'No. I understand your question perfectly.'

'Well?'

Better stall a little longer. This might be hell ever-after. Headquarters will certainly be told about this conversation. Can't afford the Third Programme to broadcast this, at all.

'Well, Miss Goolam. I've nothing against you as an Indian. Really.'

'Go on, Mr Sobert.'

'I do think you're a stuck-up type, though.'

'Stuck-up type? I think the same of you. Go on.'

'That's about it, Miss Goolam.'

'Well, would you like me to tell you what I think of you?'

'I think it would be only fair. Yes.'

'I dislike you very much indeed, Mr Sobert. I think you're a rude individual. Boorish. Insulting. And maybe a little mad.'

'Is that all?'

'No.'

'Well?'

'I don't trust your kind of people, if you want the plain truth, Mr Sobert. I've always tried to steer clear of Negroes wherever I meet them. I detest them. And I would be glad if you'd be kind enough to forget that you ever spoke to me, or that we ever met. I've been living in this house for a long time, much longer than you have, and I absolutely refuse to leave because of you. Or anybody for that matter. And least of all, because of you!'

I'm sure this calls for a bit of rape, you know. Deep South style, at that. It's a pity that Goolam Chops is so bloody brown! It wouldn't do to pull it off with her. Might even start a new vogue in American problem novels. Might upset the colour values so dearly cherished. Still, it would be a treat to read of 'off-white women' getting it for a change.

'We know where we stand, now, don't we, Mr Sobert?'

'I suppose so, Miss Goolam.'

'Goodbye, Mr Sobert.'

'Goodbye, Miss Goolam.'

Door slams. Brisk carpeted footsteps.

What should I really do with this blasted eiderdown? It's such an eyesore.

5

Larry's barbershop. Smelly and overcrowded always. Get here at nine-thirty and you leave by three o'clock. Larry and his assistant moving like tired millionaires at Black Fast.

'Oh Lawd! Bless me eyesight! Is really you that, me own friend?' Larry's stentorian greeting.

'Yes. Larry. Same one.'

'Then tell me what's happening, nuh, Jamaican Johnnie!' Larry's stentorian request.

'Not a thing, man.'

'But you see this, Jamaican Johnnie! He like to starve the barber, too much you know. Just gaze on the head of hair he carrying round with him! Is starve he starving the barber why he looking like something out of the *National Geographical Magazine*!'

'What's my position, Larry?'

'Position?'

'Yes. Number thirteen, as usual?'

'No man must ever use that number in this shop. It don't exist on these premises, Johnnie. Anything that need numbering go as far as twelve and stop. The next number after twelve is fourteen. Don't you know that, man?'

'All right, Larry. What's my number then?'

'Scratch your name on the pad and add one to the last total, nuh. Watch out for the banned number though.'

Name. Position on list is number eleven. That means one-thirty, maybe two o'clock.

'How's Britain's only coloured millionaire?'

'You fellers hearing this Jamaican Johnnie? Me's a millionaire, eh? This Johnnie well understand me poverty and still he beating me with big tease in the bargain. Never mind. I going to live to see the day when all you displaced black people learn to respect me as a gentleman of means and plenty leisure.'

Guffaws from everybody in the shop. Shouts of 'True word. True word, that!' ring out and die away just as suddenly as they were uttered. Larry puts down his No. 1 cutter and scissors on the narrow mantelpiece. The customer draws up his knee and sinks down into the chair. He knows he'll have to wait while Larry lays down the law.

Larry snorts quietly and begins. 'Now, listen to me, all you immigrant rubbish! We's all black together. Some brownish, but don't let that phenomenon bother you, at all. We's all suffering from the same tar-brush disease in this Britain place. Listen to what I hear last night. I tell you when I hear it, I nearly drop down on me knees with shame in me heart. See God there!'

A sprinkling of sighs from the customers. Larry's assistant downs his scissors and comb. Always does this out of sympathy. When Larry stops, everybody stops with him. The two half-trimmed heads barely peeping above the chairs look like sculpture rejects.

Larry lights a cigarette.

'Me dear sir, when I come to this country during the war as a R.A.F. man I did meet a boy from Saint Lucia, name Cecil Linton. Me and the man getting on well together. We was great friends and almost like brothers in certain ways. After the war, we drift all about the place together. We hunt skirts together. Some of the times, we share one between the two of we. Such is the big bond we hold for each other! Well, I get a job up in the Liverpool place, nuh. So the partnership between me and Cecil break up, because he didn't want to leave London. As a matter of fact, before I go off to Liverpool, Cecil get himself a real nice girl name Pauline. Nice Irish thing, man! Real good skirt! I was very happy for him. Well, now, I go off for me job. I write Cecil. No reply. I write two, three times. Not a word come back to me from Cecil. I decide to write the skirt. But I get foxed. Didn't know her surname. I say to meself, perhaps, Cecil making her use his name like they married and all that. Next thing, I send off a letter to Mrs Pauline Linton. No reply, as usual. I give up, at last. Yet, one thing that disturb me was that I wasn't getting back the letters from the post office. And that is why I start to think that the letters did well reach.'

Larry takes a long drag on his cigarette. Turns slightly to his left, looks at the customer in the chair and pats his half-trimmed head. 'Coming back to you, old man. I must tell this one. It have a deep-deep moral in it.'

The customer grunts affably.

Larry turns away and says loudly: 'Real nice boy, this. He respect a story with a moral, and that is much more than I can say for the lot of you here today.'

He abuses the cigarette again. Rather like a Benzedrine inhaler. A doubled fist. A series of clutching movements, up and down from his face, followed by roars of exhalations.

Finally settles off.

'Well, last night, after all these years, I hear the truth of the matter. I hear the dead happenings of Mr Cecil and Miss Pauline.'

Hesitates grandly.

'You know what happen?'

Smiles.

'You know what make me sick?'

Pause. Cigarette again.

'Cecil and Pauline did get the letters all right, yes. They did want to answer, too. But they was planning a big deal, and it never include answering my letters then, at all. They ups and get married off decent-like in truth. Then they pack them things and go straight to Saint Lucia like they hear gold down there. Things run smooth-like for a few months. She admire the climate and the seaside life and even the food. Then, sudden-like, Miss Pauline jump up and says she want to go back to England. Cecil begin to feel like a fish in a frying-pan, so he and she take a boat and come back to the fog. As soon as she touch the turf at Southampton, she make a beeline to her parents and leave Cecil all on him lonesome. Cecil try to contact the bitch because after all she's him lawful wedded bitch and all that. No success. He go up to the house and the parents tell him on the doorstep that their daughter doesn't want to see him any more. The parents tell him that if he want to contact Pauline that he must write her solicitor. Imagine a piece of impertinence like that, eh? A man have to see lawyer-office before he can talk to him lawful wife. Well, final things come to a head on one Bank Holiday. It seems like Cecil corn-up in him rum and beer plenty. Must a-been drinking for two whole days. He decide to pay a social call on him wife and him wife parents in that drunken condition. He get refused and still he standing outside bobbing and weaving like a punchie. Sudden-like he break down the front door; run inside; grab the father and bang him all about the place like football; grab the wife and batter her little bit; and then he set fire to the house. The house burning wild while Cecil and the father rolling all about, and the wife and the mother hollering like a pair of butchering pigs. Police and fire-engines and ambulance come to clear away the mess that Cecil and him bad rum cause. And the ending of the story is that Cecil get five years for arson. Five years, I telling you! And for a real out-of-the-way charge like arson! I don't think another West Indian name on the books for that quality of offence.'

A long pause. Barbershop's dead still.

'And that is why I feel sick when I hear it last night. Poor

65

unfortunate Cecil serve him time and beat it afterwards to America. And is only last night that I hear that him is a big shot in some Negro Insurance Company, or the other. He making dollars like a bookie! Hand over fist, like he mad!'

The customer in the chair swivels the chair on its pole and faces Larry before I'm able to look up and see what he's doing. The customer says: 'Look, nuh! Larry! Moral or no moral, I have to go 'bout me business. All you doing is provoking me like how Cecil gal did provoke him to do the arson thing on the house! So, come nuh! Finish the head.'

The customer's holding an open razor brandishing it in front of Larry's nose. Larry shakes his head in disgust and says: 'Is why you taking a serious thing and making a joke of it? Your brains must be water and mud or what? Put down what don't concern you and shut your black mouth. I don't finish the moral yet. If you can't wait hop out of the chair and find a next barber to finish you off. Now, just fade out and make me tell the last part.'

The customer sighs cynically; puts the razor on the mantel-piece and slips heavily into the warmth of the chair. Larry smiles and pats him on both shoulders. Larry's assistant winks at the customer. Tenseness grips Larry. Main-speaker twitchings all over his face. He lights another cigarette and drops his Ronson in his overall pocket.

'Well, back to Pauline. You must be wondering what happen to her, nuh? I going to tell you, now. She's very much in the picture. Right in the dead centre of it, if you ask me! Why I say so? I say so because is she herself whom I meet last night and is she same one who tell me the story with her own mouth! And, what's more, she not ashamed or embarrassed up, at all. She talk like she never was implicated in the business. Like she was stranger to all the worries. Believe me! She really baffle me with her outside treatment of the story.'

Larry flicks the ash from the tip of his cigarette and hesitates for the big moment.

'Gentlemen: This is what I have to announce, at last! Pauline get a divorce and every connection with Cecil and herself wipe away nice and clean. But! Pauline is now a common prostitute! On the Bayswater Road, of all roads!'

No response.

'And more than that! She keeping a boy from Saint Lucia and loving him plenty on top of the bargain!'

Not loud cheers, but a certain flutter of approval.

'Retribution! That's it as I see it.' Larry stirring the session. 'She going to get fix good and proper this time. I just know that her new man going to prove to be her downfall. As sure as rain come down in Manchester!'

Larry's assistant asks, 'What 'bout the moral?'

Larry straightens up and recites, '"Our deeds shall follow us from afar, and what we have been, shall make us what we are."'

Customers' chorus: 'True word, Larry! Most true word, that, old man!'

Larry's customer shifts in the chair and calls out boldly, 'Ready to finish me off, now?'

'Yes, man. Coming back to you in a second.'

He stubs out his cigarette and saunters over to the mantelpiece. Gentle coughing and side discussions ensue.

'Still working down the club, Johnnie?' Larry calls to me. Not turning. Clipping the half-trimmed head furiously.

'Still there, boy.'

'Holding on, eh? Best thing that. This Britain call for a slow and steady treatment of most things like jobs. Not like the States where a man can chop and change as him fancy.'

'You're telling me!'

'Is a good thing for a man character, though. Don't you think so, Johnnie?'

'Could be, Larry. Could be.'

'You don't sound sure, countryman. What happening?'

'Nothing at all.'

No more communication for about three minutes. He's devouring the head like an expert in a hurry. Customer's looking thinner every minute. Discussions. Left and right of me. Missa Manley. Busta. Federation. Bauxite. Chaguanas. De-waste-a-time Colonial Office. Tax Rebate. Arrival of more immigrants. Skirts.

'You know something, Johnnie?'

'Not until you tell me, Larry.'

'Still got your sense-a-fun, eh?' Guffaws.

'What's on your mind?'

'Well, Johnnie, I was thinking of a certain plan.'

'Yes?'

'Is a real big move, countryman. Real big.'

'Listening.'

'You know anything about the house business in Britain? What I driving at is this: Real-estate investment, man! I going in for it, but with a syndicate of fellers behind me. I want to buy up all sort of old house and fix them up and rent only to coloured people who come up on all these extravagant excursions.'

'What you really want to do, Larry, is to exploit them as much as possible, don't you?'

'Not so loud, countryman!'

'Well?'

'Shh! Don't talk too much about that word "exploit", Johnnie boy. That word is a Spanish machete, you know. Cut both sides. Look now in a place like Brixton! In Brixton, you'll find all sorts exploiting on a high scale. You'll find the Jew man, the few clever Gentile ones, one or two Englishfied Orientals, and even the odd African! All of them doing one thing, and doing that thing well. They catching the coloured people like flies on flypaper. Is just as my poor old teacher in the Jamaica bush school used to say, Johnnie. He used to say: "Lawrence Denton, you're a fairly bright boy. And because of this I want you to know that 'Necessity is Invention mother'." You following me, Johnnie boy?'

'Yes. Count me out, though.'

'Why?'

'Simple. No money to spare on shares, Larry. No! Lawrence Denton and Co. Ltd. That's better. You will have a sort of limited liability, won't you? Anyway, you'll be contributing to every-body's happiness and misery, all at the same time.'

'You're a difficult bugger to talk to, these last months! Why?'

'D'you think so?'

Larry dries up. The customer's almost ready to be sprung loose. Takes a look round the room, and Larry bangs his head back into position. That head was mine, I bet.

Autumn pavement's certainly working out successfully for Larry. Had to come here to wake up like the rest of us, no doubt.

Pity's not for him, as Biddy would say. Pity? Who wants that old-fashioned thing, anyway! Surely not Larry. Must take a packet out of the shop; what with the gambling sideline, the American 'doubtfuls', the miserable hustlings of one thing and another. How many free days left for Larry? I wonder. Don't think he's been inside, yet. Won't forget what I was told when I first got here. 'Boy! It's an achievement when a coloured man stays out of prison for a whole year. A first-class achievement!' Told to me by a recidivist. The voice of experience. None better.

Claustrophobic cross-talk in shop for about three hours. Involved only twice. Another achievement! Second thought about achievement, today. Must guard against a thought like that. Could get depressed. Could get ideas about improvement. Could even get in the frame of mind to join Larry's 'houses for niggers only' soirée.

'You quiet, bad, today, Johnnie!' A thrust from Larry's assistant. 'Milking the Yanks, eh?'

'No more than they deserve!' A Barbadian quickly adds. By far the most simian nig in the shop. And the only one with *coolth*.

Larry's assistant: 'True word, Ringo! True word.'

So the Barbadian's Ringo. Ringo, the progressive Hyde Parker. Always heard of this one. Never met him before. Might be interesting to sound him. He's supposed to be the boy with the silver spoon in the mouth. West Indian intellectual on permanent loan to Britain. What's he made out of?

'You're Ringo, are you?'

'Yes. And you're Jamaican Johnnie, I've been hearing about.' Bright black.

'Never seen you at the club.'

'Don't like clubs.'

'Like my mother. She loathes clubs. Houses of iniquity.'

'I don't think anybody's mother should be dragged into this discussion.' Never a conversation, always a discussion: student-mania.

'How long have you been in England, Ringo?'

'Twelve years. Why?'

'Studied Law?'

'Among other things. Why?'

69

I hope he keeps on asking why. I'll just ignore it and press on. I'd love to introduce this one to Shakuntala. Not to Fiona, or to Biddy. Only to Shakuntala.

'What other things, Ringo?'

'Oh, I've studied Journalism…'

'Where?'

'Regent Street Poly. Why?'

'What other things?'

'I've read Economics. Right now I'm interested in Politics and Philosophy.'

'Quite a well-linked set of subjects. What will you do after Politics and Philosophy? Go back home?'

He hesitates. Looks angry, to me. Good! Very good, indeed! Let's see the kind of silver his spoon's made of. The Barbadian's a little Englishman all along the line. Must remember this. One sure sign so far. He doesn't think very much of Yanks.

'Why d'you ask that?'

'Curious, that's all. A man with a string of qualifications like you ought to be an asset somewhere or the other.'

'What you really want to know is whether I intend to return to Barbados and enter politics. That's it, isn't it?'

'Well, yes.' Trying desperately hard to sound doubtful.

'I suppose I could do that, if I felt like.'

'What do you feel like doing, then, Ringo?'

'Not sure, yet.'

Things seem to be petering out. Must salt his tail. Better drag Larry into it. How? Ah! Make it simple and direct. The only way.

'Larry!'

'Yes, Johnnie.'

'If you had all Ringo's qualifications and experience, would you want to go home?'

'No question about it at all, Johnnie boy. And that's for sure, as the Yankee man would say.'

'Why are you so certain, Larry?' Ringo asks.

'Well, listen to me, old man Ringo. It's a simple thing. I would want to go home for the big-time pickings. If a man have plenty letters behind him name, that is the time for him to get into the swim and make the presence felt. That's the time for him to set up a new class division with all the might and main he have at his disposal. And when I say that, I mean a real brand-new class division.'

'But, why the new class division, as you put it?'

'That's a foolish question, Ringo, me student friend.'

'Why?'

'Well, I mean to say, man, who going to go back with letters behind him name and be contented with a working-class house, or for that matter, a working-class mother and father, or a working-class skirt, or a working-class pub, or a working-class anything? You tell me that right now. Which man in him right mind, provided that he have the necessary letters shining behind him name? Which man?'

'I would, Larry.'

'Ringo! Don't make me laugh, old man. Why didn't you say, "I will"? Make it definite, nuh. Tell me that you will go back to your tenement yard in Barbados and rot. Don't say, "I would". It's too easy to say a thing like that under the circs.'

'All right, Larry. I will.'

'Don't believe you, at all, at all.'

'That's also easy to say, Larry. Isn't it?'

Deadlock. I like Ringo, in a way. Not a bad nig. But I don't believe him, either. Think I'll put in my ninepence at this point.

'Tell me, Ringo and Larry! Don't you believe in the West Indies and the Federation thing? Don't you think there'll be big things happening there very soon? Money's going to be spent wisely. Jobs opening out. Improvements being made right and left. Grievances being aired. Investments from outside being invited.'

'Isn't that too much of a rose-coloured view, Johnnie? We're both living over here, and we don't know the whole story. Hundreds are still coming, especially from Jamaica. Hands are still tied by powers outside the West Indies. Even poverty's not forceful enough to egg them on to do some serious thinking. It's a farce!'

Larry bristles and says: 'Well, I going to tell you and Mister Jamaican Johnnie something for your own good, now. I feel that there's something fishy about that politics that going on in the intellectual circles of Jamaica. Things look too selfish to me.

71

Things look like they want to glorify one man instead of the dream nation that everybody dreaming about. Is a funny thing, but I can smell out a man who want to go down in history as a big-time independence-bringer. As I see him, so I know him. Pure selfishness working behind the Jamaica part of this business. And this is why I feel that there's lots of pickings going. And you'd be foolish to waste your good-good letters and qualifications on a mere job at a desk back home. Or anywhere for that matter.'

'Larry and the word "exploit" – inseparable pals, you know, Johnnie. He never sees beyond the black market or the private deal.'

Must talk some more to Ringo. He has the kind of faith that I envy. A kind of vision that seems like a strength. What the hell's his vision exactly, though…? Despite the love of degrees and all that, he has a calm that I envy. How did he come by it? Barbados is a bastard of a place for Ringo's type in many ways, too. Must have found the calm over here, somewhere. Possibly he's that way because something's dead inside. I'll get that way in time, I suppose. Does he really care? Could be putting on an act. Hyde Parkers can rise to an occasion. Ask him round to the club on Tuesday. Slack night, Tuesday. Can talk as much as we want without being disturbed too often. Might even introduce him to Biddy, if she promises to be cute and charming as she always is to the more privileged customer.

When will Larry ever get around to me? Almost one o'clock already. No use depending on his assistant. Looks as if he's on Black Fast, again. What'll he do when Larry becomes Lawrence Denton and Co. Ltd.? Go back to hustling with black jack and Coon-can, I bet.

Larry's off again. Going to the door to talk to a man on a bicycle. 'Sweepstake vendor,' somebody mutters. 'Irish and Jamaican.' Where were they printed? I wonder.

That was quick! Larry's back. All smiles. Left back pocket bulging. Assistant leans across and whispers to Larry. Larry nods. Assistant nods vigorously and whistles under his breath. Approval, no doubt. Mixed, may be, with a feeling of regret at not having been in on it.

Ringo's reading a textbook and stopping every now and then

to make notes in the margin. Legs crossed. Head bent. Lost to the world of hustlers. Brows furrowed. Yet another qualification on the way.

A blonde reports silently at the door. Stands and waits. Heads turn towards her. But not Larry's. He remains perched over his customer's head.

The blonde's still waiting. Larry tells her to come back at three o'clock, not to forget 'de t'ings'; post the pools; call at the laundry. All these commands, without turning round to face her. Impressive show! Tough gent, our Larry!

Of course, he's got a reliable barber's mirror. Conveniently placed, too.

6

Monday evening at the club. Still thinking about Ringo's calm. Larry's back-yard ethics. His aplomb. His blonde's sepulchral patience. Fiona's warmth. Fiona's stupidity. Sandra's. Biddy's brainy manoeuvres.

My position in all this?

Nothing special. Merely a part of the flow. That's all. Nothing more important than that. Unless every little crawling sufferer has a voice in the total shout. Unless I relinquish my position as a 'protected' colonial drifter and see the shout as a thing to which I could contribute with gusto and retaliation. Unless somebody takes me seriously; takes the business of being a black man with a certain seriousness and fondness.

Crap again! Black man, my eye!

Why should anybody who's going about his living stop and go about my own for me?

That reminds me – met a man on my way back from Larry's. Latimer Road Tube station. Said to me out of the clear blue, 'Where d'you come from?'

'Jamaica.'

'Oh, really. I had a cousin and a brother stationed in British Guiana, some time ago.'

'British Guiana, eh?'

'New Amsterdam, as a matter of fact. Lovely and warm! Envied them a great deal, I can tell you.'

'Yes.'

'How're you making out, over here?'

'So-so.'

'Come across much prejudice, at all?'

'A bit of ignorance, now and then. Why?'

'That's not the same thing, is it really? Ignorance is a different matter, don't you think?'

'Causes prejudice nine out of ten times, though.'

'Of course. Yes.' Hesitates. 'What you chaps need, in my humble estimation, is to be respected before you're accepted.'

'I don't understand.'

'Simply, respect before acceptance.'

'How?'

'For one thing, I'd object to the B.B.C. putting on Coon shows.'

'Yes?'

'Doesn't help one bit, you know. Your people are already late in starting, and programmes like that only show you up in a bad light.'

'How would you stop the B.B.C. from putting on Coon shows?'

'Write letters. Deputations. Anything with strong representation.' Pause. 'The trouble with you chaps is that you *do not* come with a concerted voice. You must have that to make an impression in this society.'

'I see.'

'Sure. The Coon shows ought to be stopped.'

'What about the entertainment the shows offer to viewers? The jobs of the actors and so on?'

'They'll get by, don't worry.'

'You think the shows are harmful, don't you?'

'Very much so. Aren't they to you?'

'We've had our own Coon shows in Jamaica.'

'But there's a difference, isn't there? Over here, on television, the Coons are white men blacked up. Can't you see the insult to your people?'

'If I strained a point, may be. Or, perhaps if they were actually pushing the coloured population of Britain farther down the social scale. On the other hand, if you wanted to get to the root of the prejudice and really do a thorough job, I could understand your argument if it included textbooks in schools, advertisements, sayings like "worked like a nigger", documentary films improperly slanted, B.B.C. features and plays, West End plays, novels, the bloody lot!'

'You're a strange man!'

'You think so, do you? Well, that's the way I look at it. Take away one thing like the television Coons and there's bound to be more harm caused than anything else. Even resentment. In any case, I can't see where they're big enough, or significant enough, or odious enough to warrant the action that you're suggesting.'

'I would think that television is the strongest weapon of propaganda – in certain instances – even stronger than the National Press.'

'Yes. But are the Coon shows as damaging as the hundreds of thousands of old-fashioned Geography texts being used in British schools? Textbooks with fantastic accounts of family life in Africa and the West Indies are read year after year, and never revised unless –'

'That's nonsense!'

'– unless some busybody with a conscience decides to make recommendations and the usual red tape which might take ten years to see the light of day.'

'What sort of books, d'you mean?'

'Books with information like this, for instance: "Father; Mother; Child: Brave; Squaw; Papoose: Pappy; Mammie; Pickaninny." Don't you see anything harmful there?'

'Do they still have that sort of bilge?'

'They do. They most certainly do. You try getting the average English child to think of himself as a native of England and listen to what he says. As far as he's concerned, the word "native" means a black man. And not only that, it means a black man who's as wild as hell, running amok with painted face and curare darts, tribal markings and distended ear lobes.'

'Incredible, isn't it?'

'And if the children are fed on that nonsense, plus the superstitions of their parents, there'll be another generation of fanatics rearing to take over the myth. O.K.?'

'Why?'

'Why? You ask that, in all seriousness?'

'Yes. I do. Why?'

'Well, they have policies on other important matters. A host of them, if you ask me.'

'Matters like what?'

'The police, for one. The Church. The Royal Family.'

'They have a host, eh?'

'Most certainly. Why can't they tighten up on programmes which are offensive to outside races?'

'Nice term that, "outside". "Outside races", at that. Must remember that one.'

'I find it difficult to talk to you. I can't quite understand your attitude.'

'I thought you were trying your best to. Anyway, that's not important right now.' Slight sigh. Pause. 'Would it satisfy you if the B.B.C. included, out of the blue, a coloured character in *Mrs Dale's Diary*? Or even a complete West Indian Dale's Diary, for that matter?'

'Might be a damn' good thing. The public would see a coloured person suddenly in his true relationship to themselves – in other words, just as a human being.'

'Yes. True. But isn't that forcing it a bit? How would you work him in without sniggers from people like me and others who'd smell a rat? I mean, Mrs Dale and her crew belong to a world quite removed –'

Interrupting fiercely. 'Removed? Removed from what? Dr Dale could have a coloured patient. Any coloured man could be employed by all sorts of people in the serial. The thing that the B.B.C. would have to watch is the business of making too much of his appearance in the plot.'

'Intrusion would be the better word, don't you think?'

'Rubbish!'

'All right.'

'I'll tell you what's wrong with the colour problem! People like you! People like you, the so-called enlightened ones! Your kind are obviously pulling the effort apart at the seams. I've often found this true. Absolutely true. The enlightened coloured man is nothing more than the black man's Judas!'

And that's the end of me.

My position in all this? Obviously something special. Very special. Stumbling blocks are. So, I'm more than merely a part of the flow after all.

'What's up, Johnnie? Can't you hear your public clamouring for you?'

'Where, Sandra?'

'Over by the dartboard, dear boy. Hustle them up, will you? Tonight's a drag as it is already without your adding to it.'

Leave her for the table by the dartboard, and faintly overhear her on the subject of daydreaming waiters: '…if only these waiters had to pay the rent of this place, they'd soon realize the necessity of keeping on their toes. Heaven knows, the job's easy enough as it is, and when they don't even try to…'

The rest is lost in a babel of eager G.I.s, eager to prove their existence, eager to prove that they too are acceptable presences. And, where? In the white whore's society. They're doing their best by competing for the highest-priced drinks, by ordering mammoth rounds and by throwing away the 'craziest' tips.

So they're throwing them my way! What am I to do? Refuse them? Give the boys safe counsel? Lecture them about their resented dollar, their attractive dollar, their life-giving dollar? Say to them, 'Brothers under the skin!' (Doesn't matter if mine is darker or browner or blacker or more freckled, as long as the word 'skin' is used. Wonderful leveller, that word! Warm and therapeutic.) 'Hold on to your money and spend it in Africa and the West Indies where you'll be truly appreciated. They know how to treat members of the "inside races"?'

So, I go and get my share of the pickings at the table by the dartboard. I go and get my share and Sandra's share for her, too. Enlightened nig putting the pressure on a few eager suckers for his own benefit and for a waster's, as well, while buddha cash register sits like a lump of joy and gets paunchier and paunchier.

Nig playing the game with nig for a packet of chips and rent money in the long run.

It's the same G.I. with the mania for a 'fix'. Seems calm tonight. Must have got one, somewhere.

'Hey, man! You go grab your boy a whole mess o' pot, Johnnie-O?'

I was wrong. Droopy-drawers is still upset. Still hunting. Must have had too little between yesterday and tonight.

'Drinks, first, Pres. What's it going to be?'

Soft soap, rich in lather. Stings their eyes and blinds them, and me, perhaps.

'Dig, man! Dig the normal, Johnnie-O!'

'No, Pres. Nothing doing. I told you about me, last night. Didn't I?'

'Aw! Come down our lane, Johnnie-O. Help relieve the tension, man.'

'What about trying something else?'

'Like what, for instance, Doc?'

'Double Scotches.'

'Jump off my back, will yer! Can't afford to get wasted in that way, daddy-o. What's burning way down inside has gotta be put out with fire. Fire! Dig? A whole basinful o' hooch wouldn't dent the fever. Gotta be the fix or nuttin'. Vous dig?'

Of course, I dig. I dig and I'm moved to tears of red, clotted blood over you, man. Hysterical, in fact. Drooping with sympathy.

'Come on, Pres. What d'you want to drink?'

'O.K. Make it beers, man. Beers slighted molested by three gins and two Scotches. Sling the rocks. Don't be long, now. Me, you and the night's got a whole mess o' business to see through, daddy-o. A basinful o' joy. Yes, sir!' Biddy's hellishly subdued! What happened last night? Her Highness seems more lowlife than ever. Suppose she couldn't find anybody to love and slop over. At least, one of God's little acres got a rest for a Sunday. The rest isn't doing her any good, either. Too quiet and gentle for my use. Better puncture the calm and see what stirs beneath that decaying heart of hers.

'Step on it, Biddy! Are you going to take all night to open five beers? I remember when you could do a dozen in half the time!'

No reply. Strange. Try again.

'Come on, old hypocrite! Stir yourself, will you.'

'Why am I suddenly an old hypocrite?'

'So you can actually talk, Biddy-O?'

'Not so much of the Biddy-O, big head!'

'Coming to life, eh, Biddy-O.'

'The name's plain and simple Biddy. O.K.?'

'Yes, Miss Snobbish.'

'What's wrong with you?'

'The world's calm, Biddy-O.'

'Idiot!'

'Ah! Got you, now. Something's up. What?'

'Nothing you can change, thank you.'

'Now, seriously, Biddy. What have I done you?'

'Nothing you can avoid, Johnnie-O.'

'All right, wasp! What have I destroyed, then? Another illusion?'

'Skip it.'

'Sure.' Must get a nice stern tone. 'Let's have the drinks on a clean tray for a change, will you. Thank you.'

She hands me a nice dirty tray. Almost flings the drinks on it, she does. Spills all of them and shouts the total in my face. Looks near to tears, to me. Dante's Inferno's nothing compared with this hell-hole. But nothing!

Back to the table by the dartboard. Serving the drinks against croaking cross-chat, back-chat, sex-chat, and heady effluvia from Luckies, Pall Mall and Parliament. The 'fix' pipes up, again. Is ignored. Pipes up once more. Is told to stow it by one of the girls.

'For Chris' sake, Johnnie don't do that sort o' hustling, Pres. How many times must I tell you that?'

Sweet whore's defence.

Lots of thanks for the tip. Moving back to the bar. Almost getting there, when the 'fix' shouts: 'Maybe later, 'gator, huh? Maybe.'

Is ignored, again. Like nothing.

Back to Biddy.

'Look, tell me what I've done, will you?'

Drily, 'Why?'

Silence. Wounded. She can keep it for all I care. Keep it warmly nursed in her gaping heart. Miss Bloody World!

Look away slowly. Quick movement might betray me. Nothing like turning one's back on defeat especially when a woman is the conqueror. Especially when she's the one returning from the wars with your bloody head impaled on her tongue.

Think about something. Anything. Not Biddy for a moment. Not Biddy for eternity. Not her, for God's sake. Of course, I'm licking the wound like mad. Better lick something else. Ah! Yes.

Yes! Think of Judas Johnnie. *Mrs Dale's Diary.* Policy.

Crap!

Go serve other suckers and forget the man at Latimer Road; forget the 'fix'; forget Biddy's bleeding heart. And mine, incidentally. Do the rounds and do them like an earnest thief.

Doing them and not getting any orders. Might as well give up and go back to the end of the bar. Not Biddy's end. She'll come to me, in time, if I wait long enough.

For an anxious type, I'm a prince of waiting long hours for consolation. Must have got it from somebody or the other. Whom? The old lady? Could have. Could have been the old man, for all I know. I wonder what he'd say to that? Me. Actually taking after him in some murky detail. Wouldn't believe it, I bet. No, sir! Not the old man. Not that 'real man'. That hard-working, level-headed bulwark. Must have got it from an aunt on my mother's side. Or the grandmother. Quite possibly. True. Mother's mother. Gong-gong, the real force.

Bitch of a thing, this waiting business!

One thinks of all sorts. One thinks of a father who's a hurricane that never ceased blowing dutifully through one's nightmares, one's thoughts and actions. One thinks of him as something very special. On some other planet. Next to mine. Yet one feels the impact of love, or is it duty and all that accompanies it? A planet, according to Larry, is a world of hope cut off from earth intentionally. And Panama was like that. Panama's the old man. Panama is a strange world to a child who sees an airmail envelope being delivered every so-and-so of the month. Dutifully arriving. Appreciated on receipt. And more than that. A father is a force. Within a mother's world. Or so the man said. But when an airmail envelope means a father's presence, then there's bound to be a problem later on. Much later, maybe. For child and mother. Poor mother!

'Johnnie!'

You do that, girl. Call and call, again. Not going to answer you one damn. I'm on another planet, Biddy girl. Another planet, and another time.

If only I'd been on the old man's planet with him…? Would there have been any changes of tempo? Would there have been any changes in my bastard middle-classery? Would I have been the successful boy? The lad who's most likely to become a top line 'native civil servant'. Would I be here, now? Native civil servant, my arse!

'Johnnie!'

Call again, bitch. Call until your tubes give out. I'll be waiting to hear them go whistling to a stop. Scream the name louder.

I suppose the old man's right after all's said and done. I suppose he had the right life saved up for me. The life of endless respectable pursuits and conventional patterns of behaviour. Not that the old man would have insisted. But 'the others' would have prescribed a girl three to four shades lighter than myself. Respectable people are married people. Shade's the thing. Could very well be the reason for my coming to England where I can get a girl a million shades lighter than myself. Just to show the Jamaican and Panamanian middle-classery where it gets off. Crap, again!

Nevertheless an airmail envelope is an airmail envelope if even there's a real handsome draft in it. If even it feeds, clothes and educates you. If even it buys houses and hires servants. If even…

'Come here, a minute, Johnnie!'

Why don't you take a running jump into the cash register, girl of my dreams? I ain't listening and I ain't coming, either. I'll come in my own great, good time, said the man. Just come down from the hill and leave off, will you!

A father is an important ailment to have as a child. He may be any type. Doesn't matter. Having him around completes the shape of things to come. Having him on another planet is also an ailment, butter on bread but not quite the same like other boys' ailments, if you see what I mean. Yet a grandmother is an ailment, too – matrilineal society and all that effort. Grandmothers are forces, warriors, pre-war calm and post-war neuroses.

Didn't have two. One seemed too much. Dynamic. Bigger than a dozen airmail envelopes arriving on the same Saturday. Her influence was her magic. Her magic, her life. And her life was everybody else's around the place. Even the servants'. Strange word, that one. Not 'servants', but 'even'. It makes an arse of a noise in one's conscience, doesn't it? Depends, I would imagine, on the size of one's conscience. Some are too vast. Sounds get lost in their multiple middle-class convolutions.

'Johnnie!'

Much nearer to me, now. Pretend not to hear her. Burn Sweet Biddy, burn! All of your feminine cussedness. All of it, you twisted bar lily.

> But I can give thee more;
> For I will raise her statue in pure gold;
> That while Verona by that name is known,
> There shall no figure at such rate be set
> As that of true and faithful Juliet.

If Juliet's dead, so are you, Biddy-O, and my father certainly wouldn't think of erecting a statue for you, sweet misery. Call again, from the dead, Biddy-O. Call, love!

'Johnnie!'

'What?'

'Nothing.'

Oh, no! Not cat-and-mouse. Ain't that just like a woman? She's been sticking like a leech and now it's nothing. Ain't that something?

'Johnnie?'

'What d'you want to say?'

'Are you ready to hear it?'

If I say yes, I'll throttle her, so help me!

'Well, Johnnie?'

'What d'you want to say?'

'Are you ready to hear it?'

If I say yes, I'll throttle her, so help me! For the second time.

'Well, Johnnie?'

She's attacking again. I'll surprise her. I'll be real sweet and chatty. If it kills me, I'll surprise her. Nothing like an unexpected swing of the pendulum.

'Yes, Biddy. I'm sorry. I'm ready.'

'Are you really, big head?'

Thought as much.

'Why did you accept Sandra's help, Johnnie?'

'So that's it!'

'Isn't my money good enough? You spoke to me first, remember? And I promised to let you have it.'

'That's it, then. Is that the reason for the blue mood?'

'You haven't much decency, have you, Johnnie?'

'No, I haven't, Biddy. Where d'you think I'll be able to get some? The chemist's shop, perhaps?'

'Shut up!'

'Had a bad night because of that, I suppose?'

'Mind your own business.'

'Anyway, what have you against Sandra?'

'Nothing.'

'Oh, yes, you have. Had I borrowed it from anybody else, you wouldn't have minded, at all. Would you?'

'You're dreaming again. Sandra means nothing to me. Nothing, I tell you. Absolutely nothing!'

'O.K. What do I mean to you?'

'Less than nothing. Didn't you know?'

So that's what I've been waiting for! Nothing. Nothing which is something. Something, at least, to Biddy and her whore's heart.

Misogynist? Who, me? Of course not. Just hate being crowded. You can't fight affection. A white woman's affection included. Fight it and you're bait for any tyro's couch. Especially the kind of affection that intends putting 'things' on a level with decency and fair play, a sort of all's-hunky-dory-between-races-of-this-upset-world affectionate crap. Atonement if you like. Biddy is the prayer book that's left behind on the pew and never taken with you out into the street.

'Where are your devil's horns and tail, tonight, old son?' Sandra glides up to us and stops amidst a tinkle of bracelet charms. Obviously coming up for air.

'What d'you mean, Sandra?'

'You look so angelic, dear heart. That's all.'

'Don't feel it though.'

'Have you hustled our members in the corner?'

'Yes.'

'Try again.'

'O.K.'

Off to chew the Yankee dollar. Sandra's turning round to Biddy. Poor Biddy. Sandra's the boss every time.

What new poison can I offer these half-dead suckers? Surely they're accustomed to Sandra's usual. They'd love some Jamaican white rum, if only Sandra stocked it. Change of colour would boost the sales if nothing else. Reminds me of this coat of mine. Tired of its whiteness, its shortness, its distinction. How's Biddy doing? Take a sly and figure it out. Both of them chatting like rivers in spate. Both at arm's length, though. Hope they wash away each other's sins when they're about it. Pity that water's the birth symbol, too.

Nobody's buying a damn' thing. Not even a light for a cigarette. The lighter trick is the easiest. Nothing to it. Cuts the waiter's embarrassment by three-quarters. Of course, it's the customer's good sense and decency being appealed to. These are not always available. Presidents catch on too quickly. And why shouldn't they? They've had enough practice in sucking up and crawling – not all, but the majority in this crab-hole, at any rate. Yes sir, boss man! Now you see de light and then you just don't! De quickness of de hand deceive de eye, as de man done say from time of ole!

Back to the bar.

'Any orders?'

'No, Sandra.'

'Life's like that.'

'I suppose so.'

Cool pause. Biddy positions her ears for an intake of God knows what. Sandra has on her expensive look tonight. Expensive smell, to match as well. Could have been close to Sandra if she hadn't her middle-classery wrapped so tightly about her. Guess I'm too much like her. Still, I'm close enough as it is. At least, Biddy makes me think so.

Funny thing about Sandra is that every now and then she exposes the girl-come-to-London side of her like a badge of office. From the provinces to this smell of success along the way. Wonder what her mistakes were like?

'What's happening later?'

'Home for me, Sandra.'

'Want to do a job for me?'

'Where?'

'At home.'

'What's the job?'

'The usual.'

'Well, Sandra, I –'

'Well, nothing. I'm having a few officers and one or two others up for late supper and cards. You could make a packet if you care to come along. Serve drinks and help clear up.'

'Can you let me out this time?'

'O.K. No skin off my nose, Johnnie. It's their money and your tips. Nothing to do with me.'

'I know, Sandra. But –'

'Just thought you'd like to earn a little bit on the side. Considering tonight's haul, you'd do well to come up later.'

'I can't tonight.'

'Anyway, it's your pocket. I'd better go down and ask the other Rockefeller, I suppose.'

'Sorry, Sandra.'

'Not to worry, Johnnie.'

'D'you think you'll make out all right?'

'Sure. Prefer you, actually. But what to do?'

A tiny chuckle and she glides away. Tinkle of bracelet charms, again.

I know Biddy's beaming like a lighthouse, right now. Won't give her the pleasure of facing her. Play it low and cool. She's on top of everything, now. Sandra draws a duck and Biddy rejoices. Better not stay around the bar. Think I'll walk over to the 'fix' and stomach some of his dialogue, instead. Anything to dodge the clammy hand of – call it what you may. Heave away from the bar and head straight for the table by the dartboard. Almost there, when –

'If you aren't going to Sandra's, why don't you come back with me for something to eat?'

Over the shoulder like a ping-pong shot: 'Right. I'll do that. Thanks.'

Now why did I have to do that little stupid thing? You've done it, boy! You've goofed like the rest and you'll suffer like a whale harpooned through the eyes. Why did I think of a whale? Could have thought of a rat in a trap; a dog in a kennel; a moth round a lamp; fish on a hook; anything. I suppose a whale's more my size of fool.

Oh Lord! Biddy's the big wheel for ever and ever. Damned ass! She's the cream. Plans for action must be running in at this very moment. But why shouldn't I adore every second of it? It's free, unexpected, tested, approved, and not on the game. Ha!

I'd prefer to be in the cabin talking to Fiona, and don't I know it. Talking to Biddy is like – said it before, in any case. Fiona? Strange desire to listen to her madcap story about Joseph, the off-white Provider, all over again. Maybe there's more to come. About the baby. About her parents. About goof-balls Gerald. About Fiona herself minus the rest. I wonder what Fiona would be like minus the rest? So many women minus the rest are dull and smelly as hell; that's the trouble, really. Maybe it's just my nose or my imagination. Or just my fear. Mother always warned me about my unpreparedness to face up to stark realities. Bless her and her warnings! Unpreparedness, fear, disinclination, or anything she'd like to call it!

'Hi, Pres! Come a-here, my man!'

That's the 'fix'. On time. Saved in the nick. Might need to be saved from him, too. Anyway, later for that.

The fast-talking 'fix', again: 'Hey, look! We can't talk with these hanging on like Christmas buntings, daddy-o. Let's shift outside and make it private-like, man!'

'Sure.'

The 'fix' and I creep out. The noise tails off all catlike and cute, as the 'fix' might have put it. Outside looks minus. He sinks his fists into his trouser pockets and assumes the Pres posture – shoulders hunched, head drooping, and feet doing a stationary soft-shoe shuffle. Bojangles in the blood!

'Now dig, Johnnie. I got me a pile o' loot tonight somewhere all stacked up and waiting to make with the good times, man.'

'Where?'

'The man's got it, Johnnie-O. All safe and sound. I've just gotta say the word and we're in business. Like that!'

'Like that, is it?'

'Sure thing, Ace. How much can you rustle up between now and closing time?'

'I can't.'

'Don't gimme that, Pres.'

'Honestly.'

'Why?'

'Not my line, that's all.'

'Come off, Ace. Git off my back, will you! You're my boy for the fix and you knows it.'

'I'm not. And I don't intend to start the racket for you either. Understand?'

'No, Pres. No. Capital N-O!'

'Well, that's your lookout, isn't it?'

'Tell you what – things are cool, Ace. Drop a name and we're still in business. O.K.?'

'Not even that.'

'Man, you're the brakes. The very brakes, daddy-o. Can't you see them broads waiting for the concert? Can't you push it so we all live nice and easy, man? We've got a ball on our hands later and the time's gotta roll but smooth, baby. How's about a turnabout?'

'Can't help you, Pres. Sorry.'

'So that's the final rubber stamp, eh?'

'Yes, Pres.'

Leaving him. Heading back to the bar. He follows, hopping rhythmically and muting an imaginary blues trumpet. Gone! The man's real gone! High for the lack of a fix. It's all in the mind, as the man says.

Biddy's more than cool. She's easy. She's gliding and hoping for heaven. Two tables begin a jazzy clamour for service. Biddy smiles at me and prepares for an onslaught. The orders are coming, roaring at me – in all, ten Scotches, three gins, three lagers, two light ales, and twenty cigarettes. Almost forgot – two Scotches for me.

Biddy's hands are pistons. The trays are dry and nearly shining. The girl's a wonder! She has grabbed a man. That's why.

Then the lull.

Everybody sits it out and the waiter's dead for another half an hour. So is the tightfisted late dropper-in who parks himself by the dartboard. Maybe he's the man the 'fix' is waiting for. Who knows? Maybe he's the man with the loot. The 'fix' daddy.

Hoof around slowly and empty a few ashtrays. Take a peep at the latecomer. Thought as much. The provider himself. Drooping eyeballs, the lot. Will save himself some money tonight, though. Might be depending on the 'fix', for all I know. Certainly looks the type that would knock the hell out of anybody who lets him down.

The 'fix' looks at him, winks and shakes his head from side to side. The latecomer blinks and shuffles towards the door. He shuffles back again, and stands with his back to the table. The 'fix' gets up and walks to the door. The latecomer joins him. Both glide through the door.

Last orders! Big shout. Another onslaught. Bottles clink and clank as Biddy prepares herself. Orders all over the place. Pushing 'shorts' like anything.

The 'fix' returns. Unaccompanied.

Bottles away. And the suckers are being hustled off the premises. The 'fix' is high against his will. He hasn't given up, though. Crouching low, he slides between Biddy and Sandra. Biddy's locking the door and Sandra's patting her hair into shape at the back. She winks at me and moves away slowly. Biddy straightens up and grabs the 'fix' round the waist. She jerks him to and he snaps suddenly erect and attentive.

'What's up with you, now?'

'The ball is on and I'm off, Biddy-O. We're all off, God-damn!'

'Is that all?'

Biddy-O, that's not all, no how! I'm in trouble. Real trouble, girl. The works.'

Biddy looks at me and sighs. Sandra looks at Biddy and shakes her head disconsolately. The 'fix' says nothing more. Finally, he sags.

I'm beginning to feel released. I know what's happening to Biddy's bleeding heart. Of course, I do. It's bleeding profusely at this very moment. Bleeding for a displaced, 'fixless', weak-kneed, bilious G.I.

'See you later, Johnnie.'

'What's wrong with you?' As if I don't damn' well know.

'I must take him home, Johnnie.'

'Why?' As if I'm not greatly relieved.

'Because it wouldn't be wise to let him go off like this. I think he's in some sort of trouble or the other. Might even get picked up by the A.P.s, or anybody for that matter. You can never tell.'

'What about his friends?' Sandra asks calmly.

'And what about our supper date, Biddy-O?' I ask viciously.

Sandra chuckles as if she's found us out – the dark secret. She adds, 'So that's why you're busy tonight, Mr Rockefeller.'

About face. She gets no answer. She chuckles again and is forgotten.

'He's got no friends. They've left him, as you can see,' Biddy snaps back.

'And me?'

'Tomorrow, Johnnie. Any time. You know that.'

Our little gathering breaks up. Tight, nervous, little gathering, as it is, simply disintegrates like nothing. Sandra waves down a taxi. I walk away, relieved and slightly peeved. Maybe a trifle nauseated.

Wonder what name the 'fix' travels under? Bet it's something to do with Booker T. Washington, or Abraham Lincoln, or William Edward Burghardt DuBois, or John Brown 'of Osawatomie'.

Couldn't care less, really. Or so I feel anyway, right now.

Down Oxford Street.

Not happy as a lark, either. Tips aren't too bad. Enough to hold on to. Ought to be able to pay back the fiver sooner than I thought.

What gives with Biddy? Her open-house heart annoys me no end. I'm sure it annoys Sandra, too. Could easily be the rub between them. Sandra, the eternally selfish one, and Biddy, the fool with a gaping wound for a heart and a feather pillow for a head.

89

So, she says that she'll take me any old time… 'Tomorrow, Johnnie. Any time. You know that.' She's damn' ready to accommodate all comers – suppose it's her way of getting as much out of the job as she's able to with rivals like the professionals around the place. Yet, she could be paid for it. Don't think she'd know how to ask. She's the original, aimless, giving type – country girl who's come down to town and remains a country girl for eternity. Must have had a man at some stage – a man around the house, a man who's pretending to be there for keeps, or to be kept by her for keeps.

Could introduce Ringo to her. Might develop nicely and fruitfully for all I know. Might even flow along into marriage and a house in the country. But, what if it were disastrous? Surely both would weather it. They're made that way. She's always giving and he's always calm and prepared. Always prepared to accept benefits.

Could introduce her to the man at Latimer Road Station. I bet she'd soften him up a bit. Would be interesting, very; he being all *Dale's Diary*, and she being terribly G.I.-and-P.X.-conscious. Certain she'd drive him mad. And a good job, too.

Passing Selfridge's. Quick glimpses of the windows. Round the corner like a bee. Heading for a No. 13.

Hell's loose! What's all this? Somebody's shouting my name. Careful now. Car-full of them – of us, I mean – black, brown and indistinct – all shouting for me. Larry's there, too.

Cross over to them.

'And why're you coloured chaps such happy people?'

Appreciative guffaws from all.

Larry speaks up, 'Listen, old man, you'd better jump in and make we take you down the hole, nuh.'

'Where to, Larry?'

'Down a little place in the back o' the Circus, father. Just back o' Regent Street, nuh.'

'The Egg?'

'Same place.'

'What's on down there tonight?'

'Special happenings, man. Specialities, Johnnie.'

'Leave me out, Larry.'

'Why?'

'Money. That's why.'

'Simple matter, Johnnie. We can fix something at the door. What we want don't need money, countryman.'

'All right.'

'Get in, then nuh.'

Door opens. Masses of bodies. Cigarette mushrooms all over the place. Distinct aroma of 'fix'. Not to worry, really. The boys will be boys if it kills them.

'What's the attraction, Larry?'

'Listen, Johnnie. It's G.I. pay day, and you know what that mean to all of we.'

'Had a few in tonight at my place, but they weren't exactly giving it away. What's so special at the Egg? How's it they're shelling it out there and nowhere else?'

'Because they're always ready to spend on things that count plenty to we hustlers, down at the Egg, Johnnie. We got the control of operations down there. Not like at your place where we can't get no breaks, father.'

'What kind of goods have you got to hustle, Larry?'

Let's see if I can take the rise out of him, a bit.

'More than you'd be able to handle.'

'I see.'

No more conversation. The car rumbles and jerks. It bows and screeches Hollywood style. Finally, the Egg. Easy pass-by at the door. Not a word said. Busman's holiday for me – so I suppose it's all right by everybody. The doorman behaves like a punchie by imitation rather than by profession. Can just imagine how much he pockets!

Down the hole with Larry. He begins his big hustle exercise. Rounding up a gang of girls. Four to be precise. The way to acquire Lawrence Denton & Co. Ltd. I suppose.

I dislike this place intensely. Still, I'm always dropping in. Dislike the master of ceremonies, too. Nasty piece of work from the Lucea bush in Jamaica. The type who falls in love with London and never has anything to give in return but a babble of stories about the upper-class types he's mixed with during the war. He's always got a sordid story about some unfortunate Lady this-or-that whom he had on a string. Bet he only held her hand, if the truth be known. Yet, that must be his way of contributing to the effort.

Speak of the devil, or rather think of the devil and he bloody well appears.

'Well, well! Mr Sobert.'

'Hello, Maxwell.'

'D'you know something, dear boy! Most of my crowd refuse to visit me any more. They're afraid of coming down here. I just don't know what this club's coming to. Marvellous spenders, too. And talking about class! They give this place so much class, that you'd believe you're in the Colony Club in Berkeley Square.'

No reply. Stand tight and wait. There's bound to be the trimmings after this.

'I could build this club on the right lines. I could build it on their patronage alone, if things were left to me. No trouble whatsoever. Manners perfect! Lovely people. Give me those every time. D'you know Lady Catherine Daws-Blacken came down here the other night and…'

Babble on, crap-hound. Maxwell, you're a tall, consumptive, unintelligent ponce. Shut up! Upper classes, drinking glasses, stupid rasses…you make me sick!

Good! Being relieved, at last. Some rotting whore wants him to put her in the floor show. Slip away before he's got time to re-wind.

What makes him think that I'm not one of the stinkers? Finds me every time and depresses me with the trials and tribulations brought down on him by our 'black brothers' and their unwanted presence. Old man Arnold is a godsend to Maxwell. How he puts up with all this upper-class propaganda and pays him on top of it, I can't understand. I'm sure the old man could do better than Maxwell. Must be a damn' good reason why he's holding on to him. Maybe he, too, has a touch of upper classery in his sooty veins.

The moth-eaten band looks tired and dejected. The G.I. mass is getting thicker and thicker. The girls, smellier and smellier. Larry's on to another bunch of them near the bandstand. What's up?

Think I'll go over and pump Larry gently.

'What's the crazy air-lift about, countryman?'

'Johnnie boy! You's watching a skirt-lift if there's ever to be one. And when you hear from the shout, your friend Larry will be collecting for his flawless delivery and a little nearer the millionaire class.'

'Or better still, Larry – nearer the Lawrence Denton & Co. Ltd. class?'

'I tell you what to do, Johnnie. You watch how I handle the proceedings and see if I don't hustle like a dream, old man.'

'Where's the skirt-lift bound for?'

'My place.'

'How many?'

'Six and six.'

'Twelve of them? In your tiny barbershop?'

'Yep.'

'But there's hardly room enough for four –'

'We ain't dancing down there, countryman. We're meditating and we're going to hold a proper meeting house.'

'And you expect them to leave a luscious floor show for that?'

'Of course. Why not? They'll be private and happy as the day's long, countryman.'

'You mean you're holding a –'

'All right. Don't publish the blasted thing!'

'But, Larry, that's begging for trouble.'

'Don't we all.'

'What d'you mean?'

'Don't we all ask for trouble when we leave home and come to this country, countryman? Don't we all willingly expose weselves to the traditions of this England when we turn we back on The Rock? And what's more, it's worth it, Johnnie. Ten bob a head, and the "thing" is five bob a stick. Now, you is a ready reckoner, so reckon that for a party of twelve!'

'I see.'

I've had it! Maxwell's heading my way, again. Stand your ground, boy. Can't be long before the floor show starts anyway. Just look at this pompous ponce!

'You know, Sobert, you should have been in London during

93

the war. Lovely time. A really lovely time. D'you see this mess, here? Could never have happened then. No, sir! Never. There'd be no room for them.'

'Why?'

'Simply because no club owner or secretary would have had them. A few would be allowed in for atmosphere, that's all.'

'How did you get in?'

'Not as atmosphere.'

'As what, then?'

'Well, for one thing, I was friendly with the Duke of…better not call any names. I used to take out a duke's niece in those days and she was deeply interested in jazz and African drumming. So, we went all over the place in search of what she called, "the real thing".'

'Weren't you enough!'

'Wait a minute! Don't you ever make that mistake, Sobert! Don't you ever mix me up with this lot.'

'Were they better behaved in those days?'

'What days?'

'The halcyon days, Maxwell.'

'Of course.'

'I wonder why?'

'The G.I. influence wasn't as corrupting. And the majority of us, West Indians, Africans, Americans, were in the Services. At least, there was a job to go to after the spree. Nowadays the spree is the job and there's a long day's rest afterwards.'

'How d'you stick it down here, Maxwell?'

'What d'you mean by that?'

'I mean, after all's said and done, a place like this should be purgatory for you. What with all the filth and working-class dullness about, I would have imagined that the Egg's the last port of call for a name-dropper like you.'

'My job is to build up a first-rate clientele for the old man. And that means I'm in charge of weeding out all these hustlers and whores, as expertly as possible. After that, my crowd will be introduced one by one.'

'Your crowd? What's it like?'

'Come down in three months and you'll see the difference. My dear Sobert, I'm telling you, you won't recognize all this filth when the right people are in it.'

'In it, is right!'

Pause. He looks at his watch and straightens his tie. Inspects his shoes, twirls his cuff-links into view, and clears his throat.

'Sobert, my man, I'll have to leave you, now. The floor show is due to begin in a few minutes. Hell of a job, you know! It's no joke trying to keep a pack of savages amused for one hour.'

'Maxwell, you're a must for Mrs Blount's next tea-party. She'd love you, boy! You might even end up owning the house, or something equally rewarding like that. You crap-hound!'

Where's Larry? Ah, yes. Got his sixes in line. Clever little barber of Oxford Circus, you! What's the time?

'Larry.'

'Yes, Johnnie boy.'

'Got the time?'

'Near one o'clock, I think. You going already?'

'Think so.'

'You can join us if you get a bitch to come along, you know.'

Sure. I know. I'd love to get Mrs Blount, if only she'd come. What an imperialist party we'd have: she on the floor, and the blacks exhaling 'happiness' in her face.

'You haven't answered me, Johnnie. You going to get you a girl and come down with us? You don't have to pay a farthing.'

'All right. See you there, later on.'

'You will find your way without any bother because the car will be outside. How you going get there?'

'The all-night bus, I suppose.'

'O.K. See you, countryman.'

Maxwell has called his savages to order. The band sounds tired and confused.

Oh Lord! He's using his wartime accent. Can't take this.

Working my way to the exit. Enough of Larry for one night. Enough of Maxwell, too. Enough of the West End.

Late as it is, there's nothing to keep me down here. Think I'll stroll along and window shop. They're not lighted; at least, most of them aren't. Better than listening to Maxwell and his slop.

95

7

Tuesday already. A few hours and it'll be six o'clock, August Tuesday, another hit-and-miss day four thousand miles away from a little place affectionately called The Rock.

The Rock of what? That's what I'd like to know. Perhaps, the tourist guide books know how to explain it attractively. Something like The Rock of Pleasure. Or The Rock of Sunshine and Romance. Or, simply, The British Rock.

Carpet on the stairs seems to be a presence. Everybody's sleeping. Even Trado the Courageous. Even Shakuntala the delightful Orient Express. And as I'm about it, even Mrs Blount the Locust.

Wish Fiona would visit me.

Strange need for her company, suddenly. Wouldn't it be marvellous if she's in the cabin waiting for me? Of course, it would be marvellous.

Just right, at this hour of the morning.

I'm coming, Fiona. Coming to hear more about Joseph, Gerald and all the sordid details involved. Just sit tight, girl. I'm coming like a panting dog, Fiona. Coming to be melodramatically yours, Fiona. I'm climbing the stairs right now. Hold on. Don't give up.

An empty room.

Hoping for the skies. But doesn't everybody at some time or the other? In a way, I'm relieved she's not in here. Yes. Really relieved. More than that. Positively at ease.

Throw myself across the bed. Can't be bothered to undress. Do that later. Lovely without the glare of the top light. Morning's oozing in: funny little shadows on the ceiling. Elfin shapes. Shapes of mother elf, father elf, and a string of baby elves...

'A whole day, son! Imagine! You've wasted a whole day. Do you think that's the way to pass an exam? When I was your age, I had very few of your advantages. I had to look after a large house, five young children and a great deal more besides. I've never regretted it. It's a discipline that has done wonders for me, son. My mother always had a baby to occupy her time, and I had to take over from her and run the house. All this, plus school work to cope with. And both were done. Both were well done. Exams were passed and the family was looked after. D'you see what I mean?'

'Humm.'

'Is that all you can say?'

'Yes. Why? You wanted more?'

'Do you think that running aimlessly in and out of people's backyards will get you a first-class pass in the Senior Cambridge Certificate Examination? Do you?'

'I don't know.'

'He doesn't know! Of course, you *don't* know. Believe me, son, you're heading for a fall. The world's geared to certificates, diplomas, degrees and the rest. It's a specialist world, and you're right outside it if you don't get the necessary qualifications. The Senior Cambridge is a start. It's not much, but it's a start. It's a good practice for the stiffer ones, later on. How're the theorems getting on?'

'So-so.'

'Only so-so? Mastered Theorem 29, yet?'

'What's that one?'

'Are you joking or something, boy?'

'No. I'm not. What's 29 about?'

'So you can find time to gallop about the streets like a dray horse but you can't retain a simple theorem. D'you realize how important that theorem is?'

'No, Mother.'

'So it's *Mother*, now, is it? Soft soap, eh? You know as well as I do that that word hasn't passed your lips for nearly three days. Why the effort all of a sudden?'

'I think I'd better go to my room.'

'Why?'

'Got to get a piece of valve rubber for the front wheel.'

'That bicycle's the curse of curses, believe me.'

'I know.'

'Are you being impertinent?'

'No.'

'I suppose you're going out?'

'Yes.'

'Yes, what?'

'Yes, Mother.'

'That's better. Now, where to?'

'Down the road.'

'Where down the road?'

'Oh Lord, Mother! Give us a chance, will you.'

'It's easier to say, "Give *me* a chance".'

'O.K. Give me a chance.'

'You'll never make the grade, Johnnie. Never. Not at this terribly slow rate, son. You can depend on that, my boy. Never. Never…'

She ought to see me, now. Fully dressed, shoes and all, sprawling across the bed. A lighthearted reminder like, 'A little gentleman never lies down in his clothes' wouldn't mean a thing, at this moment.

Funny little shadows on the ceiling aren't elfin shapes any longer. They're blobs of light and shade, big blobs, angular blobs, blobs without romance or fancy.

Might as well turn on the light and get undressed.

These pyjamas ought to be thrown away. Not one pair with a sound seat or any warmth for that matter. Make do with this red one. Not too bad as ripped arses go.

And who's bloody well knocking, now?

'Coming. Just a moment.'

Talk about being caught with your…might be Fiona. No. She wouldn't make a habit of it, being as desperately English as she is and all that. Rubbish!

'Coming.'

Pause. Gripping the pyjama trousers round the waist and stretching to reach the door knob. Hoping the damn' thing doesn't slip down.

'It's you. You're up early.'

'I've just got in, actually. I saw your light; silly, I know, but I thought I'd come up for a chat.'

'Fine by me, Dick. Fine. Sit on the bed.'

'Thank you.'

'Where've you been?'

'The Dorchester.'

'Inside or out?'

'Where d'you expect?'

Can't say I like the look of his eyes. Strange kind of hurt look. Funny how raw his lids are. Dick's a bit of a puzzle. I'm sure he knows that I think so, too. Why should I like him as much as I do? That's a hell of a thought, anyway. Well, I suppose it's all right for a man to feel sympathetic towards another man without the world having to come to an abrupt end.

He's pink and raw around the mouth. Lower lip twitches. Tousled hair. Reminds me of what people used to say about the English population at home: 'Massa! When it rain don't you ever walk too near any of those limey people, you hear. If you ever does forget the warning, you will get such a surprise that your nose won't stop paying for it for days. And is purely because they won't bathe like ordinary people. Rawness is the English people smell after the rain done fall. True word!'

'What's the time, Dick?'

'Five-forty-five.'

Short and sweet. Doesn't want to talk. Looks as if he's wrestling with his ghost or something. I'm glad he has come up to see me. He must have had a damn'good reason for doing so. Yet, nothing's nothing, as Larry would say. Nothing's quite apparently something. How do I squeeze it out of him? Might as well wait and see. Or rather wait and hear when the man's ready to give. Come on, boy! Give from the bottom of that dark soul of yours. I'm listening like a recorder. Think I'll just prod a little. Not too menacingly, though.

'Been out drinking, Dick?'

No reply. He's fumbling for cigarettes. Walks to the window. Looks out and sighs.

'What's worrying you, Dick? What's wrong?'

'Oh, nothing.'

Nice, cold, and flat. Of course something's wrong. Something's eating something, as Larry again would say.

What's he looking for at this hour? I wonder if he has smashed the car?

'Got the car outside?'

'Yes.'

99

'What're you looking for outside then?'

'Nothing.'

That was short and sweet: bang-bang, bang-bang! Doesn't matter. I'll get around him, somehow. I'll get a layer or two of his pink rawness scraped away before long.

'D'you know what?'

'No. I don't, Dick. What's eating you?'

Clammy silence. Sulking kind of silence. Pouting. Bellow him out, that's the treatment.

'Well!'

'All right. I'll tell you, Johnnie. I'll tell you the whole gory business.'

Slight dramatic pause. Disgusted look.

'That filthy woman's decided that it's my time to be seduced.'

'What woman?'

'My employer.'

'Oh, yes?'

'Oh, bloody yes! She sank her talons tonight, all right; and I wasn't co-operative. She screamed the place down and behaved like a maniac. Answer that one, now, Johnnie! And what's more, she'll do it again. That's what I'm terrified of. She'll obviously try it again without batting an eye.'

'Fine. So she'll try it again. She'll probably try a hundred times more, over and over again. And she'll succeed, as well.'

'You don't understand, do you?'

'I do.'

'Well?'

'Well what, Dickie boy?'

'Don't call me that; I hate it.'

'You're hating a lot of things, lately, aren't you?'

No reply.

He seems a little less perturbed. Thank God for that, too. He is being a fish-face; or isn't he? Almost hysterical.

'I think I'll go to bed. See you later. Thanks for listening, Johnnie.'

'Thanks for nothing. See you.'

Hell! Was I too rough? Played it like a novice in search of a coach, as Biddy would say. I'd better write him a note. Shove it under his door. I'll be contrite and nice. I'll be honest: not nice. I'll do that, now. Right now. I'll say I'm sorry; didn't really mean to be unreasonable; understand everything, actually; very sorry. I'll do it just like that. Might just be the thing for both our anxieties…putrid, ever so smelly anxieties…oh, poor, rich us! Anyway, it is the thing to do. Might even make me sleep less jaggedly. And, of course, I want to write him a note of apology; I want to badly; I will; I must.

My Dear Dick,

About our little tiff: forgive me. I didn't mean to be nasty to you. Clumsy, I know, but it's my way of trying to help out. What I really wanted to do was to…

Sounds like a string of gasping inanities. The whole thing is as sincere as the colon between 'tiff' and 'forgive'; ready made and fatuous. Rip it up and begin again.

Dick,

Do forgive my inconsiderate behaviour…

8

'You're up bright and early!'

'Good morning, Fiona. Yes. You, too.'

Sounds neighbourly and perky this morning. Wonder what's behind the mask? Where's the dark problem gone to? Trado the tragic ponce must be dead or something. She may have done him in for all I know. UNMARRIED MARRIED MAN FOUND STRANGLED IN BED: UNMARRIED MARRIED WOMAN HAS VOLUNTEERED TO BE OF HELP TO THE POLICE.

'Going out already?'

'Just a little stroll.'

'Where to, Johnnie?'

'Up to the Heath inevitably.'

'I'll come with you, if you can wait a few minutes.' Prettyplease pause. 'All right by you, Johnnie?'

'Sure, Fiona. I'll go on ahead, slowly.'

'Fine. I'll catch you up.'

Why does she want to do this little mad thing? She may want to prove something…try out a new form of punishment on Trado the Centurion…cause alarm or some blooming chaos…or even a little intrigue.

On the other hand, she may want to talk to me. She may genuinely want to go for a walk across the Heath. She may want to escape Trado's first yawns, etc. She may want to escape an early-morning row; escape me never, says Trado the Flypaper-man.

Think I'll tell her that I expected her last night. After a bit of nonsense chatter I'll slip that one in as if nothing's happened. I'll tell her how disappointed I was not to have had my dream come true. (Christ! That sounds fruity and insincere.) Anyway, what impression would that make? None, I bet! And who wants to make an impression? Dream? What bloody dream?

I suppose I will find something to say to her. Something conversational. Something simple and in ordinary everyday taste. Nothing excessive and insincere.

★   ★   ★

'It's always lovely up here at this time, Johnnie. No heavy traffic, very few passers-by, and above all no earnest dog-lovers.'

'Fiona, you aren't as selfish as that, are you now?'

'Could be.'

'It's everybody's Heath, isn't it? Our own big rock garden, eh?'

'Not big enough for me, Johnnie. Not half as big as I'd like it.'

'Sounds like the Heath's a world.'

'Could be. Could very well be.'

So that's it. She's in her John Donne mood, is she. I'll play along. Anything to please. Anything to forget Dick for a while.

I do hope he received the note in the right spirit. He might just be further put out by it. Can never tell: Dick, the driver of the rich; Dick, the driver of the poor; Dick, the hell-driver.

I suppose there's more to it than my feeble hope can cure. Anyway, I want him to take it the way it was meant when I wrote it. Words are such bastard dissemblers. Ancient convenient

102

hypocrites. Still, we got to live by them, toe to toe, consequence for consequence, hurt for hurt, and so on right down the flaming hill.

'Let's squat here, Johnnie.'

'O.K.'

'Still afraid of me?'

'What's up? Who told you that, anyway?'

'Aren't you?'

'I don't think so.'

'Give me your hand.'

Yes. This is the treatment, all right. This is what the Heath's for. All bloody Heaths. All over the panting world. Why do the decent bitches all behave like B film actresses...a sort of slap-happy busman's holiday the whole way through?

Yet, it may not be a busman's holiday act, at all. She may well want to be affectionate...maybe Trado the Trappist doesn't give her the chance to be 'sweet' to him.

It's no use; I'm completely outside this one. I just don't know. Never will, either.

Dick ought to be up by now.

'I'm going to tell you a story, Johnnie; but you'll have to promise me something.'

'What?'

'Not to think me a jackass.'

'O.K. I'll not think you a jackass, Fiona; only a girl with a story to tell. A girl with a history of mysteries.'

'That's a charming way of putting it. Very charming, indeed.' Mercurial pause. 'Yes. Very charming.'

For luck's sake, who's seducing whom? Oh, man! My dearest Trado, the Discobolus, ought to be here to witness our little matutinal frolic. Wouldn't he tra-la-la all over us with both his big feet! Wouldn't Trado, the Tightrope Traditional-ist, simply spit fireballs into dear Matuta Fiona's aching bifur-cation (crotch is really the better word...still, you can never tell...can you, now?) and then make a mess of me with his screwed-up Sunday newspaper. Or would he use a more impressive weapon?

Don't suppose Dick would like it any, if it comes to that. Two

103

different problems altogether. Dick, the man with a thousand routes to the West End. And Trado of the Thousand Cuckolds, appropriately decorated for valour in facing up to the enemy without assistance from his Sunday mantelpiece or from T.P., i.e. the pub. Still licking my wounds; but that's all right – not to worry. I'm getting the benefit, or so it looks to me.

'Come back, Johnnie. You're with me; remember?'

'Yes. Sorry. What's the story that's threatening to change you into a jack?'

'I'm wondering whether I ought to or not.'

'I think you must be about to expose a mammoth slab of *This is Your Life*. Aren't you?' Cold reach-me-down laughter.

'No. Not that world-shaking. As a matter of fact, nothing seems important, any more. Nothing is nothing is nothing is nothing, any more, really.'

'What's it about?'

'You.'

Aha! She's coming out of her John Donne and entering, with aplomb, her wicked Gertrude Stein mood, now.

Bloody admirable for so early on a Tuesday morning. How much will it cost? Not overmuch, as Larry would say. I hope.

'When Gerald was making love to me last night, I slipped up and called him Johnnie, at a most crucial moment.'

'You did, did you? You called him by my name.'

'Yes.'

'That's a blow for somebody's ego; and a compliment for another's, isn't it?'

'Is that all you can say?'

'What should I have said, Fiona?'

'I don't know. I'm sorry. But you do make me feel a fool.'

What's she getting at? Of what use can I be to her? Does she sincerely hope that she'll find in me some sort of rest cure from Trado? How can I be of use to her?

That's a silly thought, anyway. Of course, we can use each other; and be of even greater use later on, perhaps. Later on when our sordid commitment starts to split at the seams. When, alas, the woman has to stand up for the man, and defend him passionately. For the words 'to stand', I could have written, 'to walk up and down her beat'. There must be a decent streak somewhere in my charcoal-grey soul, mustn't there? Marvellous, incurable conceit; but never mind. The dream's like that. Always.

Dick's on the brain, again. What would be his solution? And only Dick knows. He's a funny bastard of a friend, really. Stiff upper for most of the way and then, suddenly, a plasticine breakdown, sodden and lumpy. I like him, though. Feel easy with him…much easier than ever I'd feel with Fiona or Sandra or Biddy or Shakuntala or Mrs Blount or…

'Your hand is burning, Johnnie.'

'It's true, isn't it?'

'What?'

'A warm hand, a cold heart.'

'Just words if you ask me.'

'I asked you.'

'And I answered you, Johnnie.' Happy pause. 'What's happening to your humour?'

'Happened you mean? Left it!'

'Where, may I ask?'

'Where it shan't be easily exhausted.'

'Johnnie…Johnnie…please, don't do that to me, now. For God's sake, Johnnie…Johnnie…please…'

Aha! The ninth hour. Woman breaks out of shell and flings albumen all over the bloody place. Woman in her egg-flip mood!

'I'm sorry, Fiona. I didn't mean to hurt you. Forgive me.'

'Oh, Johnnie, if only you'd realize that you're not the only one with a thin skin. If only you'd try to understand people stripped of their politics.'

'Forgive me.'

'Kiss me, Johnnie. Kiss me. Just this once.'

Go ahead! Kiss the woman. It can't hurt you, boy. She has taken off her politics, in any case; dive in, boy-o! Give her a pleasant surprise.

What if she slips and calls me Joseph?

Doesn't matter. Quits.

All right. A kiss it'll be.

One crazy worm that gets the early bird for a kiss on 'appy 'Ampstead 'Eath. And why not? This is the life, isn't it? Illicit kisses,

105

illicit embraces, illicit albumen all over the place. Marvellous! We're alive!

Yet, I hope she doesn't say 'thank you' or any embarrassing thing like that. You can never tell what that sort of gratitude might make a man like me do, in order to cover up my small rotten modesty. Hah!

I've got to say something, now. What in hell's name must I say? How do I grant this crazy favour?

When the kiss is over, that's the moment of terror. What do we say to each other? Do we kiss again for the want of something intelligent to say?

A kiss is a bit of a betrayal, isn't it, really?

Not true! It's lovely. It's peace. It's understanding.

Poor bloody Judas!

'D'you know something?'

'Humm.'

'I was expecting you last night.'

'You were, Johnnie?'

'Yes. I imagined you up in the cabin waiting for me.'

'Is that what you call your room?'

'I imagined you waiting there to tell me more about your Gerald, or Joseph and yourself. I imagined you just sitting there waiting for me to come in.'

'Your imagination was ill used, Johnnie.'

'Why d'you say that?'

'Well, quite possibly, at that very moment Gerald may have been making –'

'Yes, I know. And you may have been blurting out my name. I know.'

'You sound hurt. Or are you just peeved? After all's said and done, you're the one with the imagination, aren't you?'

A sweet trickle of humour. Controlled chuckles.

'Right again. Aren't you the perfect Miss Reality? Even on the Heath.'

'Miss Reality, eh? D'you really think so, Johnnie?'

What's she doing now?

Talk about a mixed-up piece of fluff and there's one right in front of you: The Penny Proud and The Pound Profane.

Crass description. Crass title. Can't say I didn't attempt to capture the moment in words, can you? Never mind. It's usually easier on the second or third trial; or so they say in the business (or is it 'the trade'?).

Kiss once again.

Kiss and something's solved for Fiona. Something's pigeon-holed. Something's properly identified, and then documented, and then filed, and then forgotten. And then?

Don't ask me. I wouldn't know, would I now?

Little bouts of malevolence between each kiss, and we expiate everything. Just like that. She might even call me Gerald this time. Who can tell?

What I mean is this: she could easily do that because she wants to expiate, or shall I say simply, she wants to make amends for the sin she committed against Gerald, last night.

Another gap to fill.

I wish we could be interrupted. By anyone. Except Gerald, of course. Maybe Dick. These gaps are depressing. If only I could jump her and kiss her and not worry about it, I'd be more than all right, believe me.

I could try a clever dodge. And I most certainly will. I could try to recall a long poem. Taste it in the memory and in the mouth as mother would say. Something like what, though?

Something with the hop-skip-and-jump rhythm of 'The Ancient Mariner' or for that matter, 'Kubla Khan'. That might help to fill the gap. Of course it will. How do I begin?

Oh, yes. I know something even easier than that: I'll try recalling 'To A Young Ass'. How does it begin? Can't remember, at all. Something about a poor little foal and something else. What's it, now? Oh, hell! What's the first line?

Ah! Got it!

> Poor little Foal of an oppressed race!
> I love the languid patience of thy face.

Marvellous beginning. Just the sort of beginning to make me feel nice and self-pitying; very warming indeed. Let's see if I can get the rest of it.

And oft with gentle hand I give thee bread,
And clasp thy ragged coat, and pat thy head.

Can't remember the rest, though.
Something like…? No. Maybe it's…?
Ah, yes! It goes on I think to…

> Do thy prophetic fears anticipate,
> Meek Child of Misery! thy future fate?
> The starving meal, and all the thousand aches
> 'Which patient Merit of the Unworthy takes'?
> Or is thy sad heart thrill'd with filial pain
> To see thy wretched mother's shorten'd chain?
> And truly, very piteous is her lot –
> Chain'd to a log within a narrow spot,
> Where the close-eaten grass is scarcely seen,
> While sweet around her waves the tempting green!'

'You seem so withdrawn, Johnnie. Why?'
'Nothing.'
'Aren't you enjoying me?'
What the hell does she expect me to say to that? I suppose she wants me to purr affectionately, curl up beside her and say:
'Yes, Mummy darling. You make Cream of Wheat the *bestest* in the whole wide world.'
Enjoying?
It's such a quiet, intimate word, isn't it? Entertaining, too. Enjoying what?
Enjoying hot soup? Steak? Soufflé? A saucer of milk? Sleep?
'Aren't you with me, Johnnie?'
'Sure.'
You bet I'm with you, Jezebel, Ramona, Dolores of the lonely hills. I'm with you like a thorn in the backside. I'm with you in the same way that Dick's with me. It's all in the mind, as the man in the Goonery department would say. It's all cold pork slices and celery stalks. It's inexpensive at that.
So this is the world's idea of spending an early Henry Miller morning on the Heath? Conventional. Illicit and conventional. Happy.
Enjoying you, too, girl. Like a visit to the dentist.

I must tell Dick about this. Perhaps his Dorchester séance might seem trivial in comparison.

No. Better not compare notes. Betrayal is bad enough without confession thrown in as a gay selfless gesture.

As a small boy all this appeared to be easy and in keeping with ageing adults. (In those days, people aged after fifteen, in some strange way or other.) What was a kiss except a slip between the cup and lip, as a smart-alec fourteen-year-old would've proclaimed, plus accurate gesticulations of male and female in the advanced stage.

A slip?

A slip is just a sweet hour on the Heath, or in the nick of time between illicit bed-sheets, or on the third party's night-off, day-out, odd morning lie-in.

Poor odd morning lie-in Trado!

> Since those we love and those we hate,
> With all things mean and all things great,
> Pass in a desperate disarray
> Over the hills and far away:
> It must be, Dear, that, late or soon,
> Out of the ken of the watching moon,
> We shall abscond with Yesterday
> Over the hills and far away.

Till the whole wide world is smeared with albumen!

For ever and ever and ever, till the frightened cows come home. Who cares? Certainly not Trado, at this time of the morning. And that being the situation, why should I? So there we are: Fiona and I.

'Don't you feel peaceful and very self-contained, Johnnie? I do. I could remain here like this for years on end. I could give you all the solace you've ever wanted, and still have enough for myself. I could escape like this for ever.'

Thank God for that!

As long as she knows it, it's all right by me. This Fiona's no jack in the wilderness, at all. Escape, eh? So that's what yours truly is? A little escape ratchet. A clump of grass to stumble over playfully when there's nothing better to do.

It's not the same with Dick. It couldn't be. We aren't that mean, that scheming, that calm and calculating in the eye of the sex-storm. We're different. We're as near happiness together as Fiona and I are cut off from it right now. Dick doesn't cheat on solace. Or does he?

Dick doesn't cheat on anything. He doesn't use and abuse the word 'enjoy'. Things are what they seem when we're talking, laughing, being together like brothers. Like brothers. Like brothers. Why does that sound like a lie? It is, isn't it?

'Kiss me, again, Johnnie. Please, darling. Deep down. Deep, deep down, Johnnie. Please. Don't stop. Don't stop, ever, Johnnie.'

That might be as alien a speech as any coming at me from across the Heath, really. She's calling the wrong boy, and calling him so expertly. I'll answer with one side and my metallic self, and remain with the silence of my other half. So easy, so very, very easy, even when you don't know how.

But something's dying inside.

'You look pale, Johnnie.' Clammy silence, or rather a clammy pause, if the truth be known. 'Haven't I pleased you? Just a little, maybe?'

Something's dead, and I know it. I'm calmly certain about it, and that's no lie. I'm certain of it.

'Johnnie. Look at me. Please.'

Doesn't she feel it? I would, if she had seizure instead of relaxed compliance to offer me. She doesn't understand her defeat. She doesn't understand Dick's victory. Dick's supremacy. Dick's gift of freedom to me. And her gift of aching, nervous tension; her gift of boring, irreponsible, conventional conduct; her cross, my cross. She understands none of it.

That sounds messy, doesn't it? Too much like the truth. Sloppy. Self-pity is a bore, anyway. Yet, she doesn't understand that I'm outside her; not in with her in any way. *I'm away.* I'm with Dick. I'm with him in a whirlwind comparison of loves, likes, dislikes, the lot.

'Oh, Johnnie, darling, if only Gerald could make me feel this way. If only he could make me want him; want him the way I want you; the way I want you to go on and on and on. Don't stop, now. For God's sake, don't!'

She's blind. She's selfish. She's happy. Aren't we all on the Heath, on the eager search for some image, some consolation, some reassurance? (Pompous rhetoric, but never mind. There must be a good reason for it.) The splendid unveiling of the…

'Kiss me, again, Johnnie. Hold on to me. Reassure me. Make me feel wanted. Deeper, Johnnie! Deeper!'

Yes.

The splendid unveiling of the naked truth is not such a splendid thing after all. It's painful. It's…

'My God, Johnnie! That's it. Just there. Just there. Oh, you don't know what you're doing to me.'

And I suppose that's the way it goes: nice and uneven, nice and one-sided, the blind leading-on the blind.

But there's nothing blind about Dick and me. There can't be. And I'm not trying to falsify our equation. Or am I? I don't believe it. Maybe I don't want to believe it. Maybe the companionship is, as *they* say, quite natural. Or do *they* say so?

What am I heading for? Do I want to make a declaration? A credo? A better way of loving:

> Behold, I was shapen in iniquity;
> And in sin did my mother conceive me.
> Behold, thou desirest truth in the inward parts:
> And in the hidden part thou shalt make me to know wisdom.
> Purge me with hyssop, and I shall be clean:
> Wash me and I shall be whiter than snow.

The answers may come. Slowly, at first. But they'll come and I'll know. I'll recognize their validity. Their contribution to (I almost said 'happiness') sanity. To normalcy. To priggish, conventional conduct. To a blind society.

Or so I hope.

'Johnnie, you've made me so happy. So wanted. So much a woman, full and desired. Don't say anything. Don't spoil it. Let it live deep down between us where it belongs. Where it won't be exposed and made ugly. Where we can go back and find it another time.'

But she doesn't know that something's dead, does she?

BOOK TWO

MORE NOTES IN THE PRESENT
FOR A TIME PAST

Concordia discors
(Harmony in discord)
                    HORACE:
                    Epistles 1, xii, 19

9

October, Saturday evening; two months later.

Sounds like a dreary television note on the progress of the action of a Sunday-evening six-act melodrama, doesn't it? Well, I think so.

Take it any way you wish. Take it to heart and believe it, or take it out to the dustbin and drop it. Drop it the way I've dropped certain illusions, certain midday dreams about people and events, certain likes and dislikes, certain failures and successes.

★   ★   ★

So I'm playing Fiona and being happy with Dick. Two months of simultaneous emotional co-starring – split enterprise. Divided we stand, the more united we become.

So Fiona is forgetting or has forgotten her witch-doctor. Every visit to the cabin is a trip away from the Joseph Tragedy and the Trado Tempest. Every trip, and I lose a little more peace of mind, a little calm. (Pompous, but that's how it is.) Every trip, and she gains in intrigue, appetite and energy – her kind of calm, I suppose. (Not so pompous.)

So I'm doing the world a world of good by contributing to its mess of indecision by my own weak-kneed indecision about Fiona and Dick. Who's it going to be? the devil asks, and his answer comes like a shock: both or nothing at all.

That sounds idiotic and of course it is. It can't be both. And it can't be *nothing at all*.

So where's the choice to be? Where's the wind blowing in the blood? the man asks. Where's the stronger call? Who waits but me!

Dick doesn't suspect a thing. He doesn't suspect Fiona. He

knows about me: we meet; we drink tea; we chat; we exchange confidences; we warm to each other's insecurity; and, if you like, we warm to each other's defeated middle-classery.

We feel we understand each other. Even each other's irascibility, if the whole story be told.

Crazy Saturday evening, and the club's roaring with Yankee wealth and British thuggery. Calm, unobtrusive thuggery.

Bright lights are not being bright lights for nothing.

DuBois B. Washington, the 'fix' (thought as much he would've turned out to be DuBois or Washington or something like that), is sitting in hope at the bar of sorrows. He watches Biddy while Biddy waywardly watches Sandra while Sandra watches the cash register while the cash register spans the world and waits.

The 'fix': 'Hey, baby! This is the first break you've had in a good while, why don't you come on over and talk to me, huh?'

Slow money stroll over to the 'fix' and she says: 'You haven't told me what you intend to do about me, have you?'

I'd better get into firing position for this. Sounds like Biddy's been caught right where it hurts her and society.

'O.K., baby. You know I can't marry you. And you know the only other sensible way out. So what's the drag, huh?'

'You've been with me steadily ever since that night I first rescued you, and I've never once put the grips on you; you know that for yourself, don't you?'

'That's right for sure, baby.'

'Have I nagged you any?'

'No, doll. You ain't the kind, and I love you for that, too. You know I do, don't you?'

Screech of tongues. Flimsy pause.

Biddy's two months of bliss with DuBois B. Washington must be paid for. They'll both pay. Isn't that the way it goes? No one-way tickets sold down there; only day-returns. Good word that. 'Return'. They might even do that to each other after the heats. Nothing like old dead ground and a knocked-down hurdle. Poor unfortunate doctor, or is it going to be a genuine quack?

Ooops! Sandra swoops down on a table to the right. Better hustle off and leave Adam and Eve to discuss Eve's latest price of apples in her closed market. If I know Eve, she'll make Adam pay away his soul. But there's bound to be more souls in storage where his comes from.

'Sorry, Sandra. Didn't notice these. Can I take an order, boys? What's it going to be?'

Sandra winks and glides out to sea. She's got the payday awareness on tonight.

A couple of West Indian con boys begin to warm up for the pickings: 'Johnnie, old man, if you hear of a deal, slip it our way, nuh.'

'We'll give you a cut according to the takings, countryman. All correct?'

'All right.'

'Wait, Johnnie man, you hear the news?'

'What?'

'You mean you don't hear that the Egg get raided, old man?'

'When?'

'Four nights before last.'

'What's the score?'

'Well, your great friend, Algernon Maxwell, get nick.'

'What for?'

'Weed, old man. Weed, of all things.'

'How?'

'Well, according to the rumours that floating round Soho, it look like they plant the stuff on him.'

'Who's they?'

'Can never tell, Johnnie. Maxwell have so many enemies both in and out that you can never tell.'

'But he's not a "smoker". And it would be the last thing for him to do as an extra hustle. D'you know him as a dealer?'

'No. But you know how this West End of London operate.'

'Yes. I know.'

'I think they going knock him hard, you know.'

'How much d'you think?'

'Oh, anything up to a eighteen or so.'

'First offence, eh?'

'The law can do anything, old man.'

Think I'd better walk away, now.

117

God knows that I can't stand a bone in Maxwell's body, but at the same time he's not a bloody dope-pedlar. And to think they'd plant the stuff on him…better take an order and vanish: Sandra expects every waiter to do his duty on G.I. pay-night, and indeed, on any and every night.

'What's it going to be?' That didn't have the desired effect. I suppose Sandra is watching the proceedings, so I'd better make it look nice and imperious. 'I'll take your order, now, boys. What're you having?'

Scream, bawl the place down, my sitting ducks. Now's the time to impress your several bits of fluff, your several cheap little bits of fluff whom you'll depress later on when the lights are low. Come on, excel yourselves. I'm here to take it off you with a smile and a bow.

'Biddy.'

'Yes, Johnnie.'

'Seven lagers, three Scotch no ice, two large gingers!'

'Right!'

DuBois B. Washington's very quiet, docile even. Woman has sun-stroked another victim. So the 'fix' gone got fixed, huh. But for good. Supermarket treatment, isn't it, when you come to think of it seriously. Help yourself all you want when you're inside, but as soon as you start walking out, there's a bill to pay. Sounds fair, even for a supermarket. Don't suppose he fully grasped the deal, though. DuBois B. Washington, the ancient mariner, looks strong, silent and cowed. Very American male description that. Good film title, too: The Strong, The Silent, and The Cowed – the story of the All-American Boy – starring the top ten Method actors and the top two Method gruntresses.

'There you go, Johnnie. Watch out now, will you! The tray's wet and slippery.'

'Bless you, Biddy.'

I'd better unload the poison and collect. Do it with style, boy. That's the way to be remembered. That's the way to earn your tips. That's the way to make your fortune. Great life even when you weaken!

'Thanks. Yes. I'll have a drink. Scotch, please.'

Great night for everybody.

Cruise back to Biddy and check the temperature chart. She's not looking too hostile, so here's my chance to dig in and find out the latest crisis on the Anglo-American front.

'Here's your lolly, love. And a Scotch for me. All right, Biddy?'

'Lucky, aren't we?'

'Not more than you.'

'Oh, yes. You can say that again. Only cry next time, will you?'

'Why cry?'

'Well, wouldn't you?'

'You in trouble or something?'

'Yes, Johnnie. The real thing, this time.'

'What kind?'

'The only kind.'

'Oh?'

'Oh, yes.'

'Who's the master, Biddy? Or is that asking too much?'

'No. The master's right beside you.'

'The "fix"?'

'That's the master, all right; and for God's sake don't call him that horrible name.'

'Far gone?'

'Not really. But isn't any stage "far gone"?'

'Suppose so.'

Time to bet on another horse. Time to shove off. To beetle off. Any of those will do: dialogue at an end. Tears may be terribly close at hand. One can never tell, can one; especially one who's forgotten how to cry for somebody else?

And who's this shouting an entrance like Rockefeller himself? I don't believe it. No. Not him.

'Gawd, man, Johnnie, how you do, eh? How you keeping you'self in this house of iniquity and shame?'

'Larry?'

'Yes, man.'

'But what's with the new gear, prosperous suit, cigar, velour hat, blonde? What's up?' Pause. No reply. 'Come on, Larry, give, man!'

'Nothing special, countryman. Just cruising like; you know what I meaning to say?'

119

'Cruising, eh?'

'Well, you know what the wicked world is like, old man.'

'No. I don't.'

'You still up to the clever college logical way of talking, Johnnie boy. Never mind, I have my set of hard-ass values and I don't have no space in my politics for polite fencing and logical speech and good manners and all that sort of thing. But, no sir. None at all.'

'I see.'

I'd better humour Larry, and be quick about it, too. He's as explosive as they come, tonight. Must have been making on a very big deal. He seems a bit brittle, though. I'd better watch it, all the same. I'm sure Sandra wouldn't approve of an outburst so early in the running.

'But I don't see you no place, Johnnie. What happening? Let me see now; it must be really nearly six or eight weeks that I don't clap eye on you.'

'I know, Larry. I've been taking things easy on the night life. A man's got to go slow every so often, you know what I mean?'

'You got a steady piece-a-tail, now?'

'Not really.'

'Not really, in these people language, is a "yes" answer, you know. Anyway, it's a good thing for a man to hitch himself to a steady piece-a-tail every now and then.'

'Ideas like that one could easily start a fashion, Larry.'

'Now what does that piece-a-college talk suppose to indicate?'

'Nothing at all.'

'Is all right. I think I know what you intending to transfer to the masses, countryman. But stop! You hear the way I using the people English grammar?'

'I'm listening, Larry boy.'

'Fun and joke aside, though. I think that a piece-a-tail is a good balancer for most any man in this man's town.'

'Is that the reason for the blonde?'

'Who? This piece-a-flesh, here?'

'You don't care, do you, Larry?'

'College talk, again?'

'Never mind.'

'Well, now, did you hear that I's now a company director, old man?'

'Lawrence Denton & Company. Really?'

'Yes. And very happy, too, in the bargain. Most happy, Johnnie boy. Most so!'

'You seem halfway to heaven as it is; but tell me something, where did you find the money and the other necessaries?'

'Oh, that! Johnnie boy, I's a man made by the good, famous Father to reach to the top and nobody's going to stop me. Not even Mr Chancellor of the bleeding Exchequer, himself, can get in my way of progress.'

'And the extra ammunition?'

'What's that?'

'The blonde.'

'Oh, she! Just a piece-a-excess-profit-tax, old man. You got to arrange a show every time, you know. The public expect it of you. And who am I to let down my vast public? You tell me that. Eh?'

'Yes. You answered that one like a man from the Ministry of something or the other. Dead professional, Larry. Great!'

'Thank you for that piece-a-praise, countryman.'

'And what's new in Moneyland?'

'I like that piece-a-Gepography...or is it Geography I mean? Don't matter. I like it plenty, man. I must use it on the boys when I meet up with them. Well, to answer that question, Johnnie, all I have to say is that the only thing new is that Maxwell get a year and six months.'

'When?'

'Friday, yesterday afternoon.'

'That was quick.'

'The law works in wondrous ways, old man. Wondrous ways and wondrous quick, too.'

A slight touch of sadness in his voice, but that's all. He sighs and shrugs his shoulders. So do I, not really meaning it; must keep my buddy's company, though – a kind of loyalty, if you like.

'Anything else, Larry?'

'No, boy. Things going on the same way all about, nuh. I pray for a little distraction but nothing come up to distract me except the rent to pay and the other expenses about the place. But, wait little bit, I nearly forget to tell you the best one of all, Johnnie. You going to dead from laughing when I tell this one.'

'Scandal?'

'You say scandal? No, man. Worse than that! This is high-class comedy, old man. I have it right here with me. Just wait till I get it out of the wallet, nuh. I have to keep it in safe-keeping. It is a real precious documentation this.'

Flick of wrist and wallet plus sundry papers are on show. Larry fusses with contents and selects the 'document' in question. He opens it out and hands it to me with a slightly nervous smile.

'Now, old man, read this and tell me if the old motherland not getting like a bad C film, nuh. Read it quick.'

'Let's have it then.'

'No. Not that side first. The other side is the starting point. Turn over. That's it. Read it now.'

In fairly large print, the pamphlet warns:

Avoid disease – avoid contamination – avoid mongrelism. Send them back to their place of origin – get them out. Keep W.11 white – keep Notting Hill white – be wise. European people generally mix well with us and add something to our life. They are welcome if they do not make worse the housing and unemployment problems. But it is no good bringing coloured people who are very different to ourselves. Oil and water will not mix. To try the mixture does no good to anyone, and does much harm. It is unfair to our own first duty which is the preservation of the British people. Our first duty is to look after them. Throw out the old Labour and Tory politicians who have betrayed you. Act now! Join us today! If you don't, you will most certainly regret it.

'Well, Larry, it looks as if we're living in a little hick town in the Southern States, doesn't it?'

'Worse than that, countryman. We living in a place where Democracy can mean most things under the sun. When I read the pamphlet, I nearly burst out laughing at the one-sided ideas it expressing. I'm sure that with all my lack of education that I could draft a warning that would command much more respect than that one you just read. Man! When I read it first, I thought it to be a most comical piece-a-literature, you know. It funny and it sad, all at the same time. The man who draft it must be a very tormented soul. I can see now why popular belief say that tragedy and comedy antics are very near to each other.'

'Where did you get it?'

'I picked it up in Ladbroke Grove.'

'On the street?'

'Yes. In the gutter where it actually belong. I had to dry it off and preserve it for posterity, nuh.'

'Are you scared, Larry?'

'Who, me? No, man. I'm just saying to myself how funny the whole business is, especially under a Democracy like ours. The whole business is like a C film, I tell you. A fifth-feature, at that.'

'Have you shown it to the blonde?'

'I read it out to her, yes.'

'What was the reaction?'

'She just laugh and hug me tight same time, nuh.'

'She's a good girl.'

'She's all right I suppose, until she ready to turn like a Black Widow spider.'

'I wonder what organization is behind it?'

'I wondered about that too. And all I can say is that whoever backing a thing like that must be getting some lolly for it.'

'I don't understand you. Money? How?'

'Listen, Johnnie boy, can't you see that some money is being earned in a situation like this? The people or person concerned is being dropped a damn' good amount of lolly, old man. This is no scare. It is only a way for a few gangsters to make a few hundred pounds. Believe me. Lots of cash involved.'

'You think so, eh?'

'I'm sure it's so, Johnnie. Very sure.' Pause. 'I going to see you later. Going downstairs for a look-see, nuh.'

'Right. See you.'

And the night drags on.

The key characters stay on parade: Biddy watching Sandra;

Sandra watching the cash register; the cash register waiting on me and *the other*; and so it goes on, drink after drink, order after order.

DuBois B. Washington looks as if he's *penned in an inglorious spot*, to me. He'll wriggle out of it, I suppose. It's expected of all prisoners. Stoically.

10

G.I. pay-night comes to an end.

The other and I have made our tips. Sandra and the cash register are friends again. Biddy and DuBois B. Washington still have their flesh-and-blood problem to discuss, later on. And I'm away like news. The club's too stifling after eleven o'clock. Too many sighs for comfort. Anyway, I'm glad Sandra's gimmicky decorations are up.

What must I say to Fiona when I get in?

She'll be in the cabin, as usual, waiting, waiting, high hopes flying, hoping to renew her escape. What do I say? Do I say nothing? Or do I say something like this:

> Our hands have met, but not our hearts;
> Our hands will never meet again!

Of course not. Why?

Because like the blind Fiona she always will be, she'll then turn round sweetly to me and coo: 'Why, Johnnie darling, that's from Hood. "To A False Friend", isn't it?'

And then she'll make an eager gesture which means that it's time to kiss her again; to kiss her for her having remembered the quotation from her dim pre-Joseph past. And I'll be nowhere as usual. I'll be suspended in air because I don't know how to live in the present; because I don't know how to make a clean break, how to be cruel to be kind, how to be honest.

★   ★   ★

'You're home early?'

'Would have been earlier had I not stayed behind for a few minutes to help her disloyal highness, Queen Sandra, put up her rotten Hallowe'en decorations.'

'She certainly provides home away from home for the G.I.s. But why so early?'

'My dear Dick, Sandra's always celebrating long before and long after the occasion. It's part of her Anglo-American hostess-mania or whatever you want to call it.'

'Clever business brain, isn't she?'

'I suppose so. Coming up to my room?'

'Yes. For a little while.'

He seems relaxed. Very relaxed. And a good thing too.

'What about a cup of hot chocolate?'

'Lovely. Please.'

He does seem relaxed. Almost worries me. I'd better be thankful for small mercies and not try to know why. At any rate, he dislikes prying and, what's more, he loathes parental supervision in any form, especially by me. And who wouldn't?

I wonder what would be Dick's reaction to Larry's pamphlet? I'm sure he'd laugh it out of court, as Ringo would say. I'm sure he'd be embarrassed, too. And that's the funny thing about that kind of pamphlet: it embarrasses both sides. Maybe that's the hidden strength of Democracy; who knows?

And what am I thinking about that for? in any case! There are other problems. A score of them. Yet, I suppose, this one touches something vitally near my own mixed-up life. (That sounds like the thoughts of a real self-pitying 'nig', doesn't it? Yet, who can escape the odd inward cry? Oh, man! How messy can you get!)

And there'll be moments of joy and there'll be moments of tranquil recollection. (That's the fattest slice of pomposity to date.)

'Somebody's knocking, Johnnie.'

'Oh, yes. Would you see who it is, Dick?'

Pause. Chocolate perfume.

'May I come in?'

'By all means, Fiona. Cup of chocolate?'

125

'Yes, please.'

This could be sticky. Could be very sticky indeed. Could be interesting, too. In a sort of bedroom-farce-beta-minus way.

'And how's Dick?'

'Fine, Fiona. Couldn't be better, thank you. And you?'

'That's a change. Isn't it, Johnnie?'

'What, Fiona?'

'Didn't you hear? Dick's fine; couldn't be better, he says.'

'Yes. It is, isn't it?'

Silly thing to have said. A sort of betrayal in a way. A betrayal of Dick, I mean.

Fiona also seems 'top of the morning' fit. Even more relaxed than Dick, if it comes to that. What will we talk about? I wonder. We'd better not be too full-blooded about it either. Could easily get a directive from Mrs Blount, the ageing manatee.

Shakuntala must be on the loose with some rancid bit of student scum or the other. Bless her little cotton sari!

Come to that, I wonder where's Trado, the Bull?

'Fiona, where's Mr Trado?'

'Out. Why?'

'Oh, just asked.'

What do we talk about? This is worse than the pause between Fiona's kisses. Far worse.

Why did I have to call Trado mister? What would I have called him in any case? Gerald? Your husband? Trado?

World-shaking question: To call Trado mister, in front of his unmarried wife or not to call Trado mister; that's the burning question. (That was a nice bit of padding. Might even get away with it. It might appear to be contributing to the action of the narrative, somehow.) I'm always evading some bloody moment, or situation, or eerie decision, or…

'This is very good chocolate, Johnnie.'

'Thanks, but the secret is, of course, in the sweetening, Dick. Or so I believe anyway.'

'What do you mean?'

'Condensed milk.'

That was a silly bit of dialogue. Yet everything contributes to the glory of the whole. Every little scrap counts. Nothing is wasted. We're all important. To our parents. To the tax-man. To the ad.-man. To one another.

Minutes come and go unused. Huge patches of sighs. Sighs of boredom. Sighs of embarrassment. Sighs of appreciation. Sighs of recognition. Gap-filling sighs. Stifled sighs. Sighs of compassion.

It's obvious that none of us knows what to talk about in front of the other; the other being the one outsider in the ointment.

'How's the job, Dick?'

'It's there, Fiona. Steady as ever.'

'Oh, by the way, Johnnie, I brought this up to show you. I suppose Dick can share in it, can't he?'

'Share in what, Fiona?'

'All right, you two, don't panic. It's just a silly pamphlet I was handed today in the Portobello market.'

'What does it say?'

'Are you sure you can take it, Johnnie?'

'Suppose so. Read it aloud if it's so funny.'

'All right, I will. Here goes:

'White people of Notting Hill! Send all coloured immigrants back. Workers! Housewives! Business men! Young people! Join your Local Defence Organization now and fight effectively for your interests.

'Amused, Johnnie?'

What's she driving at? A very strange innovation for a party piece. How do I answer her?

'I could be, if you tried harder, Fiona.'

'All right. I'll take you up on that, right now. Listen to this scorcher:

'This country's greatest treasure has been its native stock, its Anglo-Saxon blood. Its great achievements have not been accidents of nature, but results of the character of our race, results of the quality of the British stock. Every mile of Britain, every moment of her history, every facet of her national life has

127

been stamped with the character of her native white folk. Our greatest concern must, therefore, be the preservation of her native blood. Accordingly, the White Defence League has been formed to awaken the British people to Britain's foremost problem, the Coloured invasion, and to the necessity, if Britain is to survive, of an effective and immediate policy to keep Britain White by stopping all Coloured immigration into Britain and by expelling all Coloured immigrants already here.

'Amused this time, my dear Johnnie?'

'Tolerably, Fiona. Why?'

Giant pause. A flutter of chocolate sipping and leg crossing and uncrossing. Furtive looks that aren't meant to be furtive.

More unused minutes. I'm wrong about that. I suppose that they are being used, in view of what has just been read to the quorum minus two.

Dick's so much more dynamic and attractive when he's relaxed that I do wish he would remain that way all the time. Crazy hope! Fiona's the selfish one – *the girl with a history of mysteries*; and in another way, the prize borough idiot with the forked tongue and the biting remark, 'And how are you and the old lady hitting it off, these days, Dick?'

'Solid mutual respect, as ever, Fiona.'

'As ever?'

'Yes. Why d'you ask?'

'Oh, nothing serious. Just thought it ought to have been mutual respect "after our collision of loyalties", rather than mutual respect "as ever".'

'I don't understand. After Mrs Blount and I collided? Is there some suspicion on my loyalty, as you put it? You suspect my loyalty, Fiona?'

'Oh, no! But she may have in some little way.'

I'd better be quick about it. Jump in. Fill the gap.

'More chocolate, Dick? Fiona?'

If I myself may say so, that's a real first-class Blount interjection. *More tea, Mr Sobert*; more chocolate!

Dear God, don't we all play the lamb against the lion!

Insinuation, thy name is woman, nothing else. Fiona, you're all mellow woman. You're all unrelieved woman: body, bitch and trouble. Will you please climb down from your high, shaky horse, and stop whipping Dick?

So you don't like him. *You don't fancy him.* You don't see in him a cure for your Joseph dyspepsia and your malignant Tradoitis. I fill the bill beautifully, don't I? dear sick, sycophantic bitch. Well, take your claws out and leave him alone!

'I'll leave you now, Johnnie.'

'Why so soon, Dick?'

'Bed's waiting, I suppose.'

'But you wanted to talk to me.'

'Another time. 'Night, Fiona.'

'Good night, Dick.'

So you've chased him away. You've played it like any snake in the grass, any old beaten-up whore-mistress. And now, you'll have me for yourself. For your body's calling, yearning, masochistic greed. You step like a bulldozer over everything that doesn't suit you; over everything that stands in the way of your slim happiness, your slim, unhealthy happiness, don't you? And you smile! And so expertly (so defy me, you seem to say, defy me and take the consequence), so deftly, like the mincing step of a Brewer Street whore, you prepare your attack on me.

'And what's wrong with you?'

'Thinking.'

'Of me?'

'Yes, Fiona. Of you. Of your violent dislike of decency. Of your greedy, relentless, all-consuming sexuality.'

'Big words will get you nowhere, my dear Johnnie. Not even an inch away from me.' Speckled, giddy chuckles.

'Inescapable Fiona, eh?'

'Not exactly. More, much more, sensible than that, my darling perplexed lover. I like being with you.'

'You like using me, you mean.'

'And what's wrong with that, may I ask?'

'Nearly everything.'

'Like what for instance?'

'Forget it. You wouldn't understand.'

'Perhaps I understand this.'

Splotchy spasm of a kiss. Nervous. Then another. Then a grasping splash of two more. All resounding kisses of a greedy claimant who knows her strength, and her victim's. And I'm not resisting. I'm not even thinking of doing so. I'm merely there. There and here with my heavy, uncertain body, my heavy, wavering body. I'll remain in my two minds, in my two attitudes, one ridiculous and shamed, the other blind and serving her needs.

I'm sure of it. She's salivating (and without the use of mercury). Bless her!

Across to the bed, like clockwork. We're moving like dancers in the hope of the right kind of music to sweep us away from reality. I don't know exactly what Fiona's hoping, but I can tell you what I'm hoping: I'm hoping for numbness. A tight narcotic stupor would do me fine right now. Narcosis versus Fiona, and narcosis wouldn't have a chance.

Across to the bed. Light switch fumbled for and pressed down. Off. Darkness has sounds. Sounds of conscience. Sounds of remorse. Sounds of contempt and loathing. Darkness is the place in Fiona's future where she's dragging all her freelance bedfellows; where she's mistress of the house; where she's mightier than Heracles Trado; where she's omnipresent like the postgraduate prostitute she really is; where she alone can be assertive, challenging, brash, splendid.

She relaxes. Only to take off her hot, steaming dress. Her hot perspiring (no, sweating) outside. She grunts easily and begins to show her sizzling inside. Her inferno of greed and remorseless passion.

And to think that this, all this vulgar fuss, all this hectic abuse of something otherwise beautiful, all this slaughter of the nerves, all this splash, will make her a happy woman! Just this, this scrap of contact, this jerky, heaving breathing in a dark room, in a dark corner of an attic room, will take her away to protected areas of bliss and contentment. All this for free, from me without my love. From me without my permission, only submission.

Kisses of claimant come in roars of satisfied conquest. They bespatter me, sucking, gasping, choking, grasping, nervous. Baby talk, eager. Dream talk, eager, too. Promises, disclosures, exposures, unburdenings, a torrent of *inside stuff* tumbling out like maggots. Tumbling out, fat and curly like...

'Make love to me, again, Johnnie. Love me the way you loved me on the Heath. I need it so badly, ever so much, until it hurts way deep down inside me. Please!'

She's got something, a sort of trapped bee, about making love 'way deep down', hasn't she? There must be some hidden treasure (no, buried treasure; a better, much better, adjective for the occasion) down there. Whatever it is, I'm sure it's not only buried, but dead. Poor, silly Fiona!

On second thoughts, haven't we all? There's the rub! We're all bunged up with burials of one kind or another. All of us: Mrs Blount, Goolam Chops, Dick, Trado the blasted Blimp, yours truly, the whole of London, U.N.O., those United States of America, the world...

'Talk to me, just a little, Johnnie, please.'

'Suppose I left off at this point, Fiona; what would you do?'

'No, Johnnie, you mustn't, you can't, not now, darling! You must go on with it. For me. For me alone, Johnnie. Please.'

Selfish, biting, sucking, curled snake, you!

Better think about something else. Think about Ringo, for instance. How would he handle Fiona? Ringo's the man with a thousand problems and, at the same time, a thousand and one solutions. He's dead cool. He'd read colour, class, background, blood, master-servant relationship, Imperialism, little Englandism, the Empire, pink politics, blue politics, red politics, emerging black politics, anything and the kitchen sink into it. Yet he'd be engagingly civil about it. He'd be the charcoal-grey intellectual with a palate as wide and as catholic as the Atlantic. He'd stomach everything gracefully and argue, and reason, and correlate, and suggest, and eliminate, and be positive, and be negative, and be shrewd, and be hypocritical, and be generous, and be hopping mad if his freedom had to be sacrificed. So he'd get out of it, wouldn't he? And why don't I?

Lots of answers to that one. Lots of excuses: I dislike tears; I dislike scenes; I dislike being found out; I dislike not being liked; and much more besides.

131

Perhaps I lack the sophistication necessary to break the camel's back. Perhaps I have enough latent conscience. Perhaps all this is just a lot of bilge. And believe me, that's more like it. I'm sure that's about the most honest thing I could dream up to say, now. Perhaps even that isn't strictly honest. Surely there's only one way of getting out of this mess. The only way open to a coward like me, and this isn't mossy modesty either, is to run like hell. Run like hell to another set of hell-like circumstances, perhaps.

It's easy, far too easy, to say that I loathe hurting people. But I do. It's as simple as that. Always have, in fact. This private nicety often leads me into a complication of worries, frustrations, anxieties, crossroads. It's a nicety which no honest man can afford. And I try to afford it honestly. An impossibility, I know. But doesn't it make me feel that I'm giving everybody a fair break, an equal share of respect and affection, a breathing space for the development of personality other than my own? (That's another whacking slab – or is it a slice? – of pomposity!)

And there's Fiona and Dick. Fiona wants me, wants her own way. I'm happier with Dick. Dick? Well, Dick, what's your position? You've made no declaration. Perhaps you have let slip a few innuendos.

Good old Dick! I think he knows that I'm at ease with him; that he matters somewhere along the line between Mrs Blount's tenement and Sandra's hellhole. I suppose he's more observant than he makes out, and possibly more intelligent about our situation than I'd give him credit for. (We're always giving credit, aren't we? Especially when we're found out, exposed as frauds, held up to the bulging-eyed public as cheats and charlatans.)

So there it is; Fiona groans on; Dick waits; I wait. There (and the world and his wife know it) must be a decision. There'll be a conflict, a slight flutter of pretensions, then the unmasking and final unburdening, and the desired agreement – the new commitment.

I've often wondered, and I still wonder, if there are many people who have my burning, nihilistic desire to be outside the law, outside the emotions of other people, outside the respectable and respected critics, the police, the magistrates' court, the newspapers, the public conscience of the masses, the nasty fangs of the purgative lawmakers and assessors.

And then, I turn aside and ask, 'How does one do it?' And the answer is a babble of wishful thinking and hopeful grunts and speculative artifice.

'You're so far away, Johnnie. So near, my darling, but yet so very far.'

'I know.'

'I've never pleased you, have I?'

She actually sounds outside of her carnality. I don't like it. It's too sudden a retreat from her glowing selfishness. This is a bad sign, believe me.

She could be very appealing after a moment like this. Could easily get inside my own rusty shell and impress me. Impress me with her new-found selflessness. And, I repeat, I don't like it.

If I know her, she'll do just that. She'll impress her 'goodness' upon me and have me dragging behind her. But she will do that…in a matter of ten seconds from now! Go ahead, studio and recording room!

Warm, limpid Fiona scurries beside me, half on top of me, like an eager pet white mouse (regrettable adjective 'white', but there we are!) nosing about a dead kitchen stove. Half woman and half eccentric enchantress of the devil Satisfaction. The room is half my own and half the devil's right now: ideal tenancy.

'Don't you find me different tonight, Johnnie?'

I knew it. I knew it would come. There she vamps along like a whore. There she blows!

'Did you hear me, darling?'

'Humm.'

'Well?'

'Well what?'

'Am I different, tonight?'

'How different?'

'More co-operative; more involved, let's say?'

Bloody horrible word 'involved'. Especially coming from her at a moment like this. Could there be a change after all? Could she really be coming out of her miasma?

'You were all right, Fiona.'

'Is that all, darling?'

Nothing more to say. It's always the same. Being with Fiona

any length of time means drying up abnormally quickly. She's the original anti-flow girl.

Must add something to it. What? Something to take the acid edge off the blunt reply.

'Enjoyed it?'

That's a real feeble one, but it'll do for the time being, I suppose.

'I always do, Johnnie. You know that.'

'Yes, I know.'

'Why don't you tell me what's holding you back from me? There's something the matter, isn't there?'

'No, Fiona. There's nothing wrong.' Squeezing the doubt of my frail lie, holding it in check, like a coward, a master coward.

'Did I upset you with that pamphlet?'

'Not really.'

'Oh, come off it, Johnnie, I must have. Even a little bit?'

'Maybe.' Coward!

'You know I'm on your side, don't you?'

'Humm.' We're off on the wrong track. A blissfully wrong track.

'You know I read it out only because you asked me to? And of course, I did it, too, because I wanted to make certain people uneasy?'

'Oh, yes?'

'I wanted to embarrass Dick.'

'Why?'

'To chase him away.'

'How?'

'Well, you know what certain people's conscience is like?'

'Go on.'

'I knew that his wouldn't be able to take it, especially in front of you. He's a decent sort, or so they say, and naturally he would never think of staying on if I made a show of it. D'you see what I mean?'

'You wanted to clear the room for your use, eh?'

'That's rather blunt.'

'It's true, though, isn't it?'

'Yes. It is true, Johnnie. But could you say honestly that it's a bad thing?'

'I don't know.'

'You might have said "for our use" instead of "for my use".'

'I said "for your use".'

'It's the same thing, isn't it? I just changed it around.' She makes a slow grab for my waist, hugs me tightly, and mutters something into my navel. She releases me. 'My darling, won't you tell me what's wrong?'

Fine. Make it short, snappy and honest. This is the chance you've been waiting for, boy! Grab it. Use it. Correct her, hurt her, put her right, for the first and last time. Don't be a coward. This is a path straight to honesty, to clearing yourself, to freeing yourself, to a kind of new education for both of you. Don't muff it!

'I'm leaving here, Fiona.'

Now whatever made me say that?

'Leaving? Why?'

'I've got a room nearer the club.'

'Cheaper, I suppose?'

'Yes.'

'How much cheaper?'

'Ten bob.'

'I see.'

Do you? Do you really? Of course you don't. You believe only what I want you to believe, my dearest carnal cripple.

'Will I be able to visit you?'

How do I go on? Must play it out somehow. Mustn't hurt her, though. Must protect myself, as well. I'll try to be honest and yet not tell the truth.

Marvellous bit of insanity that!

'I suppose so, Fiona. I suppose so.'

'You sound doubtful. Don't I go on with you just the same?'

Where to, Fiona? On with me? To limbo? Or somewhere else like that? On with me to Trado-less regions, I suppose. Just how far does one have to go to escape? Wouldn't it be easier to stay right where one finds oneself and do all the necessary escaping without having to go anywhere? It's done every other day, I'd imagine, by those who've found the formula.

I could've remained in *Cayuna, Paradise Island*, Jamaica (they're all the same on the tourist handouts), and surrendered there. Instead, I've escaped only to surrender here. To what? To two antisocial emotions: to be of service to one, carnally; to be at ease with and to be affectionate to the other.

'Johnnie, I asked you a question.'

'Yes, I know, Fiona. But it's difficult to answer it right off the bat. There's always your monster downstairs to be mindful of, isn't there?'

'And what about your monster upstairs?'

'I don't understand.'

'Of course you don't. You only see around the corners you want to, don't you? Well, let me tell you a thing or two, darling. I know how you feel about your monster, and you know how I feel about mine. And as far as I'm concerned, we can go along on our undisturbed way quite happily; no one has to know, that is, neither of our monsters has to.'

'Who's my monster, Fiona?'

'Don't spread yourself all over the carpet, dear boy, you're wide open as it is already; and have been for a very long time. Now, shall we move on to other considerations?'

'I'm not quite sure whether we're on the same footing. I'd still like to know who you think my monster upstairs is?'

'Forget the whole thing, darling, for God's sake, will you?'

'Why?'

'I brought that up because I thought you were trying to fob me off with Gerald, as an excuse. Forget what I said, please. Please, my sweet!'

'I won't, you know.'

'Please.'

'No! I want to know, right now.'

'For my sake, Johnnie.'

'No!'

'All right! I'll tell you what I meant. I'll tell you whom you really want even more than you want me.' Pause. Gracious, well-bred pause.

'Go on, Fiona, let's have the whole gory business.'

'It's Dick, isn't it? Dick's the reason for your withdrawal. Dick's the monster, isn't he? You want to get out of my clutches so badly that you're almost beside yourself with rage and deceit and the rest of it, aren't you?'

'Your clutches, Fiona? Why?'

'That's all right, no doubt you refer to my kind of affection in just those words. You want to be free to give in to something new and exciting. You escape like nobody I've ever known, Johnnie. You're going to get so hurt, one day, that you'll…'

Tears of benediction. Tears of confession. Tears of spite. And now I'll say the word, the great balm, the panacea: I'm sorry, Fiona. And she'll be healed. And she'll be well healed. Yes?

No! I can't say it. Not that she wouldn't believe me, but because I wouldn't.

'Is he going to live with you?'

'I haven't asked him, yet.'

'D'you want him to?'

'I don't know.'

'Have you spoken about it together? Have you even dropped a hint?'

'No.'

Ominous pause. Woman's intelligence starts to work overtime. She's coming up with a master stroke, or is it a mistress stroke?

'You don't really know, do you?'

'What's that intended to mean?'

'I mean, you don't know what you want out of life. You're bankrupt, my darling. You're as dead as Gerald. Perhaps even more so than he is. What're you going to do about us? You can't drop me as easily as that, you know. I won't let you. And I won't share you, either.'

It's just as I feared: a mistress stroke! So, I'm cruel. I'm heartless. I'm frivolous. And of course, I damn' well am. And why should I take myself that seriously? Or for that matter, Fiona?

Anyway, what's all this hysteria about Dick? What's wrong with two men sharing digs? Sharing a flat? Sharing a house, if it comes to that? Men have been known to share a common mistress, a common sweetheart, a common fly-by-night popsie, a common prostitute, a common any kind of bitch. I'd better turn on the light. It might help in some way.

What's wrong with two pals sharing?

For God's sake! Fiona's imagination's working like mad. Like most women's imagination in a situation like this one. And that's that.

'You're clever, aren't you, darling?' The light makes a difference.

'I don't know what you mean.'

'Oh, yes, you do.' The light makes a witch of her. Wasted witch.

'If you say so.'

'Laughing, eh?' More a witch now, than ever before. My God!

'Cut it out, Fiona!'

Not again! I can't take this crying nonsense, twice in the same night. Oh, hell! What do I do, now? Just wait, I suppose. Hold on for the dry time, eh? I could flick the light off and on a few times. Ha!

I wonder what's hatching under those damp eyelashes. I just know that she's up to no good. I know it like the back of my hand, and maybe I'm more certain of it than I am of the back of my bloody hand, if it comes to a test. Sorry I didn't play with the light switch, somehow.

Aha! She's emerging from her senate of tears. Watch it, boy! She's coming with a brand-new set of tactics. Better think of something to block her. Anything. Anything.

'Fiona, don't you think you've stayed up here long enough? He might surprise you, you know. An early night and all that. Eh?'

'D'you know what else that pamphlet said, Johnnie?'

Just as I thought. She's away! Lovely, the way she ignored that.

'No.'

'Listen to this: "One of the chief reasons for the blacks pouring into Britain is their desire to mate with the white women of our country." That couldn't be said of you, could it, darling?'

'That blasted pamphlet's becoming a bit of a bible, Fiona. Haven't you read enough?'

'No, my sweet. I adore it. Every word. Listen to the rest of it, and congratulate yourself on being so terribly different:

'What is true is that many of the immigrants come here partly to find a white wife – often for reasons of prestige; and that most of them find means to have

138

trial runs. Obtaining white women is not only a matter of desire but of necessity as well, since comparatively few black women have come over here. Thus one of the chief results of the Coloured invasion is miscegenation and the debasement of our race.'

'Well, what d'you want me to say?'
'Nothing, my sweet. Nothing at all.'
'Anything else?'
'Maybe. Maybe not.'
'You'd feel very lost without that pamphlet, I bet.'
'Would you, darling?'
'I don't follow that.'
'Of course you don't, Johnnie. And I'll tell you why. Listen to this:

'Mentally the Negro is inferior to the white man. The sutures of the Negro's skull close quite early in life, preventing the further expansion of the brain, whereas the sutures in a white man do not close until late in life. It is estimated that the sutures in the skull of an anthropoid ape are obliterated at the age of twelve, in a Negro when he is twenty, and in a white man when he is forty.'

'That accounts for the sprawling Commonwealth, I'd imagine?'
'Sour grapes?'
'No, dear Fiona, we started late, or hasn't your pamphlet said so?'
'Don't be bitter, sweetie.'
'Am I being bitter?'
'Just a little evasive.'
'Fine.'
'D'you want to hear some more?'
'If it titillates you.'
'Big words again?'

'What're you trying to do?'

'Win you back from sodomy, darling boy.'

'You're an ass. Absolute rubbish!'

'And so is my pamphlet, I suppose?'

'Well, don't you think so?'

'Yes, Johnnie, I do. And you took it marvellously, darling.'

What next? I wonder. There can't be much more left in her charming pamphlet to bait me.

'D'you want to turn off the light? Or are you escaping me, again? Take your time, now; don't do anything you don't want to, Johnnie.'

'You on fire or something? Why don't you buy a vibrator? It'd amuse you for a lifetime, you know.'

'Don't be vicious, sweetie.'

Incurable, rotting Fiona. Detestable, starving Fiona. Desperate, silly Fiona. Insane, lights-out Fiona. No wonder Trado's a traveller. That man's sensible, absolutely sensible, believe me.

I suppose she's counting on this one as the farewell thrust and parry. The one for the road! Just like that. Christ!

I seem to remember having said earlier on that I was anxious. Well, I still am. And that's about the size of it.

Thought I'd never get rid of her. Of her petty trickery. Of her 'one for the road' passion. Of her mock grief. Of her 'don't leave me' moans and gyrations.

I don't suppose it's too late to visit Dick. I'd love to talk to him. About Fiona's trampish treatment earlier on. About something, until I'm sure that he wasn't hurt by her ghoulish temper.

Does he want to be disturbed? I wonder.

Might need his sleep. Might have to be up early in the morning to transport his Dorchester failure across a field of hairdressers and face-lifters.

I'll take a chance and see how it works out. Can't sleep with it on my conscience. I don't suppose he can either.

Tiptoe through the tulips of Mrs Blount's frayed carpet, and rap ever so gently on Dick's door. Mustn't disturb the sleeping lions below.

'Humm!'

'It's me – Johnnie. Can I come in?'

'Yes, Johnnie. The door's not locked.'

'I've come to make peace, Dick.'

'About?'

'Fiona's boorishness.'

'Oh, that.'

'Yes, exactly.'

'I shouldn't worry too much about her, if I were you. She's a very unhappy person, you know.'

'Wretched, if you ask me.'

'Tell me, did she upset you very much with her racial nonsense?'

'In a way, yes.'

'What way?'

'I didn't like the purpose for which she used the pamphlet, Dick. She doesn't believe a word of it, you know. Thank God, she's no Hampstead fascist! But she had a good reason, anyway, for her behaviour. A damn' good reason.'

'And what would that be, as if I don't know?'

'You do know, then, do you?'

'Of course I know, Johnnie. It's as obvious as that, isn't it?'

'I'm sorry, Dick. Very sorry, indeed.'

I meant that. Every word of it. It came easily but it also came honestly. That's the thing about our friendship, our suspect 'band of angels' if two are able to form a band; it's the freshness and sincerity of approach to each other which Fiona refuses to understand. Dick owes me nothing; I owe Dick nothing. There's no sycophancy, no sweaty allegiance, yet there's a kind of loyalty, a bond, which doesn't make slaves of us or anything like that.

That idea that Fiona caused to occur to me – the one about taking a room nearer the club – is a damn' good thing, I think. I must discuss it with Dick.

Shan't ask him to come in with me and share, but get his opinion for what it's worth. And I'm sure it's worth plenty, being a one-roomer and the sort of exile as he most certainly is.

It's too late for that sort of talk, anyway. Another time'll do. Might just end up in boring the pants off him (wouldn't do to use that metaphor in front of Fiona, I don't think) and making him uneasy. It's a problem I'll have to tackle on my own. I can see that.

'Cup of something, Johnnie?'

'No, Dick, don't trouble yourself. It's too late anyway. Forgive me for disturbing you, but I wanted to find out whether you were upset by our lady of grace downstairs or not. Now that I'm not haunted anymore I suppose we can all get some sleep, all right?' Faint chuckles from both of us. Matter settled. No sweaty allegiance. No muck. Only loyalty. And it works admirably.

'Something else worrying you?'

'I should ask you that, Dick.'

'Why?'

'Well, you did come up to my room to talk to me, in the first instance, didn't you? And then Fiona came bulldozing her way over us.'

'Oh, it's nothing, really. At least, it's nothing that can't wait until tomorrow.'

Or the next day. Or next week. Or next never.

Something else sloppy Johnnie and Dick have in common, eh. A kind of cowardice. Not exactly childlike. Not exactly adult, either. More 'in-a-between-a' as Larry would say. Cowardice mixed with false pride and a developing adult restraint, Ringo would inform me from a great height if I ever was mad enough to ask him. It's nothing killing, Biddy would advise. Play it cool, daddy-o, 'tain't no sweat, DuBois B. Washington might say if Biddy wasn't around to hear him. It's life, my dear, would be Sandra's contribution.

And so it would go on, highly personal, and very misleading.

We're all cowards! That's too simple a statement to make. It's rather like any old generalization about the enemy: whites are all imperialist bastards; blacks are ignorant, arrogant bastards; whites are all prejudiced and fascistic; blacks are primitive and smelly.

And so it would go on, highly emotional, and very comforting.

Dick has never really told me about himself, has he? Don't suppose I have either. Would like to know a bit of his history, though. Might be more interesting than I think. Might be terribly dull, on the other hand.

Two night owls burning up a nervous friendship. Burning up fuel already fouled. Fouled by the warming hand of innocence versus experience. Fouled by living and loving and lying and deceiving and escaping and all the rest.

Two night owls without a decision. What would an audience think? Would they sneer? What would the vast reading public of Sunday papers say? Queer lot, or queer student lot, or queer bleeding idlers, they'd say. More time on their bleeding hands than sense!

'Where d'you go from here, Dick?'

'Go?'

'You know?'

'Oh, I don't know.' Sighs easily, naturally. 'Keep body and soul together like the next man, I suppose. Pay the rent; feed myself; live within the law. Why?'

'What was it like before you came here?'

'The usual thing.'

'How usual?'

'Married too young, or so everybody said after the break-up.'

'Married? Really?'

'Humm. Two children, two boys.'

'D'you see them often?'

'Fairly. Any time I want to.'

'And the wife?'

'Ex-wife.'

'Yes.'

'She's married again, actually. Happily, too, bless her.'

'Why, bless her?'

'Oh, just a manner of speaking.'

'What caused the break, or is it bad form to ask?'

'I suppose I'm to blame. We clashed once too often. It would be more accurate to say that we clashed a thousand times too often.'

'Over what?'

'The usual things, you know.'

Is that all? Is that really all? Dick the dodger. Dick the shy adulterer, the renegade with an approved accent.

I'd better leave it at that.

Married, eh?

'You wanted to talk to me?' Bold second attempt. Might play this time. Insistence might pay off; second time fruitful, as Ringo would say.

'You're trying again, Johnnie, aren't you?'

'Well, I just thought…'

'You are a bit of an investigator, at that. All you need is the glaring desk light, a loosened tie, sweat on the brow, two assistants behind you, and there we have Johnnie the terror of the Secret Service Department.' Wonderful, amiable reaction. Clear, clean laughter. Not a trace of anything bitter and twisted; no sarcasm, no venom, normal or as near normal as can be.

'Yes. I am a bit of a nuisance. But don't you want to talk?'

'Can't remember what it was, now. It'll come back to me, in time.'

'Evasion, eh?'

'D'you think so?'

Sophistication, your name is restraint. Restraint, your end-result is decadence.

Why doesn't he come out with it?

Shyness? I don't think so.

Scheming? Neither.

Fear? Could be.

'Somebody's knocking, Dick.'

'Must be Shakuntala. What time is it?'

'About two-thirty by your watch if it's still working.'

'Open the door; it might be the old lady on the prowl.'

I hope not. Yet, why should I care? To hell with her!

'Oh, it's you, Mr Trado.'

'Hello, Mr Sobert. Dick there?'

'Yes, I'm here, Gerald. Come in.'

'I say, old chap, have you seen Fiona?'

'Saw her about two hours ago.'

'I've just got in. She's nowhere about.' Nervous cover-up of sly chuckles.

'She may have gone for a walk. She usually does, doesn't she?'

'Yes. Yes, of course. She could have. Damn'silly thing to do, I

144

should think. Don't you?' More nervous chuckles. 'Sorry to have disturbed you, old chap. See you in the morning.'

Didn't even look my way. Wonder if he's responsible for those pamphlets? That's a laugh! Doubt it very much. Don't think he'd even be able to spell, much less write and edit the damn' thing.

So Fiona's walking into the night like a demented Ophelia, is she? Long day's journey into a N.W.3 night: Trado out of O'Neil by Céline Ha! I should worry.

'Are you gloating, Johnnie?'

'Over what?'

'The obvious.'

'Can you blame me?'

'Highly immoral, isn't it?' A light sprinkling of chuckles from both of us. Nice and easy, nothing to fight against. A kind of harmony in discord.

And *they* say there's something queer about a relationship like ours. *They*, the mockers; *they*, the intelligent critics; *they*, the wolf-hound boys; *they*, the…

'I imagine Fiona will have a lot of explaining to do when she comes back?'

'I couldn't care less, Dick. Frankly, I couldn't care less whether she gets a damn' good belting or not.'

'I shouldn't think it'll be anything as healthy as that. Conjugal rights may be more like it. The old boy looked randy and cheated, to me.'

'The old boy, as far as I'm concerned, can take a running jump with a concrete slab round his fat neck.'

'Pamphlet fever, Johnnie? Watch it.'

'No. I don't think that rotten pamphlet comes into it, at all. It's Trado himself. No pamphlet this time, thank God!'

'He's not a bad fellow –'

'– when you get to know him! But I don't. I don't want to know him! I don't want to know the ignorant bastard, Dick. You can have him. Anybody can have him!'

'All right, all right! Not so loud.'

'I'm sorry for the hundredth time. I'm sorry. I'm sorry.'

Oh, hell! There I blow again. Shouldn't have done it. Didn't

145

mean to. Happens every time. Every time. Lack of control. Lack of proper planning. Lack of restraint. Lack of guile. Lack of everything.

'What're you going to do, Johnnie? I think a change would do you a world of good. What d'you think?'

BOOK THREE

A Time Past

Huic me, quaecumque fuisset, addixi
(To it, whatever it should have proved, I surrendered myself)
Virgil
Aeneid III, 652

11

If only I had known is such a bastard of a thing to say, anyway. I knew all along that I was looking for more than just a choice between Fiona and Dick; between greed and contentment; between unambitious sentimentality and unambitious tranquillity; between sexuality and intelligent, ordinary living. I knew too a little about myself, not much; I knew that I could be stupidly hesitant, fiercely if not self-consciously honest, overbearingly brash, fairly considerate, resentful of being bored, riddled with pretensions, preoccupied with making a go of my escape to England. I knew that I was searching, like a hundred million other people, for something to pin my tiny flag to, in order to be recognized as a right and proper claimant to happiness, however overworked that myth might be.

I knew all that, and yet I didn't try hard enough to do anything about my condition. Everything seemed so pointless. Wasted. Finally, I realized that I was headed nowhere like a hundred million others. I had escaped a malformed Jamaican middle class; I had attained my autumn pavement; I had become a waiter in a Dantesque night club; I had done more than my fair share of hurting, rejecting, and condemning; and I had created another kind of failure, and this time, in another country.

★   ★   ★

That October was a turning point in three people's lives. That Saturday evening and early Sunday morning spent talking to Dick and spent making love and rejecting Fiona contributed sheer hell to each of our dreams.

Fiona had helped me to make my decision. She had, without intending it, put the idea of leaving the Blount establishment into my numb head. I, in turn, had deliberately infected Dick with it, and off we went, leaving Trado the Tramp, Shakuntala, the old lady, and a bleeding Fiona, into a world of freedom and blissful, wishful thinking.

We took a flat in Whitcomb Street, quite near Leicester Square. We shared the rental, which was exorbitant. We cooked for each other, and when that was becoming a bore, we decided to employ a woman who'd cook our evening meal and hover over us on Sundays.

October, or rather, the last half of it, was a joy forever. November came and went, and December installed itself with constant tingling threats of bringing us both a very happy Christmas.

I kept my job at the club.

Dick had changed his. He now worked at Harrods.

★   ★   ★

It was Christmas Eve. Ten-thirty in the morning. My mother's Christmas card and a letter had arrived about a quarter of an hour before. I had re-read it for the fourth time and was about to read it again when Laura, our flat-keeper, walked in, slightly winded, and as I expected, extremely talkative.

'My Lord! Those stairs! They'll be the death of all of us, one day. Up and down, up and down, and at my age it'll never do. And what do you get out of it in the long run? Nothing!' Pause. Staccato breathing. Final disgorging exhalation. 'Letter from home, love?'

'Yes, Laura. From my mother.'

'Nice and hot over there, I bet. All those white sand beaches, no blooming smog, and what's the place called…?'

'What place?'

'Monty…Montygo…?'

'Montego Bay, you mean?'

'Yes. One of my nieces went out there. Married to an engineer, you know. Nice boy. Steady and shrewd. Very shrewd. Clever but nice, mind you.'

She rummaged in her shopping basket and brought up her indispensable packet of Weights.

'Want one, love?'

150

'Thanks.'

'I can never understand why your people come over here. I mean to say, it doesn't make sense; all that lovely climate and being among your own kind. You can't ask for more than that now, can you?'

'I suppose not.'

'What sort of answer's that? "I suppose not?" You ought to more than "suppose not" about a thing like that. I mean to say who should miss the sun more than you? Who knows his own kind more than you?'

'Yes, Laura. You're right about that.'

'Anyway, there must be reasons, mustn't there? We all have our problems. Take your Mr Snape, for instance. A real nice young man, he is. Well brought up and well schooled from the sound of him. And where's he got? What's he got himself out of it? Nothing. Now I ask you; with looks and education as he's got he should be commanding a real big position somewhere. I'm telling you, love, that this country is turning sour for all of us. Canada is the place! Or even America. Those are the countries in the lead nowadays. I can see a lot of things from where I stand, you know. A lot of things!'

'I don't suppose Dick would like to go to either of those two places, Laura. D'you think so?'

'Mr. Snape is a young man, love. And all young men benefit from a bit of foreign travel, that's what I say.'

She picked up her shopping basket and sighed slightly theatrically. I looked away. She mumbled something else and walked towards the kitchen.

I fumbled with the air-letter form, spread it out on my knees and read it again:

My dearest Son,

Your letters tell me that there's something troubling you. You must remember that I'm good at reading between the lines. I've had enough experience; first your father, and now you. I sense a certain unrest. A certain, shall I say, nervousness and anxiety? Yes?

Whatever is the matter, my son? Can't you tell your own mother? I've always been your confidante. Ever since you were a

151

child, you've always come to me with all your little problems; and haven't I helped you to solve them?

You're spending yet another Christmas away from home and I suppose you've made plans for the holiday. Have you? Where will you have Christmas dinner? Remember to go to church on Christmas Eve night. You've never missed a midnight Mass while you were at home; don't start slipping now, son. Please.

I'm glad that you've received your pudding intact. One can never tell about the Parcel Post these days, can one, my love? They throw things around so ruthlessly that the parcels I've sent abroad have arrived on only my prayers, if you know what I mean. I worry and worry until I hear they've arrived safely. I'm still the old worrier you left behind, as you can see by this letter. I've never been able to relax; not properly, anyway. There has always been something to occupy my mind – some private anxiety, some insoluble or near insoluble problem.

I do worry a great deal about you, Johnnie. There's no use your telling me not to. You're so much a part of my life that I'm unable to live one whole day without thinking about your progress in England.

Do, son, try to make friends and not enemies of the people with whom you come in contact. You're always being watched and criticized. It's only natural that you will want to spread your wings a bit – you know the sort of things I mean – attend dances, go out drinking with your pals, take out girls, that sort of conduct may be innocent enough but you can't exactly see around corners, so be on 'the best' as I've always preached, son. Don't let down my grey hairs at this late stage.

Do everything in moderation. And above all, watch your health. Do not take unnecessary risks. Wear the appropriate clothing for the season and do not go shedding your woollen things because of freak days. That's a temptation, a great temptation, especially for someone like yourself who's so accustomed to going about dressed scantily.

I shan't preach, any more.

Write soon and tell me all.

With all my love,
Mother

P.S.

Your father sends his regards, and so do a number of your friends.

My Christmas will be uneventful as usual. If only you were with me. Christmas dinner won't be the same. It hasn't been the same since you left, and won't be until you return. God bless you, my son. God bless you and keep your path safe and steady.

When things aren't going too well, do try to remember that I love you with all my heart, very, very much, and always will. Bless you, again.

★   ★   ★

The rest of the morning cruised by me nervously, even a bit jerkily.

I escaped Laura by going for a walk in Trafalgar Square. I visited the National Gallery, stared at two Goyas, admired their sudden white lights and hurried back to the flat. Laura buttonholed me again. I escaped once more and bolted into a news theatre in Leicester Square. I emerged an hour after that and went back to the flat to find a card from Fiona. She had enclosed a note:

My Darling Johnnie,

I haven't seen you since you left me in October. I got your address from a girl who works at your club. I think she said her name was Biddy.

I came to see you last Tuesday but unfortunately it was your night off. I would have come straight along to see you but I thought better of it.

I miss you terribly, more than you'd ever imagine. I often cry over you. Indeed, even at this moment. I never thought that I'd ever be able to cry over a man. But there you are!

Can you come up to see me at about one to one-thirty on Christmas Eve day? Gerald won't be at home.

Do try to come. No ties. Purely, as they say, a social visit.

Love,

Fiona

I tore up the envelope and her note. I threw away the envelope but kept the bits of the note, which I rearranged and pasted together fifteen minutes later. I placed her card on the mantelpiece and looked at the time. It was ten minutes to one.

I asked myself: why do I want to keep her note? Why? I got no answer. I don't suppose I really wanted one. I don't suppose I'd ever admit my own confusion.

I looked at the time, again, and left the flat. The stairs seemed to creak more loudly than ever before. A kind of warning I imagined. A rebuke. I felt like the child about to steal sugar from a very tall cupboard which he has to climb to reach. I was descending. That was the difference, and I knew it.

As I walked to Piccadilly Circus, I kept squeezing and relaxing Fiona's note in my overcoat pocket, and wondering what I'd tell Dick if he found out what I had done to him in a moment of confused loyalties; in a moment of confused selfishness was more like it, I thought. I bought a train ticket for Finchley Road.

I suddenly realized that everything would be all right. Fiona could never get me to betray Dick's confidence in me. She could never make Dick take second place. She could never make me do what I didn't want to do. I was positive about that. I was adamant. The rhythm of the train seemed to help to convince me: *you know you're right; you know you're right; you know you're right.* And of course, I felt as if I knew that everything was working out satisfactorily for Dick and myself.

I began, after that, to look forward to my visit; I'd say such and such a thing, and I'd answer her questions in such and such a way. I had it all planned. We were all going to have a very happy Christmas; nobody would be hurt; Fiona wouldn't be hurt; Dick and I would be together; and the smooth surface of our individual lives would remain unruffled. Calm. Calm for all in a suspect sea of submarine fears and anxieties.

I knew it would be that way; after all's said and done, I knew what to expect of Fiona, despite her warning that it would be 'purely a social visit'. Perhaps that's why I was on my way to see her. She'd try to trap me. She'd implore. And I'd refuse. Not reject, mind you. Just gently refuse to comply. Maybe even a little bit slightly firmly if it came to that. I knew all this.

Trado's absence could mean only one thing. Again, the time of day. The day. Everything. I wasn't fooled. She may have expected me to be, but how could I? I was prepared for Fiona, the siren of a thousand loves. And this made me feel free and easy. The rhythm of the train continued to reassure me. I grabbed at it. Wallowed in it. Never wanted it to stop, in fact.

Finchley Road looked moth-eaten and raw. Very raw. After the bright lights of the West End, the old, friendly road seemed desperately sick and passive. The street lamps were too slender; the pavement was damp and dirty; the plane trees were skinny and battered.

The front door was open. Her sitting-room door was un-locked. I walked in and stood by the first armchair. There she was, in front of me, fresh and a little flushed with expectancy.

She rose and said: 'I'm glad you could make it, Johnnie. Come and sit next to me.'

To the point and warm, all at the same time. She sat beside me, turned slowly to my left, and stared at me intently. Her eyes rested on my clenched fist. I felt exposed. She had seen through me, as usual. She had unearthed my secret plan, my plan of power over her, my petty strength, my ineffectual false pride.

Everything that had given me courage on the train journey slipped away from me suddenly. I hoped I wasn't showing my terror too plainly. In one sentence: Come and sit next to me; she had established her position. She had established her assurance. She had proved her knowledge of my eggshell resistance. I was uncomfortable and I tried, for all it was worth, not to show it. Even the clenched fist was my way of not proving her right.

'You're just as nervous, just as tense, aren't you?' she said casually, scoring her point like a professional, restrained and assured, assured of her charm and intention to get to the point. A trace of a smile darted between us. She was playing her part with enviable competence. 'Now, what about something to drink?'

'What have you got?'

'A roomful. Rum, Scotch, gin, vodka, wine, sherry, port, beer.'

'Scotch'll do fine.'

She moved about quietly.

'Soda?'

'No. Straight.'

She sat beside me and threw back her head. Addressing the ceiling, she said slowly, almost tasting each word: 'Got you!' She paused for about five seconds and continued: 'So I've actually got you to come, and, I suppose, much against your better judgment?'

'What?' Stupidly, I pretended not to understand.

'I've got you, at last, Johnnie. I've got you to come and see me, I mean.'

I said nothing. I drained my Scotch with an exaggerated sucking noise. She lowered her head and smiled.

'Another?'

'Please.'

I'm going to enjoy every moment of this, I thought idly, playing with the idea of upsetting Fiona's plans for a one-woman show of grit and glamour.

I sipped my drink slowly this time.

'I don't suppose we're exactly strangers?'

' 'Course we aren't, Fiona. Why do you ask?'

She eased herself down beside me. Her thighs felt large and hard. Her hair was perfumed delicately. She knew, at once, that her whole body was being appreciated, being acknowledged; the perfume of her hair, everything about her thighs, her breathing, her manner, had become a force outside herself. She knew that they could work for her in a kind of quick magic upon my numb senses; they could take the place of words of entreaty, words of revenge, words of bitterness, words of love, even.

The room had a sad stillness about it, a stillness of brooding and resentment, a stillness that carried a message of shock and bewilderment.

'I'm pregnant, Johnnie.'

She was still all grit and glamour, despite the nature of her news. Her thighs felt a trifle harder and larger as she shifted her position to face me. She could afford to look majestically down on her captive, I thought quickly, as if in retaliation.

If only she had realized that her low cunning would be useless, impotent, I'm certain she would have tried another tack. Poor fool! She imagined she had trapped her witch-doctor all over again! Joseph had returned to be sacrificed.

156

I knew it was now time for her to say something else; the pause had been long enough for her purpose. I hadn't offered anything. Silence worked wonders on Fiona. She hated it. It unnerved her. I toyed with the second Scotch and sipped it appreciatively.

She smiled sweetly. Her performance was admirable. She had eaten the entire book of rules. She was going to win, once and for all.

'Well, my darling, how're you going to explain this to Dick?'

'I don't think he'll be interested. D'you?'

'I can't say. I don't live with him.'

Claws well bared, she sprang at that one from a great height. At last, she began to show signs of anticipation. Anticipation of victory. Very bad for her position; very good for mine. After all, this was a kind of Good versus Evil demonstration.

Her calm was going, too. She fidgeted about and her breathing had become noticeably jerky and irregular. Her wonderful poise was going. I can't be sure that she knew that I was aware of all this, but I was, and that was what really counted in our little farce of a contest of wits.

'I'm nearly three months pregnant, Johnnie.' Not exactly blurted out, but with a hint of passion behind it.

'Time does go quickly, doesn't it?' It was going to be like this the whole way through, and I was prepared to play my game as nastily as possible, as cautiously as possible.

'I'm pregnant!'

'By whom?'

'You, obviously!'

'Or Trado, or most of his friends, or the new tenant, or the ghost of Joseph come back to thrill you, or…'

'Stop it!'

'Why? Don't you want to hear how pregnant you really are? I'm willing to tell you; so listen. Listen carefully, my dearest, artful bitch! You're no more pregnant than the old dragon upstairs. You're as pregnant as you'd like me to believe, which means I don't believe, therefore you aren't. Now that we've settled that ruse, perhaps we can tackle plan number two. What else is there?'

'You black bastard!'

Obviously a personal, highly personal, translation of 'Merry Christmas to you, Johnnie'. 'And Many Happy Returns' I was tempted to reply, but thought better of it.

'Another Scotch?' Wonderful recovery.

'Please.'

She cooled rather smartly. Plan number two was in operation. And I was ready for it. I knew that I'd have to watch her closely this time. Just how far she'd go I wasn't certain.

'What's your life with Dick like?'

Here's my cue, I thought. Here's my time to play her silly; to play her like a die across a vast floor area, I comforted myself. I waited for her to return; she was taking a long time over the third drink. I hoped I'd get a drink of Scotch and nothing else. I chuckled at the thought.

She came up to me slowly. The glass was nearly full. I knew and she knew. It was too obvious. We both smiled. Huge thighs grazed against me for the third time. Must have been intentional.

'Well, Fiona, life with Dick is very uneventful. It's steady. It's relaxing and it's happiness nearly all the time.'

'A pack of lies!'

Just as I had expected. Yet, I ignored it like a bad smell in select company.

'It's simple and straightforward at the worst of times. And what's more we're very free and able to lead the life we most desire.'

'Sounds entirely false to me.'

'But it would, dear, grasping Fiona. It most certainly would. Especially how relentless you are in your own miserable, greedy, oversexed world.'

'You always rose to my greedy, oversexed moments, Johnnie. Or have you forgotten?'

'And probably will again, if you behave nicely.'

That stung her as planned. Stung her way deep down. The large-thighed parasite!

'Johnnie, listen to me.'

'I'm listening.'

'I want to save you from making a fatal mistake.'

'You do, do you?'

'I want to give you what's really yours.'

'Yes?'

'I want to give you everything. I want to be everything that Dick is to you and more.'

'What d'you think Dick is to me?'

'He's your lover, isn't he?'

'He's my best friend.'

'What d'you mean?'

'Just that.'

'Don't you make love to each other?'

'I'm sorry to disappoint you, Fiona, but we don't.'

'Don't you sleep together in the same bed, like lovers?'

'Of course we do not!'

'But aren't people like Dick supposed to be…'

'Some are, I would imagine.'

'Are you trying to tell me that Dick's fidelity isn't based on some sort of sex or the other? I suppose he's different, is he?'

'He may not be. All I'm trying to tell you is that we do not make love to each other.'

'I don't understand.'

'Of course you don't.'

'Explain it to me, then. Tell me why you left here and went off like a honeymoon couple. Tell me that!'

'I thought you knew.'

'No. I do not!'

'All right, I'll tell you. I left here to be rid of you; to be rid of your overpowering passion; to be rid of your depressing sexuality; to be rid of the old lady upstairs; to be rid of your blasted Gerald; to be rid of one bloody tenement room!'

'Is that really all?'

'No. Above all, I left here because I couldn't stand being Joseph's gap-filler. I left because I wanted my freedom. Satisfied?'

'I should ask you that, darling.'

'And my answer is yes. Yes! Yes! Yes!'

'So if the truth be known, Dick and yourself are merely sharing a flat. Is that it?'

'Yes, Fiona.' I was firm about that, perhaps too firm, too passionately firm. But I would hit back nicely. I paused. She

159

stared at me vacantly. I was waiting for that. 'Now that's settled, are you still pregnant, Fiona?'

She must have been expecting it. She smiled graciously and nodded sheepishly: 'No, Johnnie. No.'

She wasn't even ashamed. She beamed at the hopeful news and moistened her lips. She didn't ask me this time; she refilled my glass, a good double shot. We were all going to have a very happy Christmas and no doubt about it. We were simmering in it: she wasn't pregnant, and I wasn't homosexual! At least one of her needs had been satisfied. She felt all woman again. Her pride had been restored to its dizzy eminence. Her belly was crying out once more for the hot coals of a man's pummelling embrace. Her thighs were warming up dynamo-style. The agony had begun in a new vein.

We sat and talked about Shakuntala, the old lady, Trado, ourselves. Then she introduced the first positive sign of her infernal greed: she asked me whether I remembered how happy I had made her that morning on Hampstead Heath.

Well, even if I wanted to forget, I suppose it would have been impolite not to remember in the circumstance. So, I remembered. Abdication is almost impossible! And she, too, remembered the whole affair as if it had happened yesterday. And off she went in an orgy of recollection. Her thighs were nervous, now. Reckless. She fanned them carelessly; she crossed them; she lowered one and raised the other boldly; she shook them; she banged them together; and she banged me with them. She was having a wonderful time; not hers the way of tranquil recollection Oh, no! She was alive once more, and she agreed to celebrate her dingy rebirth like a carnival clown.

She was prepared, fully prepared, for her invasion; throbbing limbs, and all. I was not, however, willing to be invaded. But this didn't interfere with Fiona's progress. She warmed up with great Latin gusto.

'You haven't kissed me, d'you know that?'

'You might become just a little bit pregnant if I do. Aren't you afraid?'

'Be serious, darling.'

'I am being serious, Fiona. Dead serious.'

She made an earnest grab at something or other, missed and collided with my left kneecap. She wasn't hurt, however. She giggled wickedly, rather like a six-year-old who's after buried treasure at the bottom of the garden. She swiftly changed position and made another earnest grab. She got it that time. How happy she seemed!

I didn't resist.

She worked diligently. I watched her impassioned progress and admired her economy of movement. She brought to her activity a certain intelligence, a certain private knowhow, alarming to me at first, but to which I grew accustomed as she continued on her recklessly romantic way.

At least one person's Christmas Eve had begun with a sort of a bang. There was no denying it.

'You have come back to me, really and truly, darling? Say you have. Please.'

'I most certainly have not.'

'Don't spoil it. Please, Johnnie! Don't! For my sake!'

'Aren't you tired?'

'No. Never.'

'Aren't you uncomfortable?'

'No. Are you?'

'Slightly.'

And plan number two came into operation. I was almost whisked into the adjoining room where she'd prepared the battle-bed.

Perhaps to be too weak is a very bad thing. Perhaps to be only slightly weak is a very attractive thing: it generates hope of conquest. Fiona's animal energy thrived on it. It grew, expanded, and was bolstered by it.

Trado's battle-bed was more than adequate. Almost triumphal.

Until this day I never blamed the Scotch.

12

And so, amid a shower of promises to return; to love her for ever; to make savage love to her *ad nauseam*; to be a man and not a mouse; to face up to reality *ad infinitum*; I left Fiona on Christmas Eve at about four o'clock, and got back to Piccadilly Circus by half past or thereabouts.

The flat looked appealing. Laura had gone out.

There was a splash of mail on the mat. I sank into a chair and opened the envelopes addressed to me; I gathered up Dick's and put them aside.

There was one from Dick. Not a simple card in good taste as I would've expected from him but a rather gay and funny one. He had signed it: *With fondest regards from Dick*. I looked at the cover again. It was very funny indeed.

I laughed aloud.

Then, suddenly, I knew that I had to tell Dick about Fiona. Awkward. But admission of failure has always been an awkward exercise at the best of times, I consoled myself. Dick, I was sure, would be let down. After all, he had been trying his best to be my friend; to be an anchor; to be a bulwark against my attacks, my frequent attacks of escapism. I had let him down, and I had let myself *way deep down*; splendidly *way deep down*, and liked it, or at least the last half of it, anyway.

But I didn't feel somehow that Fiona had conquered. She had given me a lift, if you like, a cunning strength which I needed badly. She had given me something (call it resistance, call it experience), an independence. I had given in to her but had not been destroyed, as Dick would tell me when he found out what I had done. I felt that I could manage her assaults in the future. Take it or leave it was the result of our vulgar reunion.

I took out her note and placed it on the narrow ledge of the mantelpiece, the only uncluttered part left after Laura's Christmas card display. Dick would know that I wanted him to read it. He would know it was my way of making confession easy, without the usual mawkishness and waste. He would understand.

I had a scented bath, warm and bracing after the chilling time of preparing my confessional. I dressed and left the flat. I hoped that the atmosphere of the club would act as a distraction. I sincerely hoped so; the first time I ever had.

We were all going to have a through-train to happiness. We were all going to have an enjoyable festive season: a very merry Christmas, all round.

★　　★　　★

Cards. Cards. Cards. Biddy was jubilant. Sandra exultant. They were busy pecking at oval-shaped cards, elongated cards, jack-in-the-box cards, home-made cards, French, American, Danish cards, cards of price, cards of worth, cards of duty, cards of love.

'Where's DuBois Washington's, Biddy-O?'

'Mind your own business!'

'You didn't mind your own when you gave my address to a woman you've never seen before, did you?'

'She asked for it.'

'So you gave it to her like a loyal little Girl Guide. Happy Christmas.'

'Happy Christmas, yourself.'

There was a trickle of customers at the counter. They'd all been manned with gin, light ales, Scotch, etc. Youth had to have a damned good commercial Christmas if Sandra had anything to do with it! No music. No enticement. Nothing.

Sandra and Biddy and their cards. Lights weren't even turned on. Nothing. But the customers had to be milked. They had to be *tied* without being kissed. They had to be —— without the usual garish, cheap, sluttish preliminaries.

'Thanks for your card, Johnnie.'

'Thanks for yours, Sandra.'

Wonderful commercial tenseness. Everything was perfumed by it. Old cash register herself, immobile, paunchy, couchant. Even she had been decorated with cards, bunting, etc.

'And for mine.'

'And for yours, Biddy.' I didn't bother to snap at her even though it was my time to get even-stephen with her grumpy, snarling, thin-skinned manner.

We had done our duty by one another. Now, I was a waiter

once more. A server of hot reminders that the rent's got to be paid; staff to be paid; electricity bill to be paid; Sandra's gowns, personal debts, etc., have to be paid, and so on.

I idled about. Fidgeted more than idled, actually. I thought about Maxwell. Was he lording it off on his mates? What kind of Christmas will he have? Has he heard from any of his upper-middle-class wartime cronies? What'll he do when he comes out? Will he still be cocky? Will he be accepted in a new circle? Will he continue to be rejected by the old?

The minutes grazed by. Things were beginning to look up. The place was humming faintly. Biddy was losing her charm rapidly. It was draining away like wasted treacle.

Tips. Tips. Tips. I could see nothing else. And that was as it should be: Christmas or no Christmas, tips should flow, I persuaded myself. A lovely greedy sensation ran wild over everything I touched; everything I did; everything I hoped for; everything I collided with. Tips for the rental of the flat; tips for spending money; tips for the hell of it. Yet I never thought of tips for the passage back home. Why? Had I decided to face things? Had I made the grade at last? Why? And the answer came: I'm happy enough if the tips are! Then I knew that the future was a myth. I was certain that greed was the message of the age; I knew this and I gloated over the fact in my own inimitable pompous way, smiling and feeling as secure as ever in my filth, in my self-embrace, on my autumn pavement.

Then I thought of Fiona's greed. Another kingdom-come kind of tips greed. Similar greed. Must-get-it-at-all-cost kind of greed. Hurt everybody. Cheat everybody. Use everybody. Nobody's a friend. Nobody's in love. Love doesn't matter. Just greed! Greed's the total ambition. We escape from love to fling ourselves into the waiting arms of greed. There's nothing else to escape to. If one's truly greedy, one's on the way to the top. If one wants to be mediocre, one must learn to avoid greed, avoid ambition, avoid selfishness, avoid gluttony, avoid tips, avoid Fiona's sexuality, avoid Sandra's commercial earnestness, avoid hustling, avoid hustlers, avoid…

'Well, well, if the gentleman's son not looking like a million then I'm a blind-eye man in a blind-eye country! What happening, Johnnie?' Larry broke into my neurotic reverie. He was Christmas 'high', and out on a slender limb, at that.

'Happy Christmas, Larry boy!'

'Take the same sentiments from me too, nuh.'

'You sound well away. Where've you been?'

'All over, countryman. All over.'

'No blonde?'

'No blonde.'

'Checked out on you?'

'Call it that, nuh. Call it just that.'

He was rocking gently. I knew that Sandra wouldn't like that. I had to hide him away somewhere. If he sat, he'd fool anybody, I thought hurriedly.

'You'd better sit down, Larry. O.K.?'

'No. Not O.K., countryman.'

'But Sandra might create if she sees you in your present happy state, man. You know how it is.' A chance chuckle.

'Boy! I simply love that college English you flinging at me, you know.'

'I know you do, that's why I flung it. Grab this one and talk to me. Want a drink in the meantime?'

'If you protect me you protect yourself. Right, Johnnie?'

'Could be.'

'Peace and love, then nuh! Tell that white whore, Sandra, that I want to talk to her. Tell her that Larry want to wish her a ——ing happy Christmas. Miss whoring Sandra is who I mean, country-man. Your boss. You go tell her. Tell her that I have a first-class Christmas present for her.'

'Take it easy, Larry. It's not worth it. Have a drink.'

'No. I have a duty to perform on this very ——ed up Christmas Eve night. If you don't bring her over to me, I will call her myself, you know that yourself. I will do that little thing as easy as spitting on this blasted floor, here.'

'Look, Larry, let's talk about it quietly. Let's –'

'Sandra! Sandra! I want you!'

His shouting was electric. Sandra left the counter and came over to us.

'What's wrong with this one?' she said calmly. 'Christmas already for some people, eh?'

'You don't mind yourself about that now, Miss Sandra bitch! You just answer me this one. Why did you take it on yourself to tell my woman that I's not a suitable fellow to be seen around with? You tell me that right now, and satisfy my feelings on the matter.'

'What woman are you talking about?'

'The blonde one. My woman that I bring down here a few times ago. Don't form ass, Sandra! You ——ing well know who I talking about to rass!'

'I'm afraid I'll have to ask you to leave. Come along. Get out. And come back when you're sober enough to apologize.'

'Not so easy, Sandra! You not talking to me like that, you old whoring, cheating bitch you! I come down here tonight to give you a old-time piece-a-me-mind so just cool down off the "come along, get out" business, and listen good to what I got to tell you.'

'Johnnie!'

'Yes, Sandra?'

'Get Larry outside, will you?'

She walked back to the counter. I looked at Larry and pleaded with my eyes. He winked conspiratorially. He wasn't as drunk as we all thought. Yet his act was on top form. He got up and lurched towards me.

Quietly, barely above a whisper, he said: 'I soon go away, now, countryman. I won't give you any bothers. Me and you is one. This Sandra is something else, believe me. This ——ing pro is the one I want to settle. It won't take long. I won't even give her the pleasure of marking her face; I wouldn't even touch her. Don't worry. I soon go away.'

I pretended to hold him and turn him round. He took his cue right on time and leapt to the counter.

'Now, Miss Sandra, don't you —— round my business, again. If you do it again, I going to change the look of your face entirely. I warn you off this time, and you better thank God.'

'Johnnie!' Sandra's voice was high and shrill. She was terrified, at last. I was certain now that Larry would leave her alone. He had gained his point. All he wanted to do was to put her in an embarrassing position, and he had done so. I was glad that she wasn't stubborn about it. In some malicious way, angry as she was, and properly so, I delighted in seeing her dislodged. I liked to see her power challenged and abused, openly taken from her.

'Johnnie!' She called again. I said nothing. I didn't even move.

'Don't call him, yet. I going to tell you what you do to me, first. You cause me a whole heap of headaches. All my plans for the blonde have to frustrated because you put bad propaganda into her head. I lose a whole investment of clothes and money when she walk out and left. I lose a lot of contacts, too. In other words, you mash up my affairs in a most diabolical way. And I want to tell you something else before you get any wrong ideas. That blonde was going to be my one woman. She wasn't going on the streets as you did tell her. I'm not that kind. I've never been a ponce and never will. I wanted that woman as my girl friend. I liked her plenty, plenty. So you see what you cause, now. Understand?'

'Johnnie! What's wrong with you? I'm calling you!'

'Leave Johnnie out of this. I going, Sandra. But remember. You hear me? Remember next time not to meddle. Meddling is a nasty thing. You might not get away with it as lightly as you get away with it this time.'

He walked away normally, turned round, winked at me, and slammed the door. He had delivered his Christmas present and had left well pleased with himself. But not so Sandra. She had lost face; a certain edge to her dynamism had been made jagged; she had lost a side battle in her daily war of the Coolths – a war in which the club owner with the most coolth (i.e. the most spending money, the most elevated, the least accessible, the least outwardly worried, and the best dressed) and also the greatest poise gets the respect, indeed the combined respect, of Soho, St. James's and even Upper Regent Street. Larry had attacked all that, expertly. He had dented the shellac and tinfoil. This was inexcus-able. And in front of, if not intentionally for the benefit of, her devotees and customers. And in front of Biddy and me!

She swivelled her bracelet and the charms rattled plaintively. She ordered a drink. When she sipped it the charms sounded again; this time they were appealing and lighthearted. She had forgotten the whole affair. A drink in time saves a hell of a lot! I'm sure now, and I was then, that that was what she aimed at proving to her onlookers. But she hadn't completely recovered, however. She called me over to the counter.

'Johnnie, see to it that he never comes back here. And another thing; be more co-operative next time, will you.'

'Is that all?' I wasn't even annoyed; simply disgusted, depressed.

'Don't you come the perfect serving man with me, Johnnie! You can drop that right now.'

Of course, who wouldn't have understood? I did. Licking her wounds noisily. A bit like Fiona, I said to an imaginary jury. Perhaps even more than a bit.

The time slowed down. The customers grew wilder and more demanding. Sandra had forgotten Larry, and the bar had forgotten everything. It was old times, again.

It was after eleven. An extension of three hours had been granted and the lush-heads, half-stewed ones, rabid hustlers, the whole messy lot behaved as if they had applied for it themselves. They sprawled all over the place; laughed in any available face; spat freely; swore dispassionately; whored indiscreetly; fondled and petted indiscriminately; and 'lived up' every bloody minute as riotously as possible.

Tips. Tips. Tips. And more tips.

In a way I felt sorry for Sandra. I also felt for Larry. Between them, there was a blonde at large. And a blonde at large is an investment made and lost, or an investment about to be made and lost. Poor Larry's investment! Like Fiona's investment in me. And mine in Dick. Or Biddy's in DuBois B. Washington. Or the old lady's in the Trados. Or my mother's in me. (I've figured twice in that little emotional comparative analysis. Quite an investment I must have been: a wonder of a white hope!)

Tips. Tips. Tips.

I was doe-eyed downstairs at about two-fifteen when *the other*, his white coat looking less like a waiter's and more like a butcher's, told me that there was someone upstairs to see me.

It was a surprise. I ran up the stairs. There he was, waiting for me.

'Dick! Something wrong?'

'No, Johnnie. Not really.'

168

'D'you want a drink? Have a Christmas one on me. All right?'

'Lovely. Brandy?'

'Sure. What with?'

'Nothing, thank you.'

'Good, Soon be back.'

He looked fairly at ease. Our favourite overcoat on. And our favourite suit. We edged towards the corridor leading to the stairs. It had been such a hell of a fight to get to the bar that I bought a double brandy in order to avoid a quick return. Dick showed little surprise.

He twirled the balloon glass and said, 'Trying to bribe me?'

'Why should I want to?'

'Oh, you can never tell.'

'Come off it, Dick. What's eating at that grey soul of yours? Your visit isn't Season's Greetings, is it? What d'you want to know?'

He didn't answer me right away. Instead, he looked away and smiled, I thought at the time, a little ruefully; perhaps for the first time in our friendship I had noticed that. He turned back to me, changed his smile slowly, and sipped his brandy. He grimaced appreciatively. We both smiled.

He said calmly, 'Did you go?'

'Where?' It was too well timed for me. I was unprepared. Anyway, I caught up in time. 'Oh, I see. Yes. Yes, I did.'

'And what happened?'

'The usual.'

'Going back again after you leave here?'

'Of course not.'

'Are you sure?'

'Yes, Dick, I am sure. Is that why you've come to collect me?'

'Collect you? That sounds ominous. No. I've come because I was worried about that note from Fiona. I thought that maybe you'd gone to her and, er, well, er, forgotten to go to work. You know how stupidly sentimental reunions can be.'

'Reunion? Yes, I see what you mean.' The very same word I had used earlier on. Somehow, I made it sound like a nasty word. He had used it casually, functionally, without offending Fiona or me.

Dick's presence at the club, and at that hour, gave me a lift. The slap-happy squeals and forced gaiety seemed tolerable in a way. He asked if he could get me a drink. I refused gently. He understood. He teased me about my 'tips-gathering'. He said that he didn't mind adding to the mint which I must have acquired judging from what he saw of the semi-unconscious state of some of the customers. I agreed about the mint, and we both chuckled like fellow conspirators.

'Laura's coming tomorrow, isn't she?'

'I think so, Dick. Why?'

'I've invited someone to dinner. I'd hate Laura to let us down. Incidentally, I see she has prepared certain of her "inevitables" already.'

'Like what?'

'Oh, you know, her mammoth trifle, about fifty layers; egg-nog; stuffing; pork.' I suddenly realized that he was talking round the subject. I decided to bring him round again with a jerk. It usually worked with him. I was curious. His slick evasion would be checked if I could get in smartly.

'Who have you invited?'

'Ahh! It's a secret!'

'A mutual friend?'

'Perhaps. Perhaps not. One can never tell, especially with your likes and dislikes being turned on and off with such alarming regularity.'

'You're up to something, Dick. Yes?'

'Don't be suspicious. We'll have a jolly good time of it whatever happens.'

'Everything depends on Laura.' I wanted to draw him out. His answer to that one would be my strongest clue.

'Yes. One side of it, anyway.'

He finished his drink and left. He had never visited me before, yet I couldn't help feeling that he had somehow appeared too accustomed to what he had found: the mixed clientele, the vulgarity, the crush. He showed no surprise, no wonderment, no strangeness. He didn't even look around. Not inquisitive. Not even vaguely interested.

The morning bristled.

Didn't remember to wish Dick a happy Christmas, I suddenly thought after passing one of Sandra's G.I. holly wreaths. Then I consoled myself as I quickly remembered that he hadn't either. He must have been too concerned with Fiona's note. Maybe I oughtn't to have left it for him to read, I asked myself, not really expecting an answer, not really giving it any importance one way or another.

Tips. Tips. Tips.

I hustled with a maniacal will. The extension would be over in fifteen minutes. The fever was on. Sandra instructed her serving men to give everybody the 'bum's rush'. Her eyes looked beady and anxious. Greed wasn't even masked at that hour of the morning; she couldn't care less; let them all know that they were being used viciously, not in the least subtly. Ram them; slam them; roll them, if possible. The rent must be paid.

★   ★   ★

Still at the club. Christmas morning, half past four. Sandra had checked the till; Biddy had written up the day-book. The bottles had been filed away – filed away, because they had been 're-touched', added to and had to be kept apart from the rest of the stock. Certain clever manipulations of measures, distilled water, and close observation had also been necessary in the unique process of filing them away.

Six or seven select friends of Sandra had been allowed to remain behind: after the closing-time chores, there'd be a party, somewhere or the other. Nobody cared where. Everybody had caught a third breath – the last, if the truth be known. Things had been quite exhausting; almost twelve hours of it.

DuBois B. Washington was one of the 'allowed friends'. He was more 'high' than I'd ever seen him before. All over the counter, over everybody. Nobody minded. And who would object to a prize stuck pig whose patronage was worth nearly half of the P.X. stores, anyway? The used man was having a ball!

'Johnnie-O! I'm wailing, man! Wailing, like the man said!'

My attempt to appreciate his hilarity sounded false, but I kept it up nevertheless. I liked him. I wanted to keep his company, his drunken company, in an attempt to show the others that he was

171

a good sort. I replied somewhat inanely: 'You wail right on, Pres! Great! Real great, Mr Washington, sir. The White House is open house for all, man!'

I suddenly felt ashamed. It seemed like disrespect. I had joined the band of spivs. And, moreover, my imitation was hopelessly fraudulent. It was bad, very bad indeed. He was being attacked, I thought; and I was ashamed.

'Johnnie-O! I'm going to take your kind advice and continue to wail, daddy-o. I'm going to have me a time of crazy happenings. After all, there's nothing the dollar won't do that you want it to do, especially when the lights are low, and when I says low I mean low, man! Real cool and low! So I'll just wail on, Johnnie-O.'

Feebly I added, 'You do that.'

And he said, as if to close our duologue: 'Sure will, nice man. Sure will.'

DuBois B. Washington was overseas. And overseas he'd remain all Christmas; Biddy or no Biddy, the man was rebelling, and he didn't care who knew it. Least of all Biddy.

One of the select took over where I left off. 'You're a rebel, DuBois B.'

'Call me no names, daddy-o, I ain't with you nohow!'

'Aren't you afraid Biddy might bring down the axe?' The select jackass thought he was being helpful. I was interested to see how DuBois B. would deal with him.

'What you say?'

'Biddy. You'd better watch out. She might clamp down on you.'

'Man! She ain't nothin'! Nothin', d'ya hear? She can't reach me, now, no matter how hard she tries. I'm gone so far out that she'll have to contact me by radar, Jackson! R-A-D-A-R! You got those significant letters? And if and when she does, she's got a whole mess o' decodin' to do before she can get my twisted dialogue. You dig?'

He was freedom itself. I can see his face now: a sagging jaw, half closed bloodshot eyes, chapped lips, and nigger-hunched G.I. shoulders.

Biddy's a bitch, I thought. Yet, a clever one, though.

Sandra was ready to go. We hadn't spoken to each other since the Larry incident, apart from the 'bum's rush' she issued at fifteen to go. She pressed a fiver in my hand and wished me a happy Christmas. I thanked her dutifully.

We were outside.

The club door was being inspected by two of the select. Sandra tried it and muttered something to one of them. He nodded like Solomon, wise and bored.

Biddy came up to me.

'Why're you so bleeding selfish and irresponsible?'

'What d'you mean, Biddy?'

'I heard you and your friend discussing me. I don't like it.'

'I wasn't discussing you. And DuBois B.'s no friend of mine.'

'Since when? Why?'

Because he's chained, woman. You've caught him and caged him like a house-pet.'

'You're a bum, Johnnie!'

'So I'm a bum. I don't mind. D'you?'

'You're also bloody well finished as a man. No woman in her right senses would want to know anything like you.'

'Explain that, Biddy. Or can you?'

'I do not have to explain anything to you, and you flipping well know that. In any case, you ought to be able to explain it to yourself. You're clever enough.' She spat out every word with calculated emphasis, venomously.

'Are you drunk?' That was all I could think of saying to her.

'Never!'

And that was that. Simply. Smartly initiated, smartly concluded. Biddy had always been one for the short pronouncement which was intended to do the most damage in the least possible period of time. I wasn't quite sure that somehow she hadn't missed her target. She may have because she had been too quick about it. As soon as she had delivered her thrust, she went in search of DuBois B. who had wandered off down the road.

I thought, at the time, that she had missed her target, and yet I had a sneaking feeling that hidden somewhere in what she had said was a clue to her original intention.

So much of what Biddy said to me, day in, day out, could be dismissed as a shower of words, words of silly abuse, of faint praise, of trifling gossip, of sly cajolery, of forced resentment, of childlike spite, nothing vitally important, nothing seriously critical. For weeks on end, we thrived on badinage and nothing else.

I left the club and turned up the road. I would walk slowly, I promised myself, and try to figure out her statement; I'd try to understand it before I reached the flat.

It had been the first for a long time that Biddy had got me really worried.

I was sure she hadn't missed.

13

I was up by seven-thirty. Christmas Day had kept its promise: it had come, icy cold, slightly windy, no snow.

I dressed quickly and went for a walk. Biddy was on my mind. What did she mean by 'finished as a man'? What did she mean by the whole tirade?

Leicester Square looked haggard and spent: no gloss, no bounce, only the detritus of Christmas Eve's processions and Christmas morning's excesses. What did she mean?

Trafalgar Square. The Strand. Aldwych. Kingsway. Bloomsbury. What did she mean? 'Finished as a man'? I tried but without success. Biddy was a problem I knew I could well do without. So I set about doing without her. I tried to recall the scene between Sandra and Larry. It came back to me extraordinarily vividly. His acting had been superb; her coolth, attacked but ably defended.

Through Bloomsbury. To Tottenham Court Road. Charlotte Street. Mortimer Street. Portland Place. On to Oxford Circus. Biddy's a bitch! Sandra's a fool!

I stared up at the decorations on Regent Street and wondered at the clumsy inventions and colour schemes. They would have been quite at home in a Council-built barn, I suggested to one of the fantastic lamps whose loose tendrils were hanging perilously near the pavement. Cowardly thing to have done, really, but so soothing: lamps don't talk back at you. I muttered other inanities to most of the lamps on my way down the street. When I got to Piccadilly Circus, the Guinness clock was saying nine-fifteen. Directly under it stood Larry. He looked beaten up and doped. Late-morning driftwood. I wanted suddenly to avoid him. I wanted to change direction but I was sure he hadn't missed me; he was such a 'hawk eye' ordinarily that I decided that he had seen me, and that it would be stupid to do anything but go right up to him. After all, he had had a long shot of me: Huppert's, Barclays Bank, the entrance to Glasshouse Street.

'Happy Christmas, again, Larry.'

'You telling me that or you asking me?'

'Stranded?'

'In the middle of Piccadilly Circus? Not exactly. Just watching the morning.'

'No taxis?'

'Them don't bother me, countryman.'

'Where've you been?'

'The Egg and a few other places.'

'You sound beat.'

'Beat? Cleaned out, you mean!'

'What's wrong?'

'Lose nearly three hundred pounds last night after I left you. Three hundred pounds to rass!'

'Who was the ace?'

'If I tell you, you would call me a liar; you wouldn't believe me at all, at all.'

'Go on.'

'Ringo.'

'Ringo?'

'See what I mean? Of all people, you wouldn't expect that a student politician like Ringo would play such a role, eh.'

'No.'

'Boy!' Larry checked himself. He shook his head from side to side, and sighed heavily. 'I tell you. That Ringo is a real dark horse and no joke about it. A real first-class dark horse.' He laughed. 'I going to tell you why I laugh. I laugh because of the word dark. Ringo really black, you know. Black for true!' He laughed again, even more loudly than before.

I joined him. We both must have looked like street-corner minstrels warming for a show. Larry was performing a soft-shoe shuffle and I was trying to back out of his path. I was glad he had taken it that way.

Suddenly he stopped moving about and said: 'I have to make a merriment every now and then to shake the worries off, countryman. Good God! The boy, Ringo, pounce down and mash up the Christmas, just so. And to think that I used to believe that is only books and papers and such high things and University of London problems did fill up the boy head, eh!'

We went in search of coffee or tea. Didn't matter. Larry talked and talked about Ringo. About Ringo's ability at cards. His own easy-going nature when gambling against friends. The hardships he had had to encounter in his fight against poverty and prison. His endless ambitions. His benevolent attitudes of mind. The lot.

I listened. And he went on to enumerate painstakingly his many virtues, some well tried, some slightly passive, some hopelessly latent.

In a selfish way Larry and Ringo seemed distant, almost completely outside my own tight, neurotic world. They were acquaintances; but they really didn't touch any part of my immigrant experience. I could patronize them; feel like being with them; even suffer them in a nasty, pompous way; but I couldn't truly, honestly, have more than a passing interest in their affairs. Or so I felt, anyway, while listening to Larry's monotonous self-evaluation and self-criticism.

I had been caught up with another kind of detritus. I had entered into a peculiar contract of experience with people much more equipped for London's hustling and hard knocks than I ever could be. Yet, I knew that I was learning. I knew that I was being prepared firmly for it. I had come to it with a certain first coating, an insulation of household tricks, deceit, false pride, intolerance: a coating I often called the middle-class prerogative, the middle-class protective coloration.

To a large extent, Ringo had it; Larry would never. Sandra had enough to open an emporium. Biddy had it and tried hard, affair after affair, to forget it. Fiona had it; nursed it; buried it on occasions; resurrected it ceremonially; and frequently, when it suited her bucking sexuality, denied its existence.

Dick was caught up in it, too. He was trying desperately to escape it. This, I was certain, had attracted me forcefully. I too was a part of his escape from it. We genuinely wanted a kind of freedom. Idealistic, yet not wholly so. Or was it?

You're also bloody well finished as a man. No woman in her right senses would want to know anything like you. Something must have been showing, as the young girl's mother would have said. I may have been changing in many 'splendoured ways' which were noticeable to Biddy and Biddy alone. She must have felt terribly strong in her new knowledge: leopard-spot finder extraordinary!

Larry was still rambling on. We had had our coffee and roll and butter, when I decided to ask Larry for his help. I was certain that I could colour-hide the essential giveaway points. Larry's raw-hide intelligence, his irresponsible, irrepressible lifemanship, his courage, his abandon could be of use; could be trusted.

'Tell me something, Larry, d'you think I've changed?'

'Changed? How?'

'In any way.'

'You look a bit stouter like to me.'

'Anything else?'

'Like what, Johnnie boy?'

'You know what I mean.'

'Oh, that! Well, you get sharper.'

'What d'you mean?'

'You get sort of big-city clever up and things. You not a fool-fool back-home boy no more. Like all of we in this country, you learn quick how to cotton on to new ways of living and new ways of looking at people and them bad ideas and them good ones. You seem to me to be a sort of hard case sometimes, but a man like me can always manage to soften you up.'

'D'you think there's anything wrong with me; anything that you would consider a problem?'

'I don't think so. But what sort of talking this that the two of we boys putting down on a Christmas morning, eh?' A slight pause. 'Ah, yes! That is one thing I notice that you getting to be. You getting to be a real worry-head, countryman. You and Ringo

177

are the frown-up, thinking type of individuals. You two boys behave like you facing a brain battle all day long.' Another slight pause. 'You got woman trouble, Johnnie? You can discuss it with me, you know. I's the original Professor of Womanology, countryman. Every university college in this country is just simply clamouring for my services where that is concerned; so go ahead, shoot, and let me give you my genius in the matter.' He winked and chuckled knowingly. 'You hear my gentle approximation of college language? You hear the expert speechifier talking, boy?' He guffawed, slapped me on the back, and performed a soft-shoe shuffle to prove, I imagined, that I could take him in my confidence; that I had nothing to worry about because the whole thing was really a bad joke; that I could relax because he had had all the necessary experience in that respect and had come to the conclusion that it could be easily dealt with, laughed at if it came to that, possibly ridiculed. 'So tell me, now, if you got woman trouble or not.'

'Sort of, Larry boy.'

'What sort and description?'

'Well, it's hard to explain in a single go. It's mixed up and stupid, to tell the truth.'

'You not functioning as you think a man should, you mean?'

'You could put it that way, I suppose.'

'You have a sort of distraction?'

'Yes.'

'Another woman?'

'No.'

'No?'

Larry was excellent. He was getting it out of me like an expert. He slightly unnerved me with his sudden earnestness.

'Well, actually, Larry, I…'

'Boy! You really got a problem there.'

'You see, Larry, it's like this: I've got a woman. Or rather, she's got me. She's the grabbing, gobbling type.'

'I know the type. No worse clinging vine in the world. A clinging-vine woman is the only thing that bring all races of people on a par. Every race got their clinging-vine types, countryman. White, black, red, yellow, and indifferent.'

'She's all right, but I always want to get out of her clutches. She makes me feel caged up. Frightened. Nervous. Inadequate, if you know what I mean.'

'Used up, eh?'

'Yes. Used up would be a better way of looking at it.'

'So what line of resistance you adopting?'

'Escape, Larry.'

'As simple as that, eh, countryman? How?'

'Well, I left her and took a flat with a friend of mine.'

'A man? English?'

'Yes.'

'What sort of man?'

'How d'you mean?'

'Just that, Johnnie.'

'I'm not sure.'

'You get on well together?'

'Very well.'

'You happier that way than with the woman?'

'I'm sure of it!' Perhaps I stressed that too much; I nearly shouted it. As if in defence. As if aware of exposure. I had these second thoughts, but all too late. Larry had been given his clue.

'You think that this is bad, eh, boy? Not natural like?'

'Not really. What d'you think? D'you think it's beginning to show?'

'Show?'

'Yes. Show up in my behaviour: the way I treat people; the way I think; the way I look at things. D'you think that the more I feel guilty the more I actually am guilty? D'you think that the mere fact that I went with him to the flat is a kind of admission that I'm that way without knowing it?'

'Maybe, countryman. Maybe.'

Poor Larry was stunned. He didn't try to avoid my searching stare. It was there for him to see, and he did as intelligently as possible. We looked at each other and waited. He suggested that we had been sitting too long. He said that he needed to walk around a bit to clear his confused thoughts.

We headed towards Piccadilly Circus.

Larry was trying his best to distract me; to distract himself, too.

179

I shouldn't think he was embarrassed, but I do think that he thought I was. Everything he did or said had a touch of sympathy, a touch of understanding. After a while I began to resent it. I had to. I wasn't accustomed to it. I didn't want it. Yet, he wasn't playing the offensive game I knew Fiona would have delighted in playing herself. He was concerned. And that was enough to make me resentful.

He tried another tack.

'Countryman, you ever count the amount of Spades you see walking the streets in this London, here?'

'Used to when I first came over.'

'You know how much I just count on this cold Christmas morning, already?'

'No.'

'Twenty-nine.'

'You counted the white ones, too?'

'Them don't count, man. They belong. Cold or hot, them belong. Is the Spades I count because they look so obvious. They look obvious like they don't belong on this landscape, at all, at all.'

'White or Spade, neither belongs in this blasted cold, if you ask me, Larry.'

'I like to hear you talk like that, Johnnie boy. That is real first-class dishonest talk, eh! That is the clever side to all of we who live here long enough, you know. You talk in one big compromise fashion; just like how *they* talk to you in the first indication of racial pressure. Why should you bring the white side into it? Can't you see that you doing something that is not your duty to do? Your duty is to feel sorry for your own people, not to try to compromise. As a matter of fact, that's what I really notice wrong about you. That's the change that I notice, Johnnie. Nothing else; see God there! You look like you sell out to the other side. You look like you settle down to a real old-time Sunday dinner of compromise and blind-eye philosophy. It won't work, I can tell you right now.'

'So that's it, is it?'

'I think so.'

'D'you think a woman would be unable to put up with this new side to me?'

'She mightn't. Of course, it all depends on the sort of woman you have in mind. Some would thrive on it. The more honest ones might get fed up and tell you off and help you to reach an understanding with yourself and herself where both your lives are concerned with each other. It all depends on the make-up of woman, though.'

I felt that Larry had had too much of my needling questions, so I asked him nothing more. As far as I was concerned, he had been asked more than enough. I had given too much of myself. And so had he, of his sympathy, his ideas, his experience.

We're all parasites, I suddenly thought.

14

We wandered through the Circus, down Lower Regent Street, into Charles II Street, and across the Haymarket where Larry left me. He wished me a happy Christmas for the third or fourth time, and a 'crazy' New Year. He emphasized the word 'crazy' with his usual mock venom.

I turned to watch him, hands in pockets, shoulders drawn up high, head ducked; and hoped that he'd make out, somehow, despite his heavy gambling loss. I suppose I hoped more than that for him, at the time, but his three hundred pounds loomed so importantly that the rest seemed trivial and a little confused.

★   ★   ★

It was eleven-thirty-five when I got back to the flat. Laura was all over the place, busy, omnipresent. Her brisk, nervous movements were forbidding. I knew she'd brook no interference, not even a helping hand, not even the usual inter-chores conversation. She nodded and grunted impatiently as she passed me on the way to her Eden of a kitchen which, incidentally, resembled an expert replica of Berwick Street Market, possibly even more so like Portobello Market.

I knocked on Dick's bedroom door. He didn't answer immediately. I knocked again.

'That you, Johnnie?'

'Humm.'

'Come in.'

'Happy Christmas, Dick!'

'Thank you. Same to you.'

'You wished me that this morning, at the club. Remember? Or did you?' I was fishing. I don't know why. I really had no reason to do it, but I did nevertheless.

'Oh, yes? I did, did I? Oh, well!'

'You sound preoccupied. Something wrong?'

'Laura?'

'How?'

'She's been ordering me about all morning. You know the sort of thing: "Get out of my way; don't sit there; I've just dusted that; why don't you find something useful to do?" And that's putting it mildly.'

'Yes. I know. By the way, who's the surprise for dinner, today, Dick?'

'Surprise?'

'Don't you remember?'

'Oh!'

'Well, come on. Who's it?'

'You'll see in time.'

'Come off it! Who's coming?'

'It's a surprise, I tell you. Be patient.'

'All right, I'll wait.'

'Been out, haven't you?'

'Humm.'

'Where?'

'Round the West End.'

'Anything exciting?'

'Not really. Met a Jamaican pal of mine.'

'That all?'

'Humm.'

He was sprawled across the bed. One of his usual four-hundred-page novels was opened, his left hand fanned out to keep the place. He was fully dressed, apart from his jacket. He was wearing his favourite yellow tie.

I wanted so badly to talk to him about Biddy's remark, but something, some innate fear or reserve, held me back. I was sure that he'd be able to tell me what I wanted to know. Poor Larry didn't understand. Yet he understood another side of the question. He certainly surprised me with his snap appraisal of the matter of integration and compromise.

Dick closed his novel and sat up. He asked me to sit on the bed, beside him. I did so, and took the novel from him. The bulk of its pages felt wonderfully heavy and appealing in my hand; something to throw about, I thought; something to fill a gap with, to sit on, to stand on, to drum upon, to leave on permanent display.

'You always read these big books, Dick?'

'Not always.'

'This one's the sixth I've seen you reading.'

'I know. But it's rather simple; I like reading historical novels.'

'I've only read one. Still remember it, too.'

'Which one?'

'Can't recall the title, but it was all about Fouché and the French revolution. A translation, as a matter of fact.'

He got up and started to walk about the room aimlessly. Something was brewing, I thought fearfully; something he would have difficulty in ridding himself of.

I turned the pages of the novel carelessly, waiting for Dick to come to terms with his embarrassment. He opened the wardrobe, rummaged about, and closed it, again. Then the chest of drawers. The shoe-rack.

He stood in front of the mirror, fidgeted, and adjusted his already neatly tied Windsor knot. He patted it into shape, tugged at it gently, and smiled, half-turning towards me and half-looking at his reflection in the mirror.

Then he flung himself bodily across the bed. His head lolled over the side. His feet vibrated in rhythm with the bedsprings for a few seconds; then they became motionless, stiff. He remained in that position until Laura knocked at the door. She wanted to know whether she should serve the plum pudding hot or cold. I had told her a few weeks before Christmas that quite a lot of Jamaican families preferred it served cold with rum or port poured lavishly over it. Yet, knowing Laura as I did, I realized she

183

must have decided to take a five-minute break; and all she really wanted was a little chat to pass the time. Dick got up and suggested that she come in and sit down for a while. He wanted to make his peace with her. We smiled at each other. He offered her a cigarette and a drink of brandy. She bluntly refused both; and repeated her question. Dick looked at me and I shook my head doubtfully. She reminded us that she hadn't all day to discuss the 'flipping thing'; or was it all Christmas? I can't remember, now. Anyway, Dick made the decision.

'Serve it hot, Laura.'

'Thank God for that!' She banged the door in celebration rather than in exasperation, as she usually did when she had proved a point.

'She's a funny old stick, isn't she?'

'Humm.'

'We'd better remember to begin showering praises on her efforts before we take a mouthful, later on.'

'Dick, come clean with me. What's on your mind?'

Dick's visit to the club last night, or this morning, I thought, can only mean one thing. He's plotting something. It worried me. There was more to it than I understood. I was certain I was right about the visit. His excuse, now so many hours old, suddenly appeared flimsy and inadequate. Even the gentle use of 'reunion' seemed doubtful. His prolonged anxiety had clinched it in my mind.

He suggested that we go to the sitting room and pour ourselves a drink. He had a largish brandy, and I, almost a quadruple Scotch; more out of spite than conviviality – all things plus Christmas included. Dick's glass was all wrong for brandy, but he held it and semi-circled it appropriately.

His acute sense of 'headmastership' was at its best: he certainly kept me waiting; hanging on was more like it, tortured and a bit resentful. He threw back his head and uttered a half-stifled sigh. Perhaps he, too, was waiting, I suddenly consoled myself. Perhaps he himself was being made to wait because he was unsure of himself. He drained his glass and began to twirl it by the stem.

'Johnnie, you'll have to make a decision, very soon, won't you?'

He had released it with great tact.

I felt tired; frightened; expectant; confused. The Scotch wasn't helping me either. I tried to look composed. I must have shown some emotion, nevertheless. And he must have noticed, but being the cool interrogator he was I wasn't quite certain. I knew it was useless to try to dodge or to evade his question completely; even to evade it slightly would prove futile. Yet I tried.

'What decision, Dick?'

'Your homosexuality, Johnnie.'

Biddy was right, I heard myself say. I couldn't look at Dick. I began to top up my drink. It obviously didn't need it. He noticed that, too.

'I owe you this talk. I've owed it to you for weeks, now. Do you want me to go on?'

I attempted to brave it out.

'It's all right by me, Dick; but I'm sure I won't understand you.'

'Why?'

'Well, for one thing, you're on the wrong track about my being homosexual.' That sounded feeble and positively stupid; yet it was a try.

'Am I?'

'Aren't you?' This, I thought, could go on for quite a long time. Back and forth, back and forth, and to no avail. The whole thing was stupid, utterly stupid. I didn't want to talk about it. Dick had been too sober, too easy and matter of fact, to fight against him or to sidetrack him in any way possible.

He realized what I was trying to do. He came to the point.

'Let's stop playing games, Johnnie. How long have we shared the flat?'

'About two months or more.'

'Within that time, I've become progressively more aware of it. I've carried out my own private tests, if that doesn't sound too silly. I've watched you; checked your reactions; and now I'm fairly sure about it. Perhaps more than fairly sure when we come right down to it. At Hampstead you showed certain signs, certain signs, shall I say, of latency. I watched you carefully, but still I wasn't sure.'

185

'Watching me? What for?' Another stupid thrust.

'I watched closely for a long time, mark you, not wanting to encourage it or influence it either way. Naturally, I've been made extremely happy by your coming to share the flat with me; and I'd rather have it that way than have you still living undercover with Fiona. I'm trying to be as frank as possible, I hope you understand, Johnnie?'

'So that's it, Dick?'

'What?'

'You think that my total or nearly total rejection of Fiona's advances is the proof you've been waiting for, eh?'

'Now, don't be silly. Of course not. It's, not as simple as all that, and you jolly well know it.'

'All right. Suppose you tell me how different it is to be truly homosexual and how difficult it is for one to become aware and certain of another, especially another who doesn't know he is. Tell me that, now!'

'Don't shout, you'll have Laura barging in here and telling us not to sit on her highly polished furniture; you know what she's like.'

Dick's attempt at being nice and friendly only infuriated me.

'Oh, to hell with Laura!'

He ignored that.

'Well, Johnnie, what d'you intend doing about your predicament? It is a predicament, you know.'

'Predicament? Look, I'm no *queer*! I ought to know and that's proof enough, isn't it?'

'That was a pretty vulgar outcry.'

'Sorry, Dick. Forgive me.'

'Of course. You know – or do you – that I've been waiting on you since we left Hampstead?'

'You mean, you expected me to –'

'Try to avoid another vulgar outburst, please.'

'But surely, Dick, you don't really think that I was leading you on?'

'No. I don't. I'm only saying that I've waited long enough. You've shown no compassion in the circumstance. You even return to Fiona and tell me about it as if the whole messy affair couldn't matter to me. What about me, Johnnie? What about me? Us? Can't you see what you're doing to our relationship?'

'My idea of our relationship is obviously diametrically opposed to yours. That's all I can say.' That sounded so pompous and silly that I had to try to express myself more simply, plainly and honestly. I knew that I had to be very careful with Dick. His experience was, by far, greater than mine, and naturally he could see through every move I made or intended to make in an attempt to defend myself. I continued: 'We took this flat because of certain very simple and practical reasons. One, to be rid of the old lady's grip on us; two, so that I'd be nearer the club and that you could get a new job in the West End somewhere; three, to escape our respective leeches, Fiona and your oversexed employer, and four, because we had got accustomed to each other and were getting along well together in the face of all our mixed-up problems and anxieties. All right?'

'Purely for economic reasons, was it, Johnnie?' He sounded hurt. And, of course, he was being grossly unfair to me.

'I don't understand. Economic reasons? How?' I was going to fight this issue as cautiously as I could. I don't know what I was doing to his argument as a whole, but this point I'd ride as long as possible.

'So you don't understand. I do.'

'Look, Dick! We share things here, don't we?'

'Yes.'

'Am I living off you?'

'No. That's not what I meant.'

'Well, what do you mean by "economic reasons"?'

'D'you think I'm stupid? D'you want me to believe that our getting together was mainly to give two women the slip and to pool our resources for the rental of a flat: a matter of two living cheaper than one? Is that it?'

That was proof that I had won my little skirmish. He twisted himself out of it, but not as cleverly as he thought. I was certain now that there was more to his accusation than he had intimated.

'You're angry, Dick.'

'Do you wonder? You're a dismal failure to me, Johnnie.'

'I'm sorry about that, Dick.'

187

'You've complained of being used by Fiona; it almost drives you mad, you say. What about us? Can't you see you're doing the same thing to me?'

'Oh, don't start that, now, please!'

'Your attitude is the same. To her, and to me.'

'What d'you really want me to do, Dick?'

'I want you to return my love for you, Johnnie. And before you can do that, you've got to come to terms with what I spoke about earlier on. There's no mystery attached to it; no depravity either. I had to. Quite a lot of people have had to. Now it's your turn. If you don't you'll make a lot of people unhappy, including yourself, perhaps most of all.'

'Don't be ridiculous. I'm not bisexual. Neither am I a repressed homosexual!'

'You don't think you are, Johnnie?'

'Of course I don't think I am!'

'D'you think I'm trying to trap you?'

'I don't know what you're trying to do, Dick. Believe me.' I had cooled down considerably. I was willing to listen to him. But I was not going to be bullied into anything, nevertheless. 'I don't know what to think. You're so convincing; in theory most of what you say seems responsible and quite feasible. And at the same time, you're so utterly wrong about it all. Not really about it all, but certainly about me.'

That couldn't have been more confused and idiotic, I thought. I had lost nerve again. Somehow, I wanted to give in and have done with it. I wanted to tell him that he was right, that he was completely right. I wanted to stop talking about it; thinking about it; being so near to it, and yet so far from it. I was terribly confused and resentful and fed up.

'Well, that's it, I suppose, Johnnie.'

'I suppose so, too, Dick. But you're wrong.'

'We'll see. We'll see.'

'What does that mean?'

'It's all right. Nothing to worry about. What's the time?'

'About one o'clock, I believe.'

'Fine. Fiona'll be here in about a quarter of an hour.'

'Fiona?'

188

'Our surprise guest, Johnnie.
'But why Fiona of all people?'
'Why not?'

15

She arrived at one-twenty-five.

She looked at her wristwatch and announced coyly that she was sorry to be ten minutes late. No taxis, or something like that.

Dick bowed graciously, perhaps a trifle too theatrically, I thought at the time; but quickly assumed the informal ease and warmth of the Christmas Day host.

I wanted to ask her what she had done with Trado, but apparently Dick's dinner party had been planned for three, no more. Poor, unfortunate Trado the Trierarch would have ruined everything.

'I must say that both my former tenants, if you can be described as my tenants, are looking extremely well; even a bit prosperous.'

'I'm glad you could come along, Fiona.'

'Wonderful of you to have asked me, Dick.'

'I kept it a secret from Johnnie, just as we planned.'

'He doesn't seem thrilled to see me. Are you, Johnnie?'

'Yes. Of course I am. But what did you do with Trado?'

'He's dining with your old favourite.'

'Mrs Blount?'

'Yes. And so is Shakuntala and her current boy friend.'

'Does Trado know you're here?'

'You're worried, aren't you, Johnnie? Yes, he does. Why?'

'With Dick and myself?'

'Well, let's say with Dick and some of his friends, shall we?'

Laura went into action. She filled the room with her over-whelming diligence. Her fluid appearances, her entrances and exits, were admirable; absolutely expert. She ignored everyone; yet her efficiency hummed menacingly like a forbidding apiary.

Her dinner was highly successful; so were our sporadic out-bursts of conversation, dishonest camaraderie and coolth. We drank erratically during and after the meal. And so did Laura, who insisted that she had no appetite but only a curiously unquenchable thirst which she reminded us was utterly unlike her everyday conduct. We quickly agreed. Dick poured her some more brandy. She smiled benignly.

Fiona complimented her on a 'simply gorgeous feast'. Dick and I endorsed it handsomely, nodding and grunting and raising our glasses to the good lady, after Fiona had finished her piece.

I think we were all on the verge of being happy; certainly tipsily happy, anyway.

*   *   *

We left the table; scrambled our way to the sitting room; and flung ourselves down helter-skelter. Torpor ensued for the next half an hour. Laura, from time to time, came in on tiptoe to inspect us, the look of the victor on her flushed face.

I was glad she was happy.

Dick had poured himself a large brandy. Fiona sat up and asked for a cigarette. I gave her a lighted Chesterfield.

'We are living it up! American, eh? From your contacts at the club?'

'Humm.'

'Nice place.'

'What?'

'I said that your club is a nice place. Wake up, will you?'

'One visit gave you that impression?'

'Shouldn't take more than one visit to do that, Johnnie.'

'Depends.'

'On what?'

'Oh, on the night you went, the time of night, and with whom.'

'Or for whom, you really meant, didn't you?'

'Who's being nasty, now?'

'Isn't that what you meant?'

'I don't think so.'

Dick squirmed tactfully. Fiona and I weren't fooled. Laura's spell was wearing off. Already I had become quite clear-headed and prepared for the worst. I wanted to find out who would make the first move; Fiona had been warming up nicely and Dick had

190

had his trial run earlier on. But I was curious, much more curious than that, probably because I wanted to know just how much of this dinner party had been planned and what was the agenda agreed upon. Dick, the sly one, held his trump card splendidly, and I resented it.

I decided to make a mockery of their trial.

'Well, Dick, why don't you put your momentous question to Fiona, now, and get it over with? After all, we've eaten our death-cell meal; let's get it over with and know where we stand, eh?'

'What's all this about, Dick?'

'It's all right, Fiona. Johnnie's being his usual melodramatic self.'

I found out what I wanted to know. Fiona apparently knew nothing. She hadn't been cautioned. She hadn't discussed anything with Dick. They hadn't met. We were all starting from scratch.

Well, that was settled. I would answer her question.

'I am being helpful, Fiona. Or if you like, I'm being encouraging. You see, I'm being extremely sensitive to Dick's hopeless quandary; he has a feeling that you might be able to assist me to make a decision about myself. He's being tortured by my present twilight condition of mind, and will continue to be if I'm not brought to book. Therefore, you have been invited here today in order that you may, or might, wring this decision out of me as professionally as possible.'

'Johnnie's quite pompous when he wants to be, isn't he?' Dick chuckled into his brandy like a trained canvasser of easy votes. He was so sure of himself that I hated him for it; despised his every gesture; and hoped sincerely that he'd trip up and lose his poise. But he didn't. He went on to explain: 'Actually, Fiona, it's not as grave as he makes out. I did ask you to dine with us because I thought that you, more than anybody else we know, ought to be able to offer some advice...'

'And what am I to advise on, Dick? And why am I the important choice?'

So she really hadn't been notified as I imagined, as I feared. She was innocent. Dick was innocent. Everything was above board. She had only been invited to dinner to be used to help me make my fateful decision. There was no trap. Dick was still an honest man. Fiona was still an honest woman. This made me more resentful. I had been proved wrong again. I had to hit back hard, very hard indeed. Petty revenge was mine, and I would use it. I would make it into triumph.

I helped myself to a large Scotch.

'Now, you wait a minute, Dick. I'll answer Fiona's questions for you. What's more, I'll answer them honestly.'

Laura came in again. We adjusted our expressions and everything seemed innocent and gay. Laura asked for a drink of light ale; got it; and smiled her way out of the room. Tense expressions flitted back to our plasticine faces. I continued: 'You, my dear Fiona, are to advise me about my latent or, if you like, my repressed, homosexuality, or still better, my bisexuality. You are Dick's important choice because you are also the important threat to Dick's happiness where I'm concerned. D'you understand the situation, now? Am I to be homosexual or not? Am I to be bisexual or not? Am I to be a whole man or not? You're the one being asked to use the casting vote. It's like that, d'you see, because Dick's voted that I am and I naturally have voted that I am not. Got it?'

'Frankly, Johnnie, I do think you're homosexual, but I can't say to what extent or anything. And this doesn't mean that I don't want you as my lover. I couldn't care less. You're what I've been waiting for, homosexual or not.'

'Christ!' That's all I could have said. That's all I did say. And that was that. She had voted; and explained her choice. She even had time to explain her love for me. I don't think she was being cunning either. For once, Fiona had my respect. She had triumphed.

I hadn't really expected that from Fiona.

Dick was unnerved. Dick and the brandy; the bandy legs of his chair; the brandy and Dick! He took two, short, quick drinks; started to pace the room; and completely avoided our stares. Our eyes wanted the satisfaction of his acknowledgment. Eyes! That was all Fiona and I were at that moment. Eyes, doubting eyes, hunting eyes, hurt eyes, pleading eyes, unsure eyes, startled eyes, expectant eyes. I turned to look at her, and she eased away from me. She was uncomfortable.

Perhaps she had said more than she thought was wise. She had agreed with Dick; but also she had declared her position and mine in relation to hers. Indeed, she may have thought that she had exposed herself unnecessarily, stupidly so.

In a way, the result of the voting was: Biddy, Fiona, and Dick for; myself against. Three-one. I wondered where Larry, or for that matter, where Laura would have voted. I had a drunken urge to suggest that Laura be asked her opinion, too. After all, she was closer to the suspect than most people would ever be.

Fiona had turned back to me. She was still uncomfortable. I smiled vacantly and asked her: 'D'you think that I could be like that and not know? Is it possible?'

She shrugged her shoulders slightly and said: 'I don't know, Johnnie. I don't even want to know. I said what was honest and that's all. I've also told you where I stand in all this. It's up to you.'

'What's up to me?'

I knew the answer to my own question. Dick and Fiona knew also. Our little Christmas Day meeting had come to an end. Each would-be proud possessor was waiting on my decision. Each would-be warder of the unprotected was anxious (there's that heart-warming word, again) and tingling. Let them bloody well tingle, I flattered myself. Let them believe the tragic, the melodramatic, the whole soap-bubble of circumstantial evidence, the near-remarkable swindle.

'Fiona, tell me. You knew this all along? Believed it, I mean?'

'Yes, darling. I did.'

'And you never told me about it?'

'Yes and no. I tried to, if you remember? And then I suppose I didn't try hard enough.'

'Why not?' This was all so grossly untrue. We were play-acting again. We were being cowards, again. Fiona was helping me out with my coward's charade. Of course, she had told me. Long ago, hours and hours ago, in her own sitting room. Yet we wrestled with the truth and closed our ears, our eyes, our pores, our everything, and above all, our conscience to the cold fact that we had discussed it. And we'd continue to play our respective roles of idiocy and cowardice.

Fiona was excellent. Her reply to my 'Why not?' seemed valid and considerably above reproach; and what's more I believed her. She said: 'Call it vanity: call it pig-headedness, even plain stupidity. I jolly well knew that of the three of us I was the strongest, the least vulnerable, the best equipped to endure, if that doesn't sound too pretentious. I realized my strength, my wholeness, if you like; and therefore I was prepared to wait.'

'Wait for what?' I was being co-operative, faithfully dishonest.

'For you, Johnnie. For our kind of love. Not Dick's!'

'And you, Dick?' I had to bring him in; it was time, anyway. As far as I was concerned, it had come to a matter of 'share and share alike'. Dick's contribution would be interesting, earnest, and deadly near the truth.

'I realized nothing of the sort. I thought you cared for me, Johnnie; but that you were unable to come out and say so. I'm certain of it right now. I'm certain that you want to unmask your other self; to be free to think, plan, act as one personality, instead of two. This is the root of your unhappiness. I know this. I've seen it so often. All around me. It is that kind of freedom which you're actually hoping for. Nothing more. Right now, your bondage is making you miserable, almost antisocial. And, more or less, that's why you keep running away, Johnnie. I'm sorry if you think I'm preaching; but there we are!'

So I had been told. Well told, in fact.

It was intended that I should break down and give the right answer. They were waiting; one to snap me up, the other to retreat, beaten but still wise and hopeful: Fiona, and Dick.

I had been told identical truths: *by a woman, whose love I did not want, and by a man who wanted to love me unconditionally. In short, Johnnie was being a damn' 'hard case', and enjoying every moment of it, he believed. He was refusing, not terribly unlike Miss Otis, to dine with either of his admirers.*

In short, again, and perhaps less flippantly so, things could be summed up as follows: Fiona loved Johnnie. Johnnie was free with Dick. Dick was prepared to take over Johnnie completely if only he'd acknowledge his homosexuality and learn to be reconciled to it (it's a fact, which by its very nature, is inescapable, is and always will be, omnipresent), learn to be honest with himself and so fulfil the purpose of his thwarted manhood.

To that, all that antiseptic reasoning, Johnnie wasn't at home, wasn't admitting a thing, one way or the other! Johnnie was away! Removed so distantly that it wasn't funny!

And that was that, for the umpteenth time.

I'd make them wait for their answer. They evidently were good at waiting, so let them, I promised myself.

Never before, or since, have I wanted so badly, so earnestly, to be left alone. I wanted to be forgotten by those two edifices of tenderness and devotion. I wanted them to drop away like murky cobwebs, lose their way, murder each other, anything!

They had made a farce of freedom, my kind, anyway. My kind of freedom didn't function for them. It wasn't even a selfish thing. It was just nonexistent. They made me know, in no uncertain manner, that truly 'whole people', whatever that means, were tagged, always have been, pigeonholed, easily classified, easily lumped in a bundled mass, conveniently distributed to a waiting mob of diagnosticians, analysts, observers, recorders.

I was sure that Fiona and Dick had taken great pains to strip me, to open me up and laugh, gurgle sympathetically, at what they'd exposed. I knew that I mattered to them on that level, only. Almost belonged to them.

Their combined love actually meant nothing. Less than nothing!

16

Thank God for Boxing Day!

I went in search of Larry. I knew he'd be open, and the thought that I badly had to have a haircut was just the sort of excuse I needed. It bolstered me against all coming questions, suspicion, problems of explaining to Larry the reason for turning up on a day which he knew I'd never choose ordinarily.

The point was that I'd left it too late (the haircut, I mean); the Christmas rush; and that was all. I tried to believe this as best I could, and hoped that Larry would, too.

'What bad breeze blow you down here, countryman?'

I knew it. His sniffing nose had found something.

'Left it too late, Larry boy. Can you fix me up?'

'Not today. Closing up, now. Why you don't come back on the thirty-first? I going away today for a visit to some dealer friends of mine in Liverpool.'

'Right away, eh?'

'This very instant, boy.'

'O.K. See you on New Year's Eve, then.'

In a way, I was glad that Larry had fobbed me off. He knew all right. He knew that I wanted more than he could give me. He knew that I wanted to use him.

For the first time, I realized that I was being avoided, rejected; that I was a burden. I apologized to Larry and left. He pretended not to understand, but I knew better. As far as he could work it out, he'd swear that I was a sick man; and maybe he'd say that it was all my own fault, my own way of paying for my immigrant experience, *my new sophistication*.

★   ★   ★

I don't know why I went to see Fiona that day. I left Larry's barbershop and took a bus to West End Lane. I never even gave Trado a thought.

I rang the bell and waited. Fiona came out to me. She was surprised. She was tingling, perplexed.

'Gerald's in, Johnnie.'

'Well?'

'Can you go away while I get rid of him? Shan't take more than ten minutes; as a matter of fact, he'll be off before then, maybe; it's pub time as it is. Opening time can be a blessing, thank God! Remember, now, Johnnie, come back, will you? Don't do anything silly like changing your mind.'

She closed the door quietly. I stood in front of it for a few seconds. What kind of haircut could Fiona give me that Larry couldn't? I asked the door-knocker. (Always have liked talking to things, objects, animals, etc., rather than to reasoning, so-called intelligent people. The sick-looking Christmas decorations on Regent Street were helpful, and so was the door-knocker. They don't seem to interfere with your own freedom, your own freedom to succeed or fail. Sweet cowardice!)

I walked down the road, heading towards Trado's pub. I suddenly remembered the man, who, in August, on my way home, had stopped me and asked me to arrange a couple of *my girls* for a party at his flat in Flask Walk. I remembered his patronizing nastiness.

Perhaps I was reminded of this because waiting outside the pub was a man who resembled the Flask Walk 'monster'. He looked baggy-trousered and vulgar.

It was the same man.

I turned sharp left into a park promenade to avoid him seeing me. And to avoid Trado when he came bouncing along. I sat down on a low green chair and waited for Trado to pass; for Flask Walk and Trado to disappear into the saloon bar (don't think they'd dream of going into any other); for the way to be cleared; for all this and not knowing why I was really there, why I had bothered to leave the West End, why it was so like hypnosis of a kind.

Trado passed. The pub swallowed them both. I hurried back to Fiona. She'd be there waiting. Waiting to start another gangster's-moll playlet, another coward's charade, another fantastic orgy of make-believe. And I was prepared, from the depths of my insufferable weakness and confused personal loyalties, ambition, aspirations, I was absolutely prepared, perhaps hypnotically so, to be her gangster, to be her coward, to be her partner in the coming orgy of make-believe.

She had left both doors ajar. She was in the kitchen fixing something or other. I looked at her moving about peacefully, and wondered at her sudden calm. Only ten or twelve minutes before she had been perplexed and nervous.

I squelched myself down into Trado's favourite armchair. I felt tired, dissipated, anxious. Everything about the sitting room looked raw and diseased. The carpet, the wallpaper, the lamps, the coffee table, everything swung in to meet me. I closed my eyes.

I must have dropped off because I heard Fiona saying: 'It would be much more sensible if you went into the bedroom, darling; you'll only be stiff and miserable if you remain where you are.'

Yes. I had drifted away in my peculiar hypnosis, my own

coward's way of facing up to confusion and anxiety. She told me that I had been asleep for nearly twenty minutes. I allowed her to lead me into the bedroom. She was gentle, loving, in total command. She was confident. She was all woman. Without announcing it, she knew, and she was behaving as if she'd won a grand prize.

The make-believe was easy and fulsome.

She undressed; slipped between the sheets; and began to cry. The make-believe had now become excessive, cloying, pretty nearly disgusting. I knew what her tears meant. They were salty and ecstatic; we kissed, and I was sure. They were in celebration of my return, of my decision in her favour, of her victory; or so she must have believed.

The make-believe continued vigorously.

She said nothing. Neither did I. She felt her way over my body; and that was our only language. It made me slightly nauseated; but I bore it: we were playing, I remembered.

She worked slowly, deliberately slowly, as if she had a lifetime in which to perfect her movements, her mouldings, her rhythm.

I suddenly felt cold, unresponsive, sick. She stopped. I sat up. She jerked herself up on her elbows. We said nothing to each other. There was nothing to say. She knew. I knew.

She cried again.

This time I comforted her. I held her and kissed her neck, her ear lobes, her temples, her throat.

I was sorry.

It was her misery; not mine, I thought. Then she began to lead me gently. Ease and competence filled the room, and the devil relaxed; he had been satisfied once again, he had entered Fiona and was steadily gaining access to my indifference, to my earnest confusion.

And so it went on. I pretended not to follow; she pretended not to notice my pretence. Gently and rhythmically. She led me.

'You belong to me, Johnnie. All of you! To me. Me alone. No reservation. No holding back. No hiding. You're mine. Mine. All mine, my darling!'

Her confidence had been restored.

Her body tingled, quivered.

'Forget him, Johnnie. For God's sake!'

I was hers again. Hers to use; to amuse herself to do battle with; to manage. I was hers because I had hurt her; rejected her; despised her. I was hers because I had come to her out of the haze of her longing; out of the Christmas Day smog; out of indecision. I had come to her, not knowing why. I had come to her because I was weak; accustomed to her world of make-believe; I had come to her because I was dead inside.

Yet, I was hers, there and then, in her rumpled bed, in her sweaty, eager arms, in her electric mind, breathing in her face, breathing out my recalcitrance.

She was happy.

With all her feminine abandon, she celebrated her success, fearlessly, raucously. She shouted. She whispered. She soothed. She implored. She reminded me of the morning on the Heath. She coaxed.

She became violent.

And then she died; and I with her.

The room, its clumsy proportions, its bleakness, its irregular light and shade, its death hush, depressed me. My throat became dry, lined with grit, sore and painful.

I had the urge to go away from Fiona's panting ghost, from Fiona herself; to run away; to hide myself from her heat and shame, from Dick, from everything, and myself.

'Why don't you rest in my arms and wait, Johnnie darling?'

'Humm.'

'You'll be ready again in no time. I'll see to it. You know I can help you.'

'Humm.'

'Oh, my Johnnie, if only you knew how much I love you and want you! I want you more than anything in my whole life.'

I didn't answer. I did as she suggested. I waited. And she worked again; this time more intently, feverishly, more inventively, almost as if she had sensed failure.

And, of course, she was repaid for her maniacal effort.

Again, I had made her happy.

She slept it off, soundly. I watched her for a while; eased away from her gurgling body; got up; dressed; and left.

17

Just how much she had lost, there was no way of knowing. She'd never show it in any case. How much she had gained, I could only guess.

I told Dick everything.

From Boxing Day to New Year's Eve, we hardly spoke to each other. I hadn't tried to get in touch with Fiona, either.

I had last been with her on Boxing Day. It was now New Year's Eve. It was about four-thirty in the afternoon and I decided that I'd face Larry as arranged. I thought it would be best to find out where we stood; to find out what he had to offer; to come to terms with his particular brand of remedy, if he really had one for me. He was to be my outside opinion: yet another kind of casting vote.

It was just as I feared. The shop was packed out. Even Ringo was there. Larry was in a good mood.

'So you come back, eh? You must be badly want a haircut, countryman!'

'Why d'you say it like that, Larry boy?'

'Well, I mean there's lots of others near by to you in the West End.'

That was a feeble one, I thought. Yet, we understood each other.

'Sure. But you're my barber.'

'And maybe more than that, eh?'

It was all very cryptic and nervous. Ringo had been restored to Larry's friendship. A few of the customers referred to Larry's loss over the Christmas season but that was all. The pain had passed. Larry had grown up; Ringo was no longer the enemy.

In a vague way, nearly everything that Larry said to me that afternoon sounded as if he had decided to get at me. He used sarcasm, irony. He teased. He mocked. All in the guise of badinage.

Ringo noticed it once or twice and said certain things in order to make me know that Larry was in that 'particular frame of mind', and that it was best not to take offence. I knew otherwise. And so did Larry. He had it in for me. I had become the enemy. Ringo and I had exchanged places, I thought idly, looking at the black powder-puffs of clipped hair on the linoleum. We had entered into a game of musical chairs.

Ringo said: 'Our pioneer immigrant will soon demand to be called Mr Denton. Did you know that, Johnnie?'

'No. Why?'

Larry said: 'You two ganging up against me, nuh! You better try to think three times about it before you do it, you hearing me? Remember what happen to Algernon Maxwell? He get fixed right and proper. All the pests in this world, sooner or later, get fixed that way in accordance with their evil ways.'

He laughed impishly. Ringo and I echoed it.

'So you facing a brand-new year, countryman?' Larry demanded more than asked his question, demanded that I be shocked into terror and doubt. I wasn't worried. I wasn't even uneasy.

'All of us,' I suggested.

'And you, too, boy.'

That was pointed enough for me to feel attacked. Larry was more interested and thoughtful of my affairs than I had imagined. I'd have to be careful not to tempt the devil lest he completely expose me.

Ringo told me how important a citizen an immigrant like Happy Larry, as he called him, could become in a Welfare State. Ringo held forth for several minutes during which he asked Larry questions like: What minimum standards does a Welfare State aim to promote? What is social security? How were its foundations laid?

Larry played the intellectual and answered right back, blissfully inaccurately.

Barbershop talk fizzled out as soon as Larry's new stock of fifth-hand magazines had been distributed by the assistant who seemed much more mature and responsible than the day in August when Larry had used him as his conversational whipping-boy.

Ringo was now in Larry's chair.

I was fingering rather than thumbing through a back number of *The Tatler*. I didn't bother to get beyond the eighth page; perhaps I was too busy speculating how Larry had come by it in the first place; I don't know.

Occasional outbursts like: 'But, man! You hear what this *Daily Mirror* Cassandra man say 'bout South Africa?' 'This Britain is a real last-rate power these days, eh?' 'Biyo, boy! This Russia is a brute with her planning and long-range scheming though!' 'Is really true a thing that, you know. These things! Look at this. Is really time that these English trade unions wake up and stop stealing the workers' money. What is necessary is long-range scheming.' 'But this *Listener* magazine, or whatever you call it, is a real high-forehead magazine; I can't understand a thing in it except the pictures,' rang round the shop. All this punctuated the clipping and grinding noises of the two barbers who were working with a cold, easy expertness.

Larry was finishing off Ringo's haircut by dabbing powder behind his neck and ears. It was my turn next. Ringo sprang out of the chair. He winked at me and said quite loudly for Larry to hear: 'Watch him very closely, Johnnie. Our Larry's actually an escaped headhunter. He might turn on you at the slightest provocation.'

Larry chuckled. So did I. Ringo struggled into his duffel coat and waved us goodbye.

I was in the chair. Larry was standing behind me! He leant over me and said quietly, 'You must be badly need a talk, Johnnie boy.'

He was testing again. I'd play along.

'You must know, Larry. I've given you a hint, haven't I?'

'I want to ask you something.'

'Go ahead.'

He whispered, 'How things going for you in that die-hard direction?'

I lowered my voice. We must have looked like conspirators, or very special hustlers discussing a deal. 'The same way, Larry. The same way. Hardly any difference.'

He still whispered, 'Why d'you think that talking about it to me actually going to ease your worry, countryman?'

'I'm not sure.'

'I going to tell you what I sure of where you is concerned. I going to tell you the truth, now.'

'You sound as if you've made up your mind to surprise me. Maybe even shock me, eh?'

'Well, this is it. We, all of us boys, are approaching a brand-new year. We getting on in this country and all the rest of it on the surface. If there's a time to reflect and pass judgment, now is it. I see myself in a clear-clear light, Johnnie, and it is the same light which I taking now to see you. You're a self-seeking man. A real old-time selfish, ever-grasping individual. Take me and Ringo and the other West Indians in this country; you don't even think of us as important to your life. You only use us, you know, for your convenience. You come down here to my barber shop to get a break from your new life, your new sophistication, your new sophisticated worthless sort of existence. We don't matter to you in no way, at all. All that matter to you is your newness. But remember you not too accustomed to it and it might drag you down. Burst in your face. Mash got a potato-masher, life got it own kind of masher too, you know. That is a simple law of life.'

'If I'm self-seeking as you put it, what the hell am I seeking, anyway?'

'The usual things.'

'Don't dodge, Larry. Come out with it.'

'I'll tell you. You're looking for a sort of mirror which will make you out to be somebody worth while. You want an identity like. You want to feel that you have a nation behind you, a nation that you can call your own, a national feeling is what you looking for. You would like to walk proud like how the German or the Frenchman or the Englishman can walk proud knowing that they have tradition and a long history behind them to give them a real identity. You feel lacking in ail that because you're a colonial boy with only slavery behind you. So you bound to be confused. You bound to want to escape. You bound to get involved in all sorts of social things. Ringo, he get into political things.'

'So that's what I'm after, am I?'

'You don't believe me?'

'I don't know what to believe, Larry. Honestly. I don't know.'

'I know though. I can see the symptoms in a boy like you quite easy and natural. That's no problem for me, at all. You're discontented in a bad way. You run from this idea as if you hoping to find something to lean on for support. You dart away from your friends and countrypeople, and then you take refuge in a kind of decadent world that you don't ever derive any benefit from except headaches and frustration. You must remember that a decadent world like the one that you holding on to is a world that have its own code of behaviour and mixed-up history. You know that? That world is a meeting-house of mess! A proper rass mess!'

'I can't follow that, Larry.'

'Why?'

'For the simple reason that I'm a man who likes his freedom to do as he pleases, when and where he pleases. I want to be left alone. I don't want a blasted woman dangling round my neck; and for that matter, nobody at all.'

'A most unnatural feeling that, countryman!'

'Why?'

'You've got to assume some sort of responsibility, boy. You got to bend a little way towards the thing called conventional society and all that business. You owe it to your fellow people in the society in which you find yourself, and to yourself. Especially yourself.'

'So that's that, eh?'

'You ask me, governor, and I tell you, nuh.'

18

I left Larry at about six-fifteen and went straight to the club. New Year's Eve was going to be celebrated with Christmas Eve's decorations; the New Year ushered in like Christmas. The staleness of Christmas, its traps, its blunted enticements, its spent fever had been warmed over dutifully by Sandra, Biddy, and *the other*.

I got in just in time to assist with the finishing touches. DuBois B. Washington was there; but he had assumed a kind of dumb insolence, the only protection against the enemy's master sergeants that he could assume. The enemy's master sergeants were being their feminine worst. Sandra barked her orders. Biddy snarled and spat at DuBois B. *The other* drifted about penitently.

Fortunately their invasion couldn't reach me for Larry, for the sound of his voice which kept repeating and repeating itself, for the things he had said, for the way he had contributed to my complete exposure. And naturally when thinking of Larry I had to think of Biddy, of her: *You're also bloody well finished as a man. No woman in her right senses would want to know anything like you.* And right after that, Fiona. And after Fiona, Dick. And after Dick? Could very well be myself. Could be the New Year. Could be another way of escaping myself. Could even be my poor, unsuspecting, anxious mother.

A trickle of customers, then a small burst of prostitutes, followed by a roaring clump of G.I.s came in. Their faces looked expectant, bilious, exploitable. So they were exploited on the spot, expertly and with New Year greetings. They returned the compliment, plus tips. Who could want more than that? I asked my dripping tray.

We were all very happy: givers and receivers.

A prosperous year lay ahead.

For me, a year with a decision to make. A year in which escape would be obviously *démodé*; or would it, I asked my tray again. It only kept on dripping, mockingly, like a strange kind of truth, monstrous, eternal, independent of speculation, assured.

The evening spilled and guffawed its way along from extravagant order to extravagant tip; yet not too uneventfully. There were three instances of near-violence or, as Ringo would have put it, 'three threats of natural behaviour'. I kept out of Biddy's way as much as possible; and out of Sandra's. Tips flourished excessively. And the extension of two hours promised untapped reserves of good hustling and tips and more tips.

At about a quarter to twelve, Larry walked in; his shoulders slipping out of their accustomed stoop, his pace less and less mincing. He came straight up to me.

'I must talk to you, countryman. Spare a minute, nuh?'

We went to the men's lavatory.

'What's up, Larry?'

'Look, something's on me mind. I must get rid of it. I don't like daytime nightmares at all. And I know for sure that this thing going to haunt me same way if I don't put it right this very night, boy.'

'I'm listening.'

He offered me a cigarette from a pack of Jamaican Four Aces. He quickly explained that he'd just opened his last Christmas parcel, his fourth from back home.

He gave me a light from his gas lighter and even more quickly pressed the packet of cigarettes into my waiter's coat pocket.

'Hold on to these. I don't think you ever get the chance of a smoke off of them since you came up.'

'Bless you, Larry.'

'This is what I come to see you about. For God's sake don't take what I say to you this afternoon seriously. I was talking the truth but not to the right man. As a matter of fact, it is really myself I was talking about; talking to. You get the shower of abuse because you was haunting me with your troubles and I was more than worried about my own. And I was more than worried. You see, Johnnie, I am the one that's actually going to pieces in this man's town. I have more than enough of dodging and deceit. I almost suffocating from all the mess I have to live with. I wake up day after day to meet a set of situations that I can't cope with nohow. So what do I do, countryman? I get to work and make up my own set of tricks in order to solve that set of situations; what's more, all of them are unorthodox bad-bad.'

'And what's wrong with that?'

'Everything.'

'How?'

'You ask how. You must be never seen my set of tricks? Some of them are so low that not even a grass snake could crawl under them.'

'We're all guilty, Larry.'

'That sound like pompous talk, but never mind, I know what you mean. And if what you just said is really so, then some are guilty more than others, countryman. Anyway, you better get back now. Sandra mightn't like the idea, at all. And don't worry too much. See you next year like.'

After Larry left, I found myself worrying less and less: the coward's ease, the escapist's busman's holiday.

It was a few minutes to twelve.

Sandra was preparing to do her usual fifty-balloons-trick which she always did with great flourish and excitement. I was summoned to her side. The band stood by. *The other* darted about earnestly, probably trying to get out of Sandra's way. He did it successfully. I envied him.

'Auld Lang Syne'. Balloons, etc. Great display of joy. The new year had arrived. Sandra was at bursting point. She even looked free and happy.

Enormous circle of hands, clasped, sweaty hands. Everybody singing Burns's song (or is it his?) and frothing at the mouth with glee. The band tended to jazz it. The G.I.s co-operated diligently.

I broke away and dashed upstairs. Biddy and DuBois B. were embracing devoutly. The customers who had been unable to squeeze themselves in the giant clammy circle of good cheer downstairs had now formed their own, all over the cocktail lounge. They too were very happy.

DuBois B. looked as if he had just passed suffocation point; his black face faced west; his black face had deep blue patches about the forehead. And I supposed at the time that he, too, was extremely happy. Biddy certainly was. Up to her coming-jowl in it. Body and soul. So were all of them.

It was sickening to watch it.

Surely it was expensive for most of them; and the night was yet young, the new year hadn't even stopped its postnatal bawling. I received orders from downstairs to brave it out and break up the hugging and kissing. It was bad for business. One could trust Sandra not to be fooled by her own balloons, 'Auld Lang Syne', and sentimental slobbering. In a way, I admired her for that.

So I set about breaking it up.

Everybody was surprisingly co-operative.

Another tidal rush of mammoth orders. Biddy was her old grasping self. I hadn't changed. Tips meant the same to me, before 'Auld Lang Syne' and after. Why had they bothered to sing it in the first place? I wondered. Why had they bothered to fool themselves? Why?

I hadn't changed. They hadn't changed.

And why shouldn't they? I tried to find one good reason. I didn't succeed. Didn't want to, either.

A short, sweet fight broke out between two successful Cockney ponces. DuBois B. squashed it masterfully. Biddy beamed with pride. A very good father for her child and stuff like that may have passed through her mind. Or not. I suppose I would have liked it to, anyway.

If she had had that thought, I can't blame her really; DuBois B. had changed considerably: no 'fix', no dealing, no idiotic spending, no jive talk. DuBois B. most certainly looked like a man with a year of great promise ahead of him. Biddy had made certain about one thing, at least; it would be fun to see her mothering a baby for a change, I suggested to the back of the Four Aces packet which I held in my left hand. I threw it from hand to hand. And that's the way of the world, I consoled myself. Larry and his gift parcels! Horrible taste that second cigarette had. So accustomed to the 'mildies' in this country that the Four Aces packet may have been hashish for all I knew.

The extension lurched forwards. Lurched drunkenly. Then it fizzled to a stop. An abrupt, commercial stop. Sandra checked the till; found everything correct; passed round New Year drinks; and that was her benevolent lot done.

Biddy and DuBois B. shone blatantly white and black from the hollow of their loving-cup; and *the other* and I said 'Cheers' like mossy, modest employees, like limp, grateful servants, servants of a great white plantation mistress.

A few select customers (sorry, members!) who were ostensibly waiting for Sandra, raised theirs and grinned like appealing, toothless babies. In a few minutes, they'd be off with Sandra to help her spend the 'takings' at the place up the road. Gay parasites! All of us!

I said good night to Sandra, Biddy, DuBois B., and *the other*. I received four muttered replies. I bowed to the rest and left the club.

19

I knew that I had to face Dick's silence as best I could. What sort of mood he'd be brandishing I didn't even want to guess. I hoped he wouldn't be waiting up for me. I didn't want to hurt him.

I planned that I'd sneak in and go to bed without making the slightest sound, if possible. It would be better that way, I told the aching fear within me. I told it more than that. I told it that there had to be a break; and very, very soon we'd all be free, truly free.

Quite obviously I knew, too, that I was killing something in our friendship. I had denied Dick, inadvertently. But would I have done what Dick wanted of me was something I didn't care to ask myself. How could Dick love me? How could he, and not make me aware of it all along? I didn't understand; I didn't want to; that was my only balm, my only *out*.

I understood Fiona's kind of love. I knew that Dick understood it, too. I knew Fiona understood his for me.

I didn't want to hurt him.

I knew that that would be cowardly.

Yet I couldn't care less about Fiona. The more I thought about it, the more I realized that not even that was really true.

★   ★   ★

Oxford Circus was ragged and freezing. Yet there was something more friendly about it than the club I'd just left.

I felt the wad of notes in my right-hand trouser pocket, and the fullness of my thigh bouncing against it, as I walked across the Circus into Regent Street. A wad was easy, so very easy to come by: so many hustled shillings, half-crowns, and so on, even undrunk drinks returned to Biddy. Wonderful, easy silver converted into crisp or not so crisp fivers or pound notes at the end of a busy evening could give anybody a feeling of *new security*.

Regent Street sounded hollow under my irregular footsteps. I felt the wad, again. It had been accumulating since the 22nd of December. It felt warm and bulky. Then suddenly it felt heavy and squashy. Whatever the feeling, it was mine, all mine.

Then the crazy notion came upon me: I wanted so much more than a mere wad of notes! I wanted so much that I'd be unable to manage it all by myself. I wanted more than enough.

I became certain about what I really wanted, at that moment. I didn't want to run away from a bloody thing. I didn't love Fiona. I didn't love Dick. I didn't even love myself. I simply wanted money. Loads and loads of it!

Then, right after that, I realized that I didn't actually want loads and loads of money, at all. I merely wanted to have enough to get by comfortably.

Arrogant lie!

Or was it?

Yet the man had said, and I had believed implicitly, that London's that big cinema of a city where trees are banks and money plus freedom is as easy to come by as leaves on an autumn pavement.

Piccadilly Circus was a grey whore of lights, an open, cold storage. I wanted to get back to the flat in a hurry. I started to walk faster and in the effort to cross the Circus quickly, I broke into a steady jog. I kept it up until I reached the Haymarket. I started walking again after I entered Panton Street.

A sudden panic to talk to Dick overcame me. I decided I'd go into his room and see him. I'd wake him; I'd tell him that I'm sorry about everything; I'd try to comfort him in some way; I'd ask him to try to forgive me; I'd beg him to try to see things my way, as well as his; I'd promise anything if only he'd tell me that I hadn't really hurt him.

I ran down the last half of Panton Street, into Whitcomb Street. The sitting-room light was on. The curtains, wrenched apart by Dick's fury no doubt, looked limp and soiled.

I slowed down. I realized that there'd be no way out of it; I had to talk to him. The light was on; he was waiting. I didn't mind that. We'd talk intelligently; we wouldn't lose control. It was going to be a very meaningful New Year's meeting between two friends, two very close friends.

Dick wasn't in the sitting room. He wasn't in his bedroom. I looked everywhere. I called his name. There was no reply. I called again.

He had gone. I was certain of it. I refused to fool myself into believing that he hadn't.

I went back to the sitting room. He had left a note on the mantelpiece.

My Dearest Johnnie,

This had to happen, sooner or later. I'm sorry, very sorry. There was nothing left for me to do but to help you; indeed, to force you to make up your mind. I've left you because you're the only one able to do this; and by yourself, unmolested and completely responsible for your own decision. I had to go or I'd only torment you and keep reminding you of how hopelessly involved and in love I am with you; and this, I know, would merely further complicate things, both for you and for me.

I've taken a room at the Regent Palace, Piccadilly Circus. When you've made your decision, you'll know where to find me, or, on the other hand, you'll know where not to come. I'll give you a week to decide. Do not try to get in touch with me until the week is up. You'll need all the time at your disposal to think things out. As a matter of fact, you might well find that you'll have more than one change of attitude after arriving at what you thought was the final decision. For our sake, for the pleasant memories we've stored up through the months of partnership in the flat and before at Hampstead, for our future's sake, yours and mine, or, ours, choose, I beg of you, choose with both your head and your heart; choose intelligently but compassionately.

It's either to be Fiona or myself. It's as simple as that; and again, on second thoughts, not as simple as that sounds. It's up to you.

With all my love,

Dick

P.S.
   Happy New Year. I'm waiting for you.

I read and re-read the note about four or five times. Afterwards, I crumpled it and threw it back on the mantelpiece.

I walked into his bedroom. His bed was made. The bureau and wardrobe were empty. The aroma of his Old Spice shaving lotion was the only part of him left behind except for some traces of dusting powder at the base of the wardrobe mirror.

I went into my own room. I washed my face; dried it quickly with a few dabs of the new towel Laura had left out for me; brushed my hair vigorously; straightened my tie; and left the flat. I felt compelled to get out and go for a long walk. Anywhere.

I walked up Whitcomb Street. Into Leicester Square. Up Charing Cross Road. Up to Cambridge Circus. Left into Shaftesbury

Avenue. On to Piccadilly Circus. Into Piccadilly. And down towards Green Park.

I was heading nowhere in particular. I didn't even feel as tired as I should have, especially after the extension at the club.

I had a choice of lives before me. A choice of loves. And, perhaps, a choice of enemies.

Fiona was waiting.

Dick was waiting.

And in another way, London also was. And so was I. I knew I had to wait. For the truth about Dick, about Fiona, about myself. About my next move. That and only that was worth waiting for: the truth about myself, and the courage and ability to recognize it when it came.

It was a cold morning. Not a trace of rain, anywhere.

ABOUT THE AUTHOR

Andrew Salkey was born in Panama in 1928 of Jamaican parents, and brought up in Jamaica. A major figure in Caribbean literature, he published five novels; two collections of short stories; four collections of poetry; eight novels for children; two important travel books; and numerous groundbreaking anthologies of Caribbean writing in the 1960s and 1970s. In London from the 1950s through to the '70s, he worked as a broadcaster for the BBC Caribbean Voices programme and was later deeply involved in the Caribbean Artists Movement. In 1976 he relocated to Hampshire College in Amherst, where he died in 1995.

Peepal Tree Press is home of the best in Caribbean
and Black British fiction, poetry, literary criticism,
memoirs and historical studies.

All Peepal Tree titles are available from the website
www.peepaltreepress.com

and all good booksellers.

E-mail: contact@peepaltreepress.com

https://www.peepaltreepress.com
@peepaltreepress